Pit Bulls
in a Skirt 2

FEB 2017

FR

Also by Mikal Malone

Pit Bulls in a Skirt

Published by Dafina Books

Pit Bulls
in a Skirt 2

MIKAL
MALONE

Kensington Publishing Corp.
http://www.kensingtonbooks.com

DAFINA BOOKS are published by

Kensington Publishing Corp.
119 West 40th Street
New York, NY 10018

All Kensington Titles, Imprints, and Distributed Lines are
available at special quantity discounts for bulk purchases
for sales promotions, premiums, fund-raising, and educa-
tional or institutional use. Special book excerpts or cus-
tomized printings can also be created to fit specific needs.
For details, write or phone the office of the Kensington
special sales manager: Kensington Publishing Corp., 119
West 40th Street, New York, NY 10018, attn: Special Sales
Department, Phone: 1-800-221-2647.

Dafina and the Dafina logo Reg. U.S. Pat. & TM Off.

ISBN-13: 978-0-7582-7469-4
ISBN-10: 0-7582-7469-6

First Kensington mass market printing: January 2013

10 9 8 7 6 5 4 3 2 1

Printed in the United States of America

*This is dedicated to Cartel Publications
fans everywhere.
I love you!*

Acknowledgments

I'd like to thank all *Pit Bulls in a Skirt* fans who kept this storyline alive through word of mouth. It means the world to me. We hope you show the same support for the movie.

Mikal Malone, aka T. Styles

E-mail: authortstyles@me.com
www.facebook.com/authortstyles or T. Styles Fan Page
www.twitter.com/authortstyles

Prologue

Aleed's black Nike boots pressed against the grungy snow as he ran for his freedom. Having six warrants out for his arrest and a pocket filled with crack rocks, he knew he'd be going down for a long time if the persistent cop caught him.

"Freeze! Stop running before I shoot!" the rookie cop yelled.

The young black cop's loyalty to his job impacted his decisions. All he wanted was Aleed, the man whose picture was pinned against the police station wall, which he saw every day.

"If you don't freeze . . . I'm gonna fuckin' shoot! I'm not playin' wit you!" the cop taunted. "Stop runnin'!"

When Aleed saw the green awning over the gate in Emerald City, he felt a sense of calm. He knew that once he got over the gate, the rules the outside world lived by would not apply.

"This is my final warning," the cop yelled as they ran down the dark sidewalk, a few feet from the level of the fence. Aleed leaped over the fence.

And then the cop heard Aleed yell, "Ecilop! Ecilop!"

The cop thought the yell was weird, but he remained on his trail. He didn't realize that "ecilop" stood for police backward. It was the code word for Emerald City to lock down shop and get out of Dodge.

Instead of hopping the fence like Aleed, the cop ran through the entrance gate, past the empty guard's station, and onto Emerald's grounds. Once inside, he noticed that Emerald appeared vacant. As always, the five buildings of Emerald City encompassed a large yard in the middle. It was pitch dark and no lights were on, not even in the yard. Emerald City was in order.

"Aleed, get out here! Don't make things worse!" The rookie's voice echoed and bounced back to him off the buildings. "Aleed! I know you hear me!"

The gun he was holding shook in his hand, and the darkness and silence frightened him.

Then he heard, "What you doin' here, cop? What you doin' on EC grounds?"

The voice appeared to come from the top of one of the buildings, but the rookie couldn't see the man or his face.

"I'm a police officer, and I'm here for Aleed."

"Well, if you a D.C. cop, you should know your laws don't apply here. Leave now . . . while you still can."

The man's disregard for his shield enraged the rookie cop. "I'm not goin' nowhere without Aleed! I'm the muthafuckin' law!" the officer shouted.

The person laughed, and others laughed behind him; their voices were hidden within the night.

"Check dis out, cop. . . . Right now, the choice is yours to leave. But when I count to three, the choice will be yours no more. We run fuckin' Emerald City and everybody in it!" he yelled at the top of his lungs, sending chills through the cop's tender heart.

"One!" the voice began.

"I'm a police officer!" the rookie yelled, backing up cautiously.

"Two!" was followed by a clicking sound of many weapons upon the rooftops.

"You can't get away with this!" the officer continued.

But before he could say "three," the cop was gone. With his life in tote.

Welcome to
Emerald City!

Mercedes

We make this shit look easy.

I can't believe I'm runnin' late! I am dodging in and out of traffic, trying to make it to Emerald City on time. I should not have been fuckin' wit Derrick's sexy ass this morning. That man must've fucked me in every room in our loft-style apartment at D.C.'s National Harbor. Lifting up slightly, I tug at the seat of my Seven jeans between my legs. They were rubbing against my pussy, causing me discomfort, but damn does that boy have some good dick. It's a good thing my kids were with their father, because I'm not sure if I would've been able to keep my voice down.

I thought I knew what love was when I was with Cameron. I couldn't see the sun or the moon unless Cameron was with me. It's amazing what separation and a near-death experience can do for a relationship. Bottom line is this: Now that I've been in Derrick's presence, I know what real love is; and I'm not willing to trade it for any man in the world . . . not even for Cameron.

When I pull up to the Emerald City gate, I am immediately transformed. No longer am I a girl-friend or a mother. In Emerald City, I'm a boss! Glancing at the five buildings with green awnings circling the open field, I respect its power.

"Good morning, ma'am," says the security guard at the gate. "The other ladies just got here. They're in the field."

"Thanks, Jake. How's the baby?"

"Growing bigger every day." He smiles. "He'll be two tomorrow."

"That's right! It *is* his birthday."

"Yes, ma'am, it is."

"Well, you can have the day off to spend with your family. I'll get Amir to guard the gate for you."

"Thanks, boss! I appreciate it!"

I wait until the gates open and drive my new black Mercedes-Benz G-Class SUV inside.

Once inside, I see my girls standing outside with their cars surrounding them. It's cold out-side, and the sky is icy blue. As usual, they're draped in fur coats and diamonds; I can't help but smile. We were the flyest drug bosses in D.C., hands down! We make this shit look easy. Yvette's red Lincoln Navigator is parked next to Kenyetta's silver Lexus LS; I pull up next to Carissa's blue Porsche. I can't wait to get out of my ride and hug my friends.

"About time you got here, bitch!" Yvette yells as my girls crowd around.

"Shut your short ass up! Better late than never."

"No . . . your ass always late!" Carissa interjects.

"What is this . . . shorties-gang-up-on-Mercedes day?" I laugh. "Kenyetta, you got my back, right?"

"You know it." She smiles.

We embrace one another. Ever since we made a decision to move out of Emerald and run our operation from the outside, we saw each other less. We talked as much as we could, but we had our own lives. No matter what, we agreed to return and spend a week in Emerald City each month; and no one knew which week we'd choose but us. We did this to remain spontaneous and leave nothing to chance.

I glance at the rooftops and see our shooters in place. Whenever we are in Emerald, security is tighter than security protecting the president.

"Fuck all that bullshit! Look at that truck!" Yvette says. She traded her short, spiky hair for a cute, shoulder-length bob. "When you get that? And what happened to the car?"

"I still got my car. And if you would answer your phone sometimes, you woulda known I got this last Friday," I tell her, examining the black waist-length fur coat she wore with her jeans and black Gucci boots.

"Oh, here we go again," she says, brushing me off. "Like you always answer your phone."

"She's tellin' the truth, Yvette. You ain't the

same. Everything good with you?" Carissa questions as she tries to close her full-length chocolate coat tighter. The wind is blowing harder.

"Don't start with me, because we all have personal lives, including me."

"Yvette, we're still family, and family keeps in contact. So you tell us, how are things really going with you?" Kenyetta asks. I notice Yvette's eyes seem sad. "You ain't got no kids or no man—so what's up with you?"

Yvette looks at all of us and drops her head before brushing her hair out of her face. I feel bad for putting her on the spot, but I care about her. I care about all of them. Just because we leave Emerald doesn't mean that changes. We worth fuckin' millions! Niggas would love to kidnap one of us just to make some cash. We have to watch each other's backs.

"What's up, Vette?" I persist.

"Can we just leave it alone, Mercedes? I just need to get into my apartment, grab a drink, and relax. It's cold out here."

"Why you in a rush to go into that lonely-ass apartment, anyway?" Carissa asks, beating her feet for warmth.

"Yeah, bitch!" I tell her, looping my arm through hers. "You do seem a little anxious. You sure you ain't gettin' high on our supply?"

"I'ma fuck you up, Mercedes!" She laughs. "I'ma do better about calling when we away from Emerald. And y'all betta take that because it's all I can give right now. So, can we please get out of this cold air and go inside? Carissa sound like she in a marchin' band or somethin'."

"A'ight, bossy," I tell her. "I'ma let you off the hook for now, but you gonna tell me what's up with you."

"Yeah . . . and if you do have a man, we want to meet him," Carissa adds. "I gotta tell his ass however many times he fuckin' you, he betta increase that shit by three, because you wound up!"

We all laugh.

"Trust me, I'm gettin' sexed more than all of y'all put together. I guarantee that."

"Doubt it!" I laugh.

"That's real talk! Way more!"

"Oh . . . really," Kenyetta says. "I guess we better get inside our apartments, drop our shit off, and finish this meeting so we can hear the juicy details."

We chitchat a little longer and jump in our rides. As I pull off, I can't help but think about Yvette again. Something is definitely up.

Yvette

I love when we have drunk sex.

I'm in love! And I didn't think it would be possible after Thick died.

I open the apartment door and smile when I smell the scent of fried chicken, cheese rice-and-broccoli simmering on the stove. My girl-friend, Chris—or C. Wash, as she likes to be called—spoils me to death.

Although the relationship has its high times, I admit it's not easy being gay. The stares from people and the comments from men who see us walking in public mess my head up sometimes. But when we're alone, nothing else seems to matter. I felt dead inside before her; and since seeing her face, all I ever want to do is see her face again and again.

PIT BULLS IN A SKIRT 2

About two years earlier

Yvette was driving down Benning Road in the Northeast section of D.C., heading toward Agatha's house. Agatha was an old friend of her mother's, and she had been caring for Yvette's darkest secret: her strung-out mother. No one except Thick, whom Yvette had killed a few weeks earlier, knew that her mother was even alive.

During Yvette's childhood, Loretta was so strung-out that she couldn't care for Yvette and her two sisters. Loretta was a horrible mother. She proved it when she left Andrea, a baby, in a laundry room during one of D.C.'s worst winter storms. The infant died a few hours later. It was also Loretta who pulled over on the side of a dark road, somewhere in Virginia, to put her other daughter, Cecil, out because she couldn't afford to feed her drug habit and both of her children. So she made a choice to nurture her broken veins. To this day, Yvette still didn't know if her sister was dead or alive.

As a child, Yvette often had to lie in strange beds with her mother while Loretta had sex for money. She still remembered how the men tried to pry their fingers into her virgin womb, because sleeping with Loretta was too atrocious by itself.

Loretta thought about all of these moments from her past as she drove to her destination.

*   *   *

When Yvette got old enough to understand that sex paid, she left the small bathroom she lived in with her mother for six years and headed to Emerald City. She couldn't wait to leave the filthy conditions her mother's pimp subjected them to in his four-bedroom home.

The first day she arrived in EC, she hopped off the bus with all of her possessions stuffed into a torn blue backpack. It was a summer night and the tight blue-jean shorts and white T-shirt she wore hugged her curves, exuding more sex appeal than a young girl should have. Off the bus for two minutes, she saw her first trick pull up next to her in a shiny blue Suburban. She was immediately attracted to him.

"You wanna take a ride with me?" he asked, eyeing her huge breasts. "You don't look like you old enough to be out here by yourself."

Nervous at the man's huge and powerful persona, Yvette said, "Okay."

"What's your name, shortie?" he questioned when she got inside.

"Yvette."

"I'm Thick," he said in a voice that made Yvette's virgin body shiver.

"Thick." She giggled. "I like that."

"If you like that, I got somethin' else you'll love. I'll tell you all about it."

Thick, who was twenty-one at the time, took a sixteen-year-old Yvette into his apartment in Emerald and molded her sexually and mentally. She couldn't eat, sleep, or breathe unless he told her to. And if she showed emotion, he'd beat her.

Over time, the only problem he had with Yvette was her lack of cleanliness. She didn't know how to clean, because her mother had lived a filthy lifestyle. After a while, Thick dealt with the problem by never being home.

A year later, Loretta showed up on their doorstep, needing help, and Yvette almost fainted. Loretta had heard from drug dealers where Yvette lived and tried to extort money from them. But when Thick refused, she threatened to tell the police that he was molesting her underage daughter. Thick told Yvette to get her mother away before he placed what was left of her wretched body six feet deep. He also promised to put her out.

Yvette, who had discovered a new life in Emerald, friends, and a man, didn't want to leave the only family she'd grown to love. It took Yvette five hours to find her drug-addicted mother a home. That's where Agatha came in. For five hundred dollars, she provided a roof for Loretta and maintained Yvette's secret by not letting anyone know that her mother was alive.

And now, many years later, Yvette was bailing her mother out of trouble again.

"Agatha, I'm pulling up now," Yvette said on the phone.

"Well, you gotta hurry up! This bitch has gone too far this time!"

"Agatha, calm down. I'm coming," Yvette answered, growing impatient.

"You said that two hours ago! This bitch done tried to shoot up through a vein in her eye, 'cause the ones in her arm so fucked up! Now I know you got that good job at the phone com-

pany, so you should be fine finding her somewhere else to live. But she gotta leave here
today!"

Yvette took a deep breath and pulled up to
Agatha's house. She never told her she sold
drugs, because she didn't want Agatha asking
for more money. For that reason, she told her
that she was employed with the phone company. And since most employees were paid well
working there, she bought her story.

"I'm here."

"Good . . . she gonna be outside! Bye."

Yvette got out of her car, right before her
mother was thrown out front, wearing nothing
but a blue nightgown. Loretta's once-smooth,
chocolate skin was now as dark as charcoal and
uneven. Her body was frail, and she looked
older than her true age. Yvette desperately tried
to rid herself of the pity she felt seeing her
mother's horrible condition.

"Where am I gonna take you?" she said aloud
to herself as she walked up the five steps.

She couldn't call on her friends for help, because they didn't know about Loretta.

"Loretta, can you walk?" Yvette asked.

Her mother was lying against the door, with
her legs wide open, exposing her naked vagina.
Yvette looked around to see if anyone was looking, and everyone was.

"Loretta, come on," Yvette said as she helped
her mother up. She was as short as Yvette.

They almost fell down twice, because Loretta
was off balance. When Loretta almost caused

Yvette to fall, Yvette released her and watched her topple down two steps and hit the ground.

"Fuck! What am I gonna do wit you! Why do you have to be a washed-up–ass addict? Why couldn't I have a mother who cares for me? I hate you!" Yvette cried as she stood over her.

As she yelled at her mother, she watched a black Lexus pull up in front of the house and park.

"Fuck you doin', young?" Seven, Chris's sister, asked when they parked. Seven's tiny, neat braids dressed her head. Although everything about her mannerisms resembled a boy, she was extremely pretty and possessed a smooth brown complexion. "You know we gotta get to the Terrace and pick up that stack."

"Slim, we up the street, fall back. We gonna get there," Chris said, placing her hazard lights on.

"Oh . . . I see what you doin'," Seven said, looking at the short girl, with big titties, trying to pull another woman inside a car. "Always chasin' bitches."

"Shut your dyke ass up!" Chris said, exiting the car. "I be right back."

When Chris got out, she walked up to Yvette, who was struggling to put her mother inside her white Infiniti.

"You need help with your folks?" Chris asked, walking up to Yvette from behind.

"No! I got it myself."

When Yvette finally looked at Chris, her heart skipped a few beats. The tall girl, with light brown

17

eyes, made her melt. Yvette had never looked at another woman sexually, but she was attracted to Chris instantly. Her vanilla complexion and neat row of braids added charm to her persona.

"You sure?" Chris lifted her mother up, anyway; and with one scoop, she placed her inside the car. "You look like you strugglin', sweetheart."

When Loretta was inside, Chris looked at Yvette and caught her smiling at her.

"You a'ight, cutie?" Chris asked.

"Oh . . . uh . . . yes, I'm fine."

"You sure? 'Cause you look out of it."

"I'm—I'm . . . fine."

"Cool. . . . So what's your name?"

"Why? I'm not gay!" Yvette yelled, quickly realizing how ridiculous she sounded.

"Whoa!" Chris said, with her hands extended in front of her. "All I asked was your name, ma. I wasn't tryin' to get wit you."

"Oh."

"Not yet, anyway." Chris winked. Yvette didn't respond. "So what's your name? You do have one, don't you?" Chris smiled.

"Oh . . . yes, I'm sorry. Yvette. My name's Yvette."

"A'ight, Yvette, where you takin' her?"

"Why?"

" 'Cause I know somebody who might be able to help you get her together. My aunt went there a few years ago and she been clean ever since. Now she work there. It's a small place in Baltimore that not a lot of people know about.

The joint kinda illegal, but it works." Chris took her BlackBerry off her hip and scrolled through her contact list. "The number is four . . . one . . . zero . . ." She stopped when she saw Yvette wasn't recording the number. "You got a phone?"

"Yes," Yvette said, still caught off guard by her attraction to Chris. "I'm ready."

"Look, why don't we do this. You take my number. When you get a chance, give me a call. I'll tell you more about the spot. That way, you can make sure it's the right place for your peoples. Cool?"

Before Yvette could respond, Seven laid into the horn like she'd lost her mind.

"Slim, are you serious? I'm comin'!" Chris yelled.

"Well, hurry the fuck up den, nigga!"

Chris ignored her. "Call me anytime, Yvette. I mean that. And don't worry. . . . I know shit seem fucked up right now, but they'll get better. You too pretty to be frownin'."

When Chris walked off, Yvette didn't leave her position until Chris was out of sight. She couldn't describe the feeling she felt around her. She'd felt that feeling one other time in her life, and that was with Thick.

Yvette took her mother to the rehab center, and two large men came and took Loretta away. Yvette didn't mind taking a chance with an illegal facility. The last time she placed her mother in traditional rehab, Loretta made a crawl space under the wired fence and ripped the skin on her back to shreds while trying to escape.

After leaving the rehab center, Yvette and Chris began to hang together. What started out being days together ended up being months. And before long, they purchased a luxury apartment in Georgetown. They'd been together ever since.

Present day

"There go my bitch," Chris says as she pushes me up against the door and gives me an extra-wet kiss. I taste the liquor on her breath and I am aroused. I love when we have drunk sex. "Why you keep me waitin' so long, Vette?"

Before I answer, she takes off my coat and flings it to the floor. Once my jeans are down, she runs her warm tongue in and out of my wet pussy. I bite my bottom lip to prevent my neighbors from hearing our dirty little secret. It doesn't take long before my love oil eases out of my body. She's a pro.

"You are a trip," I say, trying to regain my composure as I pull up my jeans.

She doesn't respond. She just straightens her clothes and dishes out our plates. Placing the dishes on the new table, she says, "What are you looking at?"

"What you think I'm looking at?"

"I don't know, but if you keep staring like that, I'ma find out."

"I tapped out a long time ago," I tell her, trying to come down off my sexual high. "You are too much for me."

"Don't say stuff you don't mean." She winks.

We are eating at the table when she says, "So was today the day?"

My stomach flips and I try to act like I don't know what she's talking about—even though I do.

"What you talkin' about, Chris?" I ask, looking up from my meal.

"You know what I'm talkin' 'bout. When you goin' tell your friends 'bout us? When you goin' stop playin' games and let them know we together?" Her fork drops onto her plate and she sits back in her chair.

"I will, Chris. But you can't rush me."

"We been fuckin' wit each other almost two years now. And they still don't know 'bout me. So how is that rushin' you?"

"Chris, please!" I say, getting up from the table. I stand in front of the window and look down at our empire. For a brief moment, I question my sexuality and my life. "As long as you keep eatin' this pussy right . . . we good."

"Who you talkin' to like that?" she asks, walking up to me.

In life, I'm known as the hard-core bitch. And don't get it twisted, I still am, but there's something about Chris I respect. At times, I find myself backing down.

"I'm sorry, baby," I say, turning around to face her. "I'm just frustrated. My love for you should be enough."

"That's not it," she says, rubbing my shoulders. "I'm tired of being a secret, Yvette. I'm ready to be a part of your *whole* life."

I look into her brown eyes and feel sad about my embarrassment over our relationship.

"I'll tell them this week."

"For real?" she asks, and her eyes widen.

"For real," I say, kissing her lips. "I'll tell them before we leave Emerald." I can smell my sweet love juice on her mouth and get aroused again. "But right now," I say, continuing to walk her to the dining-room chair, "let me return the favor you gave me earlier."

As I pull down her jeans, move her boxer briefs to the side, and lick her wetness, my stomach flutters. Who knew I'd take pleasure in being with a woman? I don't know how I ended up here, but here is where I belong.

Kenyetta

"Whatever you need me to be, I will be."

I had an hour to meet my friends at the community center inside Emerald City. We had a lot to discuss about our day-to-day operations. But before doing anything, I jumped back into my car and took a drive a few blocks down to Tyland Towers to see BW. I know it's fucked up of me to be dealing with a competitor, but it is what it is. You can't help who you love, now can you? Anyway, he said he had something important to talk to me about tomorrow, but I can't wait. I have to know now! This roller-coaster relationship is killing me! At times, I wish he weren't in my life, but I'm in too deep and can't turn back now.

One year earlier

"Sir, I'm tryin' to be nice, but you're making it hard. Where is my car?" Kenyetta asked the salesperson at the counter in Sparkles detail shop.

"What kind of car you got again?" the overweight man responded. The tips of his nails were black with oil and soot.

"The red Volvo with the tinted windows."

"Oh yeah," he said, looking through a few sheets of paper on a worn-out clipboard. "You got one more person in front of you, and then you should be good."

"One more person in front of me? But I was the first one here this morning."

"Like I said, you got one more person in front of you," he said angrily, without regard for her feelings. "Wait or get your car the fuck out of here!"

Kenyetta threw her weight onto the grungy orange plastic seat and tried to prevent the tears from escaping her eyes. Dyson's funeral was in an hour, and it didn't look like she was going to make it.

The news came to her suddenly, while on the steps of Unit C.

"Hey, Yvette," Aleed said, walking up to her. "I don't know if y'all know yet, but somebody killed Dyson."

"What?" Yvette said. "Who told you that?"

"Everybody's talkin' about it," he said slowly, looking at Kenyetta. "I just thought y'all should know."

When Aleed left, the girls all looked at Kenyetta with concern.

"I'm fine," she told them before they asked. "It ain't like we were together or nothin'. It's been over between us." Although they weren't together any longer, Kenyetta couldn't wrap her mind around Dyson being gone.

Kenyetta tried to keep her head up; but when she left their sight, she cried herself to sleep. She didn't bother telling them she was going to the funeral. She wanted the last moments she'd spend with Dyson to be alone.

And now here she was, stuck in the detail shop, wondering if that moment would ever happen.

While sitting in her seat, pouting, she saw the door to the shop fling open. An extremely tall and stocky man walked in. He was wearing blue jeans, butter-colored Timberlands, and a black leather coat. His skin was dark and his hair was neatly cut. He had swag and build like Biggie did when he had money. A white hand towel rested on his shoulder; he wiped the sweat off his head with it periodically. Although Dyson was considered more attractive, the stranger still had sex appeal.

"My ride ready, playa?" he asked the man at the counter.

"You know we got you. Give me a second." Seeing this, Kenyetta stood up and walked hurriedly to the counter.

"Hold up. Why is his car ready before mine?"

"He was here before you."

"Bullshit! I'm sick of you!"

"You know what . . . I'm tired of your shit too," the salesperson barked. "Take your car and get the hell out of my shop!"

He flung the keys to Kenyetta. She snatched them off the counter and said, "You betta hope I get over this by the time I get to my car, because you don't know who you fuckin' wit."

Kenyetta pushed the glass door open and stormed outside. Without asking, she stormed into the back, disregarding everyone who was working there, to get her car. Five men who were inside moved out of the way of the line of her rage.

"Can I help you?" one of them asked.

"Get the fuck out my face. You don't know me!" She jumped inside her car and was preparing to pull off when Black Water blocked her path.

"Excuse me!" she yelled outside her driver's window. "You betta get out of my way before I run your ass ova!"

"You not gonna do that." He smiled. His teeth were white, and she loved his smile.

"I'm serious. I'm not in a good mood."

"Why don't you get out and talk to me for a second."

Kenyetta exited her ride and walked up to him. Although she was five-seven, he still had almost a foot over her—and this was even though she had on heels.

"What is your problem?" she asked, with her hand on her hip and her Louis Vuitton purse on her shoulder.

"Calm down, ma. You too pretty to be so mad."

"There's no such thing," she corrected him. "And I'm tired of niggas tellin' me I'm too pretty to do this . . . and I'm too pretty to do that!"

"Maybe you tired of hearing it, because it's true."

"No! What I'm tired of is being taken advantage of because of the way I look. All I wanted was to get my car washed, and it's obvious that's not happening."

"Hey, get that car done in ten minutes and I'll pay y'all double," Black said, ignoring her momentarily. She turned around and saw all of the men stopping their conversation to tend to her car.

"What's goin' on?"

"What you think goin' on? They cleanin' your ride."

"I'm not payin' these muthafuckas shit! I been in here all day!"

"Don't worry 'bout that. They goin' take care of you, and then you'll be free to go wherever you goin'. Cool?"

Kenyetta immediately took comfort in his take-control personality. He reminded her of Dyson in that way.

"You know what? Right now, I don't even care," she told him.

"So where you goin', Kenyetta?"

Because she hadn't told him her name, she became defensive, thinking this was a setup.

"How you know my name?" she asked, sticking her hand in her purse, touching her weapon. She wouldn't hesitate putting a bullet through his face if she had to. "I didn't tell you my name!"

"Calm down. I saw your name on the sign-in sheet inside the shop." He saw her remove her hand from her bag. "Why you so uptight? You involved in some illegal shit, or somethin'?"

"No . . . uh . . . why you say that?"

" 'Cause that's how you actin', diggin' in your purse and shit. What you got in that bag, ma?"

Kenyetta didn't respond.

"You real hostile."

"I know." She laughed softly. "And I'm sorry about my attitude. It's been a long morning and I have a lot to do."

"Let me help clear your mind," he said, taking a few strands of her hair into his hand without asking. "I love black women with silky hair like this."

"You awfully touchy-feely," she said, moving her head so that her hair escaped his grip.

"Naw, I just go after what I want."

"And what you want is me?" She sounded more hopeful than she wanted to come across as.

"I like what I like," he said, towering over her. "I also know if you got a man, he 'bout to not exist."

His comment brought her back to reality and she remembered Dyson's funeral. Although they weren't together when he was murdered, he was the last man she had.

"Uh . . . listen, I'm sorry, but I have to leave."

"What? You late for a funeral or somethin'?"

"I have to go," she repeated, avoiding his comment. She smiled when she saw her car was done. "I'll pay you back for this."

"I'm sure you will. And I got your number from Sam at the counter. So when I call, remember the name, BW."

"BW, huh?" She smiled. "I guess I'll wait for that call."

"You do that, sweetheart."

While driving to the funeral, she had to make a call. "Amir, this Kenyetta."

"Hey, boss. Everything cool?"

"Yeah, but look, tonight I want you to grab a few men and go to Sparkles. When you get there, I want you to teach the owner, Sam, a lesson."

"What kind of lesson? A permanent one?"

"Naw, but one he'll never forget. And make sure he knows the message is from me."

When she arrived at the funeral, she said her good-byes and buried the part of her life Dyson still owned. To her, it was time for the next chapter; and a part of her hoped her new friend, BW, would be in it.

There's an old saying, "Be careful what you wish for."

Present time

"I'm here, Black. Where are you?"

"I'm comin'. Just wait," he says before ending the call.

As I look at the phone, my mind wanders. He's different with me, and I'm afraid. As I sit in my car, I examine my features in the mirror. I wonder if he's going to reject me, and I pray that the beauty he told me I possessed would be enough to keep him.

He drives up next to me and I move my Gucci purse from the passenger seat of my car.

"Come over here." I smile. "I got the heat on and it's warm inside."

"Get over here and stop fuckin' around," he says.

I pout and say, "I'm comin' now."

I reluctantly get into his black Yukon and wait on his words. "What's up, BW?" I look into his eyes. "Is everything okay?"

"Naw . . . I gotta be real wit you 'bout some things."

My heart races.

"I can't fuck wit you no more. It's over."

"Huh? Why?" I'm confused at how he's talking to me. It's like he doesn't care—like we hadn't made love almost every day since we met. "Did I do somethin' wrong?"

"I'm just not feelin' the situation no more, Kenyetta." His stare is cold. "You got some good pussy and all, but you holding back, so I got to let you go."

"Please don't do this. I need you, BW. Whatever you need me to be, I will be," I say, touching his knee.

"I need a full-time woman in my life." Instantly I know what he wants: a child.

"You know what I do, BW. I have the same responsibilities as you do. Having a baby right now doesn't work for me. I have an operation to run."

"And I don't?"

"I'm not sayin' that, baby. I'm just sayin' that now is not the time for me to have a child. Just give us some time to work, please. Don't leave me like this."

"It's over, Kenyetta," he says coldly.

"Please . . . don't leave me!"

"I said it's over. . . . Now get the fuck out of my car."

I try to touch him and he pushes me away again. His rejection stings, and I don't know what to do or what to feel. And to think, I'm losing him because I don't want to have a child.

"Is it somebody else?" I ask softly, trying not to disobey his wishes. "If there is I'll be better than her. Please."

"If I ask you to leave again, I'ma lay my hands

on you." He frowns. "Now get the fuck out of my car."

Gripping my fur coat, I'm disheartened as I push open the door and hop down. The moment my Jimmy Choos hit the curb, he pulls off. The mud from the melted snow dampens my coat.

"Don't leave. . . ."

He continues to drive away; his taillights grow dimmer the farther away he gets.

Immediately I open my phone lid and redial his number. He doesn't answer, so I run after his truck.

"BW, *please!* Don't leave me alone!" I hear my high heels sound off against the wet concrete. "I'm afraid to be alone! Don't leave me! *Pleassssse!*"

He doesn't stop, and I walk to my car. My pride and heart ache so much that I can't breathe. I need this man like I need the blood in my body to move. If all he wants is a baby, I'm willing to do what needs to be done to keep him.

Carissa

"Stay out my love life."

"I'm tired of your shit every time I come to Emerald! You know I have to be here, and nothin' has changed just 'cause we got back together."

"Well, what you expect, Carissa?" he says over the phone as I pull up to the community center. "So I'm gonna ask you again. What's up with our relationship, Car?"

"Lavelle, please! If you were so worried about me, you would've stood up for me when Thick made you choose between your family and the business. Or have you forgotten that shit already?" His silence answers my question. "That's exactly what I thought. Just kiss the girls for me, a'ight? I'll be home when I can."

The line goes silent and only the sounds of my boots hitting the pavement are heard. I'm a boss bitch, and boss bitches do what they must! He has to recognize that I'm not his little naïve girlfriend anymore.

"Carissa, how many times do I have to apologize for hurting you? I was wrong for lettin' Thick convince me to turn my back on you. And if you don't want me to care about you, we can just end shit right now."

I was about to respond when the call drops.

"Fuck!" I say out loud as I shake my phone and pray for a better signal to call Lavelle back. "I hate Sprint's service!"

"You a'ight?" Yvette asks, jumping up from the table as I enter the meeting. Mercedes is right by her side, with the same concerned look on her face.

"Yeah . . . I'm okay. It's Lavelle. He still trippin' 'bout me runnin' Emerald," I say, taking off my coat before joining my friends at the table. "He gotta get over it, though."

Yvette sits back down and says, "He just cares about you, Carissa. You might as well get used to it."

"That's some bullshit!" Mercedes yells. She is the only one out of my friends who is still angry over me and Lavelle getting back together. "He shoulda worried when they almost tried to kill us for taking Emerald from them. I'm sick of Cameron and Lavelle runnin' they mouths about what we should do around here."

"Mercedes, stay out my love life," I tell her. "'Cause I sure don't get into yours."

"I'm just bein' a friend, Carissa. I'm not the enemy. But if you have a problem wit me givin' my opinion, then don't worry 'bout it," she says as she pulls her long, silky ponytail toward the back. "I'll never do it again."

"Whateva, Mercedes!"

"Whateva, then!"

"What the fuck is goin' on?" Yvette asks in an even and steady tone. She looks between us. "Whatever's goin' on y'all betta end that shit right now. We done been through too much to be arguing over dumb shit. Now both of y'all have a point, but at the end of the day, we still family. I mean . . . ain't that what you guys just told me out in the yard? And, Mercedes, you should love her no matter who she wit, 'cause I would want y'all to treat me the same no matter who I love."

Yvette's statement is filled with conviction, and I feel she wants to say something else.

Mercedes giggles and says, "Well, if you had a man, we would treat you the same, but you gotta get one first, bitch!"

Yvette laughs and says, "Shut up, winch!"

Looking at me, Mercedes continues talking. "I'm sorry, Carissa."

"I'm sorry too," I tell her, managing a light smile.

I know where her apprehension comes from, and that's why I bite my tongue. But I love him, and he's my man—not to mention we have two little girls together. Lavelle has told me he can't live without me, and I believe him.

The night Thick was killed

Carissa, Yvette, Kenyetta, and Mercedes sat around the table laughing at their ex-boyfriends. The men found it hard to believe that Dreyfus, their former drug supplier, would deal with them, considering the lack of respect he had for women.

"Yeah . . . Dreyfus is somethin' else, isn't he?" Yvette said.

"Yes, he is . . . and he doesn't work wit females," Cameron added.

"Maybe . . . maybe not," Yvette told him. "All I know is he has a badass house. I'm telling you, the waterfall was outrageous. What did you think, Mercedes?"

"I don't know, Yvette," she said as she shrugged her shoulders. "I liked his head better. He can suck a mean pussy."

Cameron's face went red with anger. "Oh, so you fuckin' Dreyfus now?"

"Sit down, playa!" Derrick shouted. "Slow your roll."

Cameron looked up at him and sat back down.

"And where are my fucking kids while you out tossing pussy at that nigga? Huh? Where my kids?"

Mercedes laughed. "Don't worry, baby . . . they weren't there."

Cameron wanted to smack the shit out of Mercedes, but Lavelle pulled him back down.

"What makes you think we'd just walk away from a million-dollar empire?"

"For one, we've doubled the salary of our soldiers so they have our backs, and Dreyfus doesn't want to fuck wit you for your betrayal in Vegas," Yvette told them.

"Y'all told him about that?" Dyson asked.

"Of course!" Kenyetta laughed.

"And how did y'all know?" Cameron added.

"Let's just say y'all should choose the female company y'all take with you on business trips more wisely in the future," Yvette advised.

Lavelle shook his head in disgust.

"So y'all have a connection wit Dreyfus and now we're out, huh? Well, what about the money we put in this shit? We ain't walkin' away empty-handed," Dyson said.

With that, Yvette snapped her fingers and one of the soldiers placed a stainless-steel suitcase on the table. She popped open the latches, looked at the money, and turned it around to them.

"It's all there," Yvette assured them, sliding the case across the table.

They looked at each other, visibly shook.

"Well, what'll happen if we don't buy this shit?" Cameron asked.

"Then you'll end up like Thick," Yvette responded.

"And how's that?" Lavelle asked.

Yvette looked around the table. "Dead."

They jumped up from their seats and pulled

out weapons as the women's soldiers placed three barrels to their heads apiece.

"Don't make this nastier than it has to be. You did us wrong, and you know it. Now it's time to step down," Yvette said. "Either way, somebody loses, but don't forget about the kids involved. If you don't step down, somebody will get killed because we won't stop fighting until the last breath leaves our bodies. And that could mean Lil C without a mother or father. Or what about Lavelle's kids? Everybody loses if these guns pop in here tonight."

"Y'all have other shops. Y'all don't need EC," Carissa said.

The looks on their faces were defeat, remorse, and guilt. They knew they had done the women wrong and they deserved Emerald City. No, fuck that—they *earned* it! The men also knew if they didn't step down, the women were fully prepared for war.

"So what's up? Do you step down or not?" Yvette pushed.

They looked at each other and grabbed the money off the table, without saying a word.

"That was a good decision," Yvette said. "Now can you do us one more solid?"

"And what the fuck is that, Yvette?" Cameron responded, still not believing everything that took place.

"Take your dead friend with you. He's up in my apartment."

When the men left, the women spent twenty

more minutes inside before exiting the building, arm in arm.

"We did it, girls," Yvette said as the cold air hit them outside. "We fought and we won!"

"Yvette, you so fucking smart! You knew this shit would work," Carissa said. "But how were you sure?"

"I wasn't. It was a big chance, but I was willing to take it," she said.

"Are you sure your face is okay?" Kenyetta asked. "That cut looks pretty deep."

"It ain't deeper than the hurt I felt by Thick's betrayal."

"And how you doing with that situation? Mentally, I mean. We know how much you loved him, in spite of himself," Mercedes asked.

"It hurts. Thick was the first and only man I'd ever been with. I'm fucked up, but what can I do? Let him disrespect me and then my friends? Naw," she said, shaking her head. "I couldn't see that. I had to push off, and what's done is done."

There was silence amongst them as they moved to the blue Suburban waiting to take them home. Four armed men guarded the truck.

"But did you guys see the looks on their faces?" Mercedes laughed.

"Yeah . . . they were crushed," Kenyetta responded.

"They should've thought about that before they did us dirty," Mercedes added. "And what about Cameron yelling, 'What about my kids?

Who had my kids?' He sounded so stupid!"
They all laughed.

"Oh shit!" Carissa said from nowhere. "I left
my keys in the community center."

"We'll all go back," Yvette said as they stopped
before reaching the truck. "We have to stick together."

"No, we don't." She giggled. "We won! It's
over now. Anyway, you can see the door from
here. So get inside the warm truck, pop the bottle of champagne, and pour my glass. We'll celebrate when I come back out."

"You sure you don't want one of the soldiers
goin' wit you?" Mercedes persisted.

"I'm sure," Carissa said, tapping her arm and
jogging back inside. "It'll only take me a second."

She ran to the office, where she had left her
keys. Once she had them, she was on her way
out, when she saw Lavelle standing in the doorway.

"Carissa, I have to talk to you."

He looked like the life had been drained
from his body. Carissa was angry that she was
there alone.

"If you hurt me, they'll see you, Lavelle. You
won't make it outta here alive!"

"I don't want to hurt you, baby."

"Well, what do you want, Lavelle?"

"*You.* I want *you,* baby. I'm sorry for all the
shit I put you through. If you leave me, I don't
know what I will do. I don't think I want to live

without you," he said, grabbing her hands. "Do you want me to die? Is that what you want?"

Carissa's heart pounded and her stomach churned. She recalled the hurt in his eyes as they sat at the table. Although everyone else looked at Yvette during the meeting, Lavelle and Carissa maintained their stare upon each other. She felt his pain, and he felt hers. They both wondered how they'd gotten themselves into a situation where their relationship was on the line.

"I'm sorry. I can't, Lavelle." She snatched her hands away from him. "It's over."

She was preparing to leave him when she heard a small thud. Turning around, she saw Lavelle on his knees with a gun to his head. *Pop!* Lavelle pulled the trigger and Carissa ran up to him.

"What are you doin'?" she screamed as she tried to take the weapon from him.

"I told you that if you leave me, none of this shit matters." He was preparing to pull the trigger again, until she wrapped her arms around him.

"Please, Lavelle. I do love you, but you hurt me so much. I don't want you to do this. *Please.*"

"You don't give a fuck about me, so why should I?"

Click.

"*Lavelle!* Don't do this! I wanted nothing more than to be with you. Why did you have to do this to me and our family?" she said as his head rested firmly on her stomach. He wrapped his arms around her tiny waist, gun still in his hand.

"I was a fool"—he wept—"a fuckin' fool, and I'm sorry, baby girl. Let me do all the things I said I'd do for you, and more. I can be the man you need me to be, I promise!"

Carissa listened, but she wondered about his recent suicide attempt. She doubted if it was real and that any bullets had been placed inside the gun.

"Okay," she said softly. "I'll give you another chance."

"For real?" he said, standing up with his hands resting strongly on her shoulders.

"Yes . . . okay. But you have to be slow with me, Lavelle. I'm not the woman I used to be. This game has changed me. You have changed me," she said, taking the gun from his hand, removing the clip next.

Carissa stumbled.

It was loaded.

"Lavelle, there are bullets in this gun."

"You thought I was playin'? I don't want to live without you!"

"Lavelle," she cried, wrapping her arms around him. "What about our daughters? You were gonna kill yourself and leave our girls?"

"I need all of you. But if I can't have you too, I don't want to live."

They spent a few more moments together; then she warned him to wait before leaving the building. If the soldiers saw him coming out, they wouldn't hesitate to shoot him.

"I'll stay behind," he said, kissing her again. "I snuck back through the side door after getting rid of Thick's body. I just had to see you before I left. Can we talk tonight?"

"Yes. But don't leave right now."

"You've made me a happy man."

"I hope I'm not making a mistake."

"You're not, Carissa. You're not."

When Carissa turned down the hallway to leave him, she ran into Yvette, who had heard everything.

"So how long have you been waiting?"

"Long enough. When you didn't come back out, I came looking for you."

"Yvette, I'm so sorry," Carissa said softly.

"Don't be. I can tell you still love him. But if he hurts you, I need you to know that I won't hesitate on killing him. Can you handle that?"

"I would have to."

"Cool, 'cause that's on my life. So, are you sure?"

"Yes."

"Well, it's settled," Yvette said, hugging her. "Congratulations."

Yvette kept Carissa's secret until Carissa finally decided to reveal it to the rest of the Emerald City women, who actually had known all along. It was the last time Carissa said she'd ever lie to her friends.

Present

"Anybody seen Kenyetta? She's never late for a meeting," Yvette says, jumping back on topic. "We have a lot to discuss tonight."

Right before we answer, Kenyetta runs through the door, obviously disoriented.

"I'm sorry I'm late," she says, sitting down. "It won't happen again." She looks at the confused expressions on our faces. "Please don't ask me what's wrong with me." Her head drops and she wipes her face with her hands. "I'm not in the mood right now."

Yvette shrugs her shoulders and says, "All right, let's get started. Where are we with supply, Mercedes?"

"I did a check before I got here, and the soldiers are stocked and supplied. The stash houses look good for at least another week. Then we have to connect with Dreyfus again."

"Cool. Any security issues I should know about?" Yvette questions Kenyetta.

Visibly upset, Kenyetta takes a deep breath and says, "The guards at the gate said that a cop came through here the other night chasin' Aleed. But they shut down the entire operation so the cop didn't find him or anything else."

"A cop came on Emerald grounds?" I ask.

"Yeah, I said the same thing. But you know the Emerald City crew ran his ass outta here. They think he was a rookie, because the vets know the rules. 'Don't bother us, and we won't bother you.' "

"Wow," Mercedes says, shaking her head. "I'm glad he had enough sense to roll out. The squad won't hesitate to kill a cop."

"We don't ever want shit to get that far," Yvette reminds us. "That's unnecessary drama."

"I agree. The vet cops give us our space. But if one of their own gets killed, all bets are off," Kenyetta says. "We won't be able to make no money round here."

"Exactly," I respond.

"But other than that incident, the fort has been tight," Kenyetta concludes.

"Good. Did everybody get paid yesterday?" Yvette asks me.

"Yep . . . Derrick made sure all the soldiers got hit off. So stop worryin'."

"Don't be too cocky, Carissa. Somethin' could happen at any moment. Just 'cause things look peaceful, it don't mean there ain't haters amongst us. I got word back the other day that a few heavy hitters in Northwest are out for us," Yvette says.

"You already know that. This is *the* most profitable operation in D.C. Wit the relationships we built, and the cops we have on payroll, we virtually unstoppable," Kenyetta says.

"Exactly, and that's why we're a target," Yvette responds.

"Be for real, Yvette. Somebody might try us on the outside, but ain't nobody crazy enough to come in Emerald," Mercedes adds.

"Is your ponytail too tight?" Yvette asks. "We

should never be caught slippin'. *Ever!* It's better to be safe than sorry."

I agree with what Yvette is saying, but I also understand Mercedes' point. We did everything possible to ensure our operation ran smoothly—from hiring extra lookouts to having our soldiers sent to the gun range twice a month for training. We had more soldiers on payroll than any other project except Tyland. Our fort was tight.

The moment the thought enters my mind, we hear gunfire outside. We jump to our feet.

"Fuck was that?" I ask, with my hand resting firmly on my nine-millimeter piece.

"Wait a minute. Let me call Derrick," Yvette says as we put on our coats.

Derrick is in charge of security. He is good at it because his men respect how he works side by side with them.

"Derrick, what's goin' on?" Yvette asks on her speaker Boost phone.

"We about to see now. Is everybody okay?"

"Yeah, we fine."

"Everybody?" he repeats.

"Mercedes is here and she's fine, Derrick. Just let us know what's up."

"Okay," he answers, exhaling. "I'ma find out what's goin' on and I'll get back wit you. Yvette, let me handle this, okay?"

"I'm gonna let you handle it, but you know I have to be involved."

"I know, just give me a head start. That's what you hired me for."

"Like I said . . . I still have to be involved."

"A'ight . . . I'll hit you when I know some-thing," he says, hanging up.

"What you think is up?" Kenyetta asks Yvette.

"I don't know, but I think we gonna find out."

It has been years since shots rang in Emerald City that are unrelated to our handing down the law. As I follow my friends to the door—all of us draped in fur coats—something in my spirit tells me things are about to change for the worse. And to think, Yvette just said not to be caught slippin'. I guess that's why she's the boss.

Emerald City

Lani & Sachi

"That's for fuckin' wit my man, bitch!"

"I knew you wouldn't be able to find his pass code!" Sachi says as she sits in the chair next to her twin sister, Lani, at the computer station.

Two huge canopy beds sit in the middle of the room, which is dressed completely in pink. The girls have everything they desire, including a sixty-two-inch plasma TV and a twenty-two-inch Apple MacBook. Their father, Craig, sells drugs and lavishes his girls with everything they want.

Developed way beyond their years, twins Sachi and Lani are head turners. With tiny breasts, small waists, and large, round butts, they are the envy at school. To add to their mystique, the twins both have long, golden, naturally curly hair.

Sachi and Lani live in Emerald City with their

mother, Margaret, and their father, Craig. Although Craig is of the street and always on them, Margaret is also always gone. (She is having an affair with her mother's new husband, and no one knows.) And since the parents are never home, the girls are always out of control.

"Shut the fuck up, Sachi! Here it goes, right here," she says as she hits the enter button and gains access to her boyfriend Lil C's Facebook account. "I betta not find out he's fuckin' around either."

"And if he is, what you gonna do?" Sachi teases. "Take him back as usual?"

"Not this time. C be checkin' for me way more than I be checkin' for him." She continues writing down his pass code on the paper next to their computer.

When Lani reads his messages, she's devastated when she sees one from her best friend, Jona. The message reads: **Lil C, i hope u liked how i sucked u off at my house yesterday. your cum tastes like my favorite candy. if you want me to do it again, just stop by before you go 2 Lani's. call me first so i can make sure my mother not home. i hope you can cum again. you gonna be mine, 2. i don't care what you say.**

"Oh shit! I should fuck that bitch up!" Sachi says, covering her mouth. She paces the room in a burgundy Juicy Couture set. "She a snake!"

Lani rises like a zombie and exits her apartment in Unit D. Marching toward Jona's apartment, which is a few doors down, she can't wait to give her a piece of her mind. The pink Baby

Phat velour sweat suit she's wearing seems like a blur in a hallway full of people. Her sister is right by her side.

"Don't do nothin' first, Lani! Let me smack her ass!"

Lani bangs on Jona's door forcefully and steps back. She cracks her knuckles, and Sachi jumps up and down anxiously. Sachi loves trouble.

"What the fuck . . . ," Jona says, flinging the door open.

When the door opens, Lani steps up and shoves the pen, which she used to write Lil C's pass code down, into her stomach.

"Owwwwww!" Jona screams, gripping her belly.

Once she falls, Sachi kicks her multiple times in the stomach and face with her black UGGS.

"That's for fuckin' wit my man, bitch!" Lani says.

"Dusty bitch! You betta be glad we ain't kill you!" Sachi adds.

Lil C and his friend Nicholas, who looks like a young Snoop Dogg, step off the elevator. Lil C sees Lani and Sachi leaving Jona's apartment; he does a double take when he sees Jona crying on the filthy floor in front of her door. Lil C, who looks like a young Al B. Sure, stands in shock. The neighbors crowd in the hallway.

"Aye, what the fuck happened?" Lil C asks, his curly hair peeking under his fitted New York Yankees cap.

Lil C is dressed warmly in an extra-large blue North Face coat. Nicholas has on a red Eddie Bauer one.

"Damn! Shortie fucked up!" Nicholas says, taking his black knit hat off and revealing his soft, bushy hair.

"Lil C, don't start wit me, 'cause this all your fault. So you betta get in here before I go off on you too," Lani promises in front of her door.

Lil C and Nicholas take one last look at Jona and follow the girls inside.

"Why are you trippin'?" Lil C takes off his cap. "You lucky I didn't go off on you in the hallway. But I ain't want my moms gettin' in the business." He wasn't supposed to be in Emerald, to begin with.

"So you fuckin' my best friend now?" Lani screams, ignoring him. "I told you if I caught you cheating, I would go off. So this is your fault!"

Although he likes her for her spiciness, right now she is irritating him.

"First off, calm down," Lil C says calmly. He always maintains his coolness.

"Let me know what you wanna do," Nicholas says, with his coat still on. "If you ain't up for this, we can roll right now."

"You ain't goin' nowhere," Sachi says to Nicholas, jumping on his lap. Whenever he comes over, they keep each other company.

"C, why are you fuckin' my best friend? I bet everybody in school knows it!"

"I don't know what you talkin' about."

"So you don't know what 'fucking' means now?"

"She saw the Facebook account, Cameron. So

you might as well stop lying," Sachi says as she and Nicholas turn on *106 & Park*.

"Mind your business 'cause you 'bout to make shit worse for your sister." He turns and looks at Lani, then says, "I ain't fuckin' wit that girl. So if that's why you did whatever you did to her, I sure hope you can handle the beef when her cousins find out."

"I ain't scared of no Tyland Towers hood rats!"

"I hope so, 'cause you know how they roll."

"What about how you roll?" Lani grabs Lil C's hand and leads him to her bedroom, pointing at the computer screen.

"Busted!" she says, with her hand on her hips. "Explain to me why she messagin' you?" she asks, pointing her manicured, red-polished nail at him.

Lil C is mad at himself for not deleting his messages. "If I ask you again to lower your voice, I'm outta here." He is trying to figure out how she got his pass code, not realizing his birthday would be the first thing she'd try. "And I ain't fuck her. She sucked my dick. There's a difference."

"Boy, are you crazy!" Lani screams.

"You know what?" he says, leaving her room. "I'm gone."

She runs behind him. "Be a man, Cameron! Don't be a pussy! If you got caught, say you got caught!"

"Nick, you ready? Lani's ass is trippin' and I ain't got time for this shit."

Nicholas pushes Sachi off his lap and stands up. "Let's roll." He places his hat on his head.

"Cameron, why are you leavin'?" Lani cries as they walk toward the door.

He attempts to pull open the door, which won't open, and she grabs his arm.

"Get off of me, Lani," he says, looking into her eyes. "Don't make me hurt you."

"Just tell me the truth." She is sobbing. "All I want you to do is tell the truth."

Lani's pain goes deeper than what Lil C realizes. With her father being in the street, and her mother never being home, she leans on him for emotional support. He has been the only person, other than her sister, whom she could rely on. In her eyes, he takes care of her, and she doesn't want to lose his love.

"I told you the truth."

"Cameron"—she weeps as tears run down her face and snot oozes from her nose—"I don't want to break up."

"It's over," he tells her.

Lani drops to the floor and goes berserk.

"Unlock this door, Sachi," he says, ignoring her antics.

"Fuck you, Cameron," Sachi responds as she bends down and rubs her sister's back. "Why you doin' this to my sister?"

Nicholas's phone rings and he steps to the side to take the call.

"Open this door, shortie," Cameron demands sternly. "I told y'all to stop lockin' us in here, anyway. Who the fuck locks a door with a key from the inside?"

"Not until you apologize, Cameron!"

"That was Ryan," Nicholas informs C. "They say they got the stuff."

"Already?" Lil C raises his eyebrows. He sold weed at school behind his parents' backs.

"I know, right? He wasn't jokin' when he said he could come through."

"That's what's up." He smiles. "Uh, Sachi, I'ma need you to let us out now. We got shit to do."

"All you care about is sellin' drugs! While you out there, you need to know she's pregnant. Now what's up?"

The room is silent for a moment.

"Pregnant?" he says, looking down at Lani.

"Yes! And you the father!" Sachi adds.

"Why you say somethin', Sachi?" Lani asks, wiping away her tears.

" 'Cause he need to know!"

"Is it true? You havin' my kid?"

"Why? It ain't like you care! All you wanna do is fuck my best friends!"

He is about to speak, when gunfire rings outside. The first person he thinks about is his mother.

"Damn! What was that?" Nicholas asks, looking toward the window.

"I gotta call my peoples," Lil C says, removing his cell phone from his pocket.

"Who?"

"My moms." He is preparing to speed-dial her number.

"Hold up! You not supposed to be in Emerald." Nicholas stops him. "If you call her, she's gonna know you're here."

He places the phone back in his pocket reluctantly. First he finds out his girl is pregnant; now shots ring out in his mother's kingdom. The day isn't going as planned; but what he doesn't realize, it is about to get worse.

Emerald City

"If somethin' happens, I'm holdin' you both personally responsible."

Derrick rushes out of the Unit C apartment he has in Emerald City. His heavy blue North Face coat is filled with a Desert Eagle and Glock 9mm, loaded and ready for action. When he enters the hallway, people are standing around. They're all looking nervous about the gunshots.

"What's goin' on, Derrick?" asks an elderly lady. Her red cat walks out of her apartment and into the hallway. Although she despises the idea of drugs being sold in Emerald, she takes comfort in how safe things have become since the girls took over. "I heard shots and I'm worried. Are the girls okay?"

"Everything's okay, Miss Key," he says, picking up her cat and handing it to her. "Try not to worry."

The woman grabs her furry cat and looks to him for more information. But Derrick moves through the hallway and toward the elevator, feeling more like a policeman than a dealer.

"Are you sure, son?" Miss Key calls to him.

"Positive," he says confidently.

"Don't lie to her!" yells the crazy old man down the hall. He always rants and raves about the future and the danger that will come to Emerald. "This is the start of hell here on earth! And it's all you drug bangers' faults!"

"Get yo old ass down the hall and stop trippin!" Derrick says. He looks directly at the vocally opinionated man, who is dressed in a brown pair of khaki pants, with a white wife beater. His nipples peek out on the sides. "Don't nobody wanna hear that shit!"

"It's true! Everyone's goin' to hell!"

Derrick ignores him and waits impatiently for the elevator. "Fuck!" he says, pushing the button to the elevator again. It isn't coming fast enough for him.

"Derrick, is everybody okay?" asks Bucky, a beautiful, dark-skinned girl, who has been trying to get with him for the longest. Although it is cold outside, she chooses to walk into the hallway wearing a tight pair of blue-jean shorts, with a ripped-up T-shirt. Every curve on her body is defined and exposed. " 'Cause I heard gunshots and I'm scared."

"Everything's cool. And you not scared, so stop faking," he tells her, trying not to look at her thick thighs and fat ass.

"I don't know why you think I'm so strong," she says, touching his arm. "If I had you, though, I wouldn't have to worry."

"Well, you don't got me," he says, shaking his head. Bucky stares him down, licking her lips.

"Not now, but I will," she responds, wiggling toward her apartment.

Derrick is relieved when the elevator finally opens. When he gets downstairs, his men are waiting.

"What happened?" he asks Bruce, Paul, Harold, and Ed as they follow him to the building's door.

"We were out here on post, when somebody said some niggas was tryin' to come through the gate. Next thing I know, the Unit B crew starts bustin' off. I ain't seen nothin' else, 'cause we ran upstairs to get you."

Derrick's phone rings; it's Mercedes. "What's up?"

"Is everything cool?" she asks.

"Naw . . . somethin' is up," he tells her. "Maybe you should go home until everything blows over." He knows she won't leave.

"We on our way out," she says, hanging up.

"Let's go to the guard's station," he tells his men.

When they get there, they see blood pouring from the large window of the guard's station. There is broken glass and meaty matter everywhere. They all aim and walk closer. They see Jake murdered and the gate left unsecure. All that remains is a uniformed body with no head. He wonders how many outsiders are in the city.

"Bruce . . . I want you and Paul to stay right here and watch the gate. Don't let nobody come through you don't know. I'ma have somebody get Jake out of here."

"Got it!" Bruce says, stealing a few looks at the bloody carnage.

"Harold and Ed, y'all come with me."

"Let me and Ed watch the gate," Harold suggests.

"Yeah . . . we got it!" Ed chimes in.

"What you sayin'? I won't watch the city right?" Bruce responds.

"Naw, but we know you won't watch the city like we will."

"A'ight, y'all got it, but if somethin' happens, I'm holdin' you both personally responsible." They nod in agreement. "Come on," Derrick says to Bruce and Paul.

Looking up to the rooftop, Derrick notices something is out of order. Where are the sharpshooters? Where are the soldiers in the field? Safety has been breached and Emerald City is in major jeopardy. Times are changing . . . for the worse.

Yvette

"We should've never abandoned our posts."

"How this happen?" I ask Derrick as we stand on the steps of Unit C.

The soldiers are back in position in the field, and the shooters are back on the roof. By the look of things, it appears that Emerald City is in order, but the trained eye can tell that things are far from normal.

"I talked to Aleed and a few others. They said a van packed with a rack of niggas pulled up, trying to get in, but Jake wouldn't open the gate. They said one of the niggas got out, ran up to him, and fired. Jake couldn't even call and warn us. After that, one of the dudes in the van opened the guard's station and then the gate. They all ran in after that."

"Where were the shooters on the roof?" Mercedes asks.

"They said everyone on our crew ran after the men, including the rooftop soldiers. Aleed told me about twenty dudes got in. When they looked for the men, they were gone. It's like they disappeared into the walls of the city."

"The soldiers in the field left post too?" I ask.

"Everybody went after these cats, Yvette. It's fucked up, but it's true," he says, dropping his head.

"This was a fuckin' setup!" I say, walking away from them momentarily. "They knew if they ran through, we'd leave the gate empty and abandon our posts. We should've never abandoned our posts, Derrick!"

"I know," he says, "but what else could they do? Just let 'em run in without *trying* to do something?"

"He's right, Yvette," Mercedes says.

"I know it's fucked up, but we never had a situation like this happen, and the men weren't prepared. I take responsibility for that. But trust . . . it'll never happen again," Derrick responds.

I know what he is saying is true, but it doesn't eliminate our problem.

"You think they still here?" Carissa asks.

"I know they are," I say, looking around. I feel violated.

"What now?" Mercedes asks.

"Let's question the neighbors. They might not tell the cops if they seen somethin', but they'll tell us. We just have to make sure we protect them."

I am still talking to my crew when Chris walks outside the building. She looks worried and my heart drops when I see her coming straight for me.

"Who the fuck is this dyke?" Mercedes asks. "I see her all the time, but she ain't always live here."

"Yeah . . . I was thinkin' the same thing," Carissa adds. "Fuckin' carpet-munchin'–ass bitch probably got somethin' to do wit this shit."

Although concrete can't melt, I feel as if I'm sinking into the steps. Not only are my friends talking about her like she is less than human, something about their words makes me feel dirty.

"Yvette, you okay?" Chris asks, moving toward me. "What's goin' on?"

"Bitch, you betta back the fuck up!" Kenyetta says, blocking her from approaching me and extending her hands out in front of her. "I don't know who you are, but you in the wrong place, at the wrong time."

"Look, I'm not tryna hurt her. I'm just tryna make sure she's a'ight."

I can't move or talk. I always wondered if she ever approached me while I was with my friends, how I'd handle it. I guess I know now.

"Yvette, you not gonna say nothin'?" Chris says. "You not gonna tell 'em?"

Derrick's eyes widen as he examines the situation. He has his hand on his heat. "Excuse me, right now is not the time," he declares. "So why don't you just go upstairs before things get out of hand."

Chris looks at him hard at first; then suddenly her expression softens. "Oh . . . a'ight . . . as long as everything cool," she says, looking at me again. "I wasn't tryna cause no trouble. Lada, Yvette." She walks away.

"Yvette, you know her?" Mercedes questions as Chris enters the building.

"Yeah, she acted like she knew you," Kenyetta adds.

"No, I don't know her," I lie, denying the love of my life.

Only when she walks away do I breathe again. I can't help but wonder if I lost for good the best thing that has ever happened to me.

Kenyetta

What I am doing is fucked up!

"Where you go, Kenyetta?" Mercedes asks as I pull up to the damaged guard's station, trying to reenter Emerald. "We were lookin' for you everywhere."

Ed and Harold stand guard while she talks to me.

"I know," I say, hoping my secret doesn't reveal himself in the backseat of my car, concealed behind tinted windows. "I just needed to get away for a minute."

"Well, you can't be doin' shit like that right now," she says. "We're at war, Kenyetta. Yvette is out lookin' for you right now."

"Tell her I'm cool. But look, let me go inside and I'll be back out in a little."

"You sure you cool?"

Harold and Ed look at me, smirk, and laugh. I wonder what that means.

"Yeah, I'm fine. Really."

I pull off before she can object, causing the sound of my wheels rolling on the gravel and dirt to penetrate my betrayal. What I am doing is fucked up! I'm bringing a member of the Tyland Towers crew onto Emerald City grounds. What surprises me the most is that he agreed to lie hidden under a thick blanket as I drove through our gates and behind Unit B.

When we park, I get out and he follows minutes later as we enter my apartment. I make him wear a hoodie to conceal his face. Once inside, I say, "Make yourself comfortable. I'ma get cleaned up."

"You know this some gangsta shit, right?" he says, taking off his hood.

I smile. "Give me a minute, baby." I gently kiss his mouth and leave.

When I come out of the bathroom ten minutes later, he's stretched out in my bed.

"You gonna stare, or are you gonna come over here and lay down next to me?" he asks, stroking his hard dick. He got comfortable real quick.

"I'm comin', baby," I say seductively.

For some reason, as I walk slowly toward him, I grow nervous. My mind says this is not something I should do, but my heart and body call for him. When I make it to the bed, I ease on top of him. He grabs my waist and pulls me onto him until my pussy surrounds his dick like a glove. My head falls back as he pushes into me.

"Damn, Kenyetta," he moans. "Why this pussy wet already?"

I don't tell him that I played with my pussy before coming out to get in the mood. I didn't want to risk having painful sex because of not being able to get into the act. After all, I'm betraying my best friends.

"You gonna carry my seed, Kenyetta?" he says, looking at me.

"Yes," I say as I push down so hard, not even air could pass between where our bodies connect. "I'ma carry your baby."

We go at it for about an hour, and my pussy is raw. BW never did cum right away. I decide to step up my dirty talk, to bring him closer to ecstasy.

"Fuck this pussy, baby!"

"You want me to fuck it?"

"Yeah . . . I want you to fuck the shit out of this wet pussy!"

"You sexy-ass bitch! I'ma knock the walls out of this shit!"

"Fuck me, daddy! Fuck your little girl!"

That really does it for him, because he shakes, and I know he's about to cum. As he's preparing to ejaculate inside me, I get scared. I can't do this! I can't have his baby. My friends don't even know about him yet, and he hasn't committed himself to me.

"Do you belong to me?"

"W-what?" he replies, on the verge of busting his creamy load inside my body.

"I said, are you mine?"

When he doesn't respond, I lift off him and sit by his side. Not trying to lose the sensation, he jerks himself until his sperm rests on his stomach.

With his breaths still heavy, he says, "So you playin' games now?"

"No!" I say, shaking my head. "Look at what I risked by bringing you here."

"Why did you bring me here if you weren't gonna do what you said?" He frowns.

" 'Cause you said this was the only way you'd be back with me. I want to be with you, Black." I touch his leg. "I just need to be sure you're mine before I have this baby."

"The baby gonna be takin' care of, Kenyetta." He sits up in the bed and rests the back of his head against the wall.

"I'm not concerned about that. We both have money, but I want to be sure you'll be in the baby's life."

"If I have a kid wit you, trust me, I'm gonna be in the kid's life. Trust me."

"What about me? Would you always be in my life?"

"I take care of all my kids' mothers. Trust me."

Did he just say, "All my kids' mothers"? Far as I know, he doesn't have any kids.

"What do you mean by 'all of my kids' mothers'?"

"Look, what you wanna do? I'm sick of playin' games."

"You never told me you had kids."

"I'm outta here," he says, standing up to get dressed. "I'm riskin' my life and now you gonna renege on a promise?"

"I don't mean to renege on anything, but you never told me you had a family."

"Kenyetta, don't call me until you serious." He storms out of my apartment.

My head drops in frustration and I wonder about everything he's ever said to me. I am so confused that I forget he can't be seen leaving my apartment or the building. As a member of Tyland Towers, he would be killed *instantly* if spotted, especially with everything that's happening now. I hop off the bed and rush toward the living room. And when I open the apartment, I see Yvette standing in my doorway.

"You a'ight?" she asks.

Sweat pours down my face and I push past her to look out the door.

"Kenyetta, are you a'ight?" she repeats, following my stare.

"Oh . . . yeah . . . uh . . . I'm fine," I say, glancing down the hallway. I see no signs of him and walk back inside. "What's up?"

"Did Mercedes tell you I been lookin' for you?" she asks, standing in the doorway.

"Yes."

"Well?"

"Well, what?"

"We waitin' on you at Unit C, Kenyetta. Why you not there?"

"I'm sorry, Yvette. I got in here and got turned around. But I'm comin' now."

"Are you sure?" She looks at my negligee. "It looks like you 'bout to go to sleep."

"Oh . . . no . . . I was just taking a quick nap. I'm fine now."

"A nap? Now?"

"Yes. But just give me a few minutes. I'll be down."

"We need you to be focused, Kenyetta. A lot of shit happenin'. And something tells me people we think we can trust are hidin' them niggas on our grounds. Are you wit us or not?"

"Don't ask what you already know."

"Well, prove it."

I exhale and say, "I'll meet you at Unit C, Yvette. Just give me a few moments."

"A'ight," she says. "Call me if you need me."

When she leaves, I close the door and lean up against it. Sliding to the floor, I try to regain my composure. Ever since Dyson left me, I've been afraid to be alone. Afraid to live my life. Dyson took care of me and protected me, even with all of our problems.

Still, I know BW is not the man for me. He's a liar. Being by myself so long has given me some time to see clearer. I'll say this, I will never love another again. *Ever.* Love doesn't work for me, and it's best not to care.

Black Water

"They have loyalty to no one."

Black hurriedly walks away from Kenyetta's apartment before she can spot him. He had planned to enter Emerald, anyway, with his men in the van. He needed to see the layout of the city for *himself,* to be able to plan his attack. So when Kenyetta said she wanted to see him, he pressed the issue about it being tonight, knowing she was there. He couldn't get inside any safer than having an Emerald City boss herself drive him in.

Black Water arrives at Harold's door and knocks twice; the hood of his jacket is still on. One of his Tyland Towers crew members opens the door and he walks inside. All of his men are present. Although the twenty men have been inside for only a couple of hours, the smell from the small apartment sickens his stomach.

"Fuck took you so long to answer the door?" he asks Jam J, after slapping him upside the head.

"Owww!" He rubs his head. "I opened it the moment you knocked."

"Next time, move quicker. Somebody coulda spotted me. Everybody, get the fuck off the couch!" Once the space is clear, he sits down. "So tell me, what's up?" Black says, looking at everyone.

Most of his men are young and expendable. He doesn't care if he's lost one of their lives. His best men are still in Tyland, safe and sound.

"Forty Deuce and Money Marter got shot. Them Emerald City boys got 'em when we were trying to get in," Cristal, the youngest member, says.

"Where are they now?"

"Red was fuckin' wit some chick in this building, so she drove them to the hospital."

"They have any problem gettin' out the gate?"

"Naw . . . Harold on duty."

"Cool, what y'all know 'bout this bitch?"

"Who? Red's girl?" Jam J asks.

"Naw, your mother's bitch!" Black Water yells. The men chuckle.

"Oh . . . far as I know, she cool. I think her name is Goldie or somethin'."

"Okay, I'ma have Harold kill her when she gets back. No witnesses. And after Emerald's mine, I'ma kill Harold and Ed 'cause they have loyalty to no one."

Jam J nods his head in agreement. "So what's the plan?" he asks.

"I'ma need three of you tonight. And the rest of you are gonna lay low for a couple of days. Harold and Ed gonna make sure you greedy muthafuckas get whatever you need to eat. And when it's time, we move to plan B."

"Okay," Jam J says as the other men nod.

"Hey, boss . . . how you get in?" Cristal asks.

"I convinced one of the bitches of Emerald City Squad to let me fuck her in her crib. She drove me right through the gate." Black Water chuckles.

"Damn! Which one was it?" Jam J questions. " 'Cause I'd fuck any one of 'em."

"Don't worry 'bout all that. Just don't move an inch, unless you hear *my* word."

"We got it. How you gonna get out?" Jam J responds.

"Ed gonna meet me round back and ride me out."

He told them the plan for later that night. His plan would be the perfect diversion for him to leave Emerald's gates. When he was done giving orders, he thought about the original Emerald City Squad. *How in the fuck did they ever give up their project to these bitches? Taking Emerald is gonna be like taking candy from a baby.*

Picking up his phone, he decides to call Big Cameron. "I'm inside Emerald."

"That was quick."

"Once I make a decision to do something, I

move. And you were right about them dudes Harold and Ed. They looked out in a major way."

"Good. So what's your next move?"

"I gotta work some things out and then I'll get back at you."

"How long will that be?"

"Soon. Why? You havin' a change of heart, or somethin'?"

"No! I want this shit to go down, just like you do."

"So what's the problem?"

"I just want you to call me before you kill the girls."

"Why?"

"Just call me."

"You'll know before I do anything," Black Water tells him, with a smirk on his face.

He ends the call.

"Niggas need to know who they can trust before doin' business," Black says softly to himself. "A lesson this weak-ass nigga is about to learn."

Carissa

"You got a lot of growin' up to do, chic. We not kids no more."

The cold air rips through my body as I stand on the steps of Unit C. It has been a long time since we had to man our post ourselves. Even when we came back once a month, we always had our men watching over things for us. But with the recent turn of events, we didn't trust this job to anyone else.

As I look around the city, I already miss the five-bedroom home I share with Lavelle in Virginia. I'd become accustomed to luxurious living, and Emerald is far from my new reality.

"Kenyetta, that shit can't work," I tell her, looking at the tiny tube filled with yellow liquid.

"I'm telling you, it does. Just one drop will put a nigga straight out of his misery."

"When would you use some shit like that, and how did you get it?" I ask.

"You know I go to this acupuncturist," she explains. "She makes it herself. She says most of her clients use it to get some sleep, and two drops will put you out for two hours. But I'ma take eight drops. I need to get some rest."

"I don't know why." I laugh. "We won't be getting a lot of rest for the next couple of weeks."

"I know. . . . I'm talkin' about when I go home."

"What's on your mind that you want to be asleep for a whole day?"

"You can't even imagine," she says.

"So what up wit you and Lavelle?" Mercedes asks me.

"Do you really wanna know?" I sit on a metal chair and tuck my hands farther in my coat pockets.

"I wouldn't ask you if I ain't wanna know." Mercedes smiles, standing beside me.

"If you must know, Lavelle's still upset about me being here. And somebody hot boxed and told him 'bout the shootin' earlier."

"I wonder who said somethin'," Kenyetta responds.

"Who knows?" I shrug. "Whether y'all wanna believe it or not, some of our men still respect Lavelle and Cameron and keep in contact with them."

"I know. That's what bothers me," Kenyetta says.

"It shouldn't. It'd be the same way if you took over a company and kept the existing employees. Some people gonna like old management, and others gonna like the new ones. Some niggas actually think we don't run things as good as the guys did."

"Fuck that! Even when they was runnin' shit, we still ran shit! And let's not forget that we pay them better than they ever did for us. We good to them," Mercedes adds.

"Exactly," Kenyetta says. "Look how long we held shit down witout error. It's been years! I bet they ain't talkin' 'bout that shit."

"I wanna know why niggas stay in our business. We ain't foldin' now, and we not gonna fold later," Mercedes says, standing up. She looks around at all of the men we have standing in the field and on the roofs. "We too strong for that."

"Mercedes, have you forgotten about what happened earlier?" I remind her. "They ran right up in here wit nothing to stop them."

"Trial and error. We tight now, and it's back to business!" Mercedes says.

For some reason, Mercedes and me had been going at it a lot lately. I had a feeling she was jealous that Lavelle was the only one who kept his promise and remained true and loyal. I know she misses Cameron.

"You got a lot of growin' up to do, chic. We not kids no more. We mothers and we have responsibilities. Stop bein' so immature."

"I'm immature because I believe that Emerald will stay strong no matter what? I'm not ready to tuck tail and run at the first sign of danger."

"And neither am I!" I yell.

"Are you sure? 'Cause you sound weak right about now."

"Mercedes, all I'm sayin' is that we need to be

smart. I would die for Emerald if I had to, and I know you know that. But I don't wanna die over no stupid shit."

"Okay, Carissa. Whatever you say," she says, waving me off.

"Where's Yvette?" Kenyetta asks in an attempt to skip the subject.

"She said she had to go inside to get somethin' to eat," I say, still looking at Mercedes. She is workin' my nerves tonight. "But that was like an hour ago."

"Yeah, it has been a minute. Should we check on her?" Mercedes suggests.

"Naw. As long as three of us are here at a time, we good," I tell her.

"I wish somebody told me that when I went inside," Kenyetta complains, pouting. "Y'all acted like y'all was gonna die without me here."

"That was Vette," I say.

And all of a sudden, I notice the expression on one of our men on the rooftop. He looks horrified. I see him draw his gun from his waist, and I follow his stare. When I do, I see three men running quickly in our direction.

"Watch out!" I yell as I draw my weapon.

Kenyetta and Mercedes pull out theirs and we all start firing. The men on the roof and the ones in the field fire as well. Why would these suicidal niggas try us? Bullets ring from everywhere; before long, two of them fall. We continue to fire, when all of a sudden one of my girls yelps in pain.

"*Owwwwww!*" she yells.

Terrified, I can't bring myself to look at who it is. Filled with rage, I hop down the stairs, two and three at a time. I want his life—with disregard for my own.

"Boss, get outta the way!" one of the men yells from the roof.

I don't stop running until I'm directly in front of him. Bullets stop flying behind me too. I know they are trying to avoid hittin' me. I walk up to him, and there are warm tears streaming down my face. He's a kid, about nineteen or twenty years old, and he possibly killed my friend. When I look at his expression, he appears demented. He's on something, for sure. I raise my arm and my gun.

He laughs and says, "Fuck you, you crazy—"

Before he finishes, I fire and hit him in the center of his face. He falls. His blood splatters on my face and white Dior coat. At my feet, I watch the blood rush from his body. Not satisfied, I shoot him a few more times, until my gun can only produce a *click-click* sound.

It is my first time killin' someone, but I'm sure it won't be my last. When the high I felt from his death passes, I'm left with the horror of finding out which of my friends is injured. Or dead.

Turning around, I slowly take the walk toward the steps of Unit C. And all of a sudden, the sensation I felt when I lost Dex and Stacia overcomes me. Am I about to lose another friend? I feel light as I move, and it's as if I'm not walking anymore. The moment I take another step, I pass out on the ground.

Yvette

I should've never left my friends' sides.

"What you want me to do, Chris? I can't just up and tell people I'm a lesbian!" I cry as I watch her fold and pack her clothes on the kitchen table. My body feels like it's sinking into the large chocolate leather sofa I'm sitting on.

"Yvette, you ain't gotta do shit," she says, grabbing a folded shirt from the pile, placing it neatly in her suitcase. "You made your decision already."

When everything is packed, she walks toward the bathroom. I quickly follow.

"Chris, please . . . give me some time!" I say, grabbing her arm. "I can't just tell my friends about us overnight! I'm not like you! I haven't been gay all my life."

"Fuck off me, Yvette! You had two years to deal with being gay. But I know what it really is," she says, moving toward the living room to grab her coat from the closet.

"What is it?"

"You never had any intentions of telling them about us. You just wanted me to lick your pussy and stay under your bed like some fuckin' sex slave! That shit ain't for me! And that ain't for us! Find another sucka-ass bitch. I'm outta here!"

She is just about to leave when I hear multiple gunshots outside. It sounds like war is taking place in the yard. Rushing toward my table, I grab my Glock and push past Chris. I am so scared—I don't stop to grab my coat. It has to be about thirty degrees outside. My adrenaline is pumping, and suddenly the time I wasted on Chris feels stupid.

I decide against the elevator and take my chances running down the stairs. My heart races as I imagine the worst. I should've never left my friends' sides during one of the most dangerous times in Emerald. As I open the door to the building, the first person I see is Carissa being helped upstairs by two of our men. Her facial expression scares me and my heart sinks. Holding the pit of my stomach, I see Mercedes lying on the ground, with Kenyetta above her, crying.

"Mercedes!" I scream, rushing to her side. "How the fuck did this happen?"

The soldier in me wants answers, but my love for Mercedes prevents me from running through the city and shooting anybody with the slightest look of guilt on his face. Stooping down, I hover

over the top of her and hope that I'm giving her comfort by being beside her. Her eyes open and she looks scared.

"What happened, Kenyetta?" I ask.

"We were on the steps, and these niggas started runnin' toward us, firin'."

I'm so angry that my hand is shaking; I place my gun in the back of my pants to prevent myself from firing by mistake.

"Mercedes . . . where are you hit?"

"In my arm. It burns a little, but I'm fine."

I open the blue North Face coat she's wearing to check the wound. She moans a little in discomfort as blood pours from her body and onto the concrete.

"I can't watch this," Carissa says as she turns around.

Lifting up her T-shirt, I see her torn flesh in her upper arm.

"Oh shit, Yvette! We gotta call the ambulance," Kenyetta says.

"No! It'll be too hot," Mercedes replies. "Plus we have to get rid of the bodies."

"She's right. Let's get her to Old Lady Faye's house downstairs," I tell them as I motion for two of the guys to help pick her up. "Kenyetta, call the Vanishers and have them remove the bodies off the field."

The Vanishers are our best-kept secret. Whenever we want a body gone, they come in this beaten-up black van and take the body off Emerald City grounds. I don't know how they disposed of the remains, but the bodies were never found.

"Carissa, tell the lieutenants we have an emergency meeting in two hours at the community center. Shit is about to get serious around here."

"Huh?" she says, staring off into space, disoriented.

"Carissa, you hear me?" I reply, walking up to her.

She doesn't move. I guess all of the action must've been too much for her. But as far as I am concerned, she would have to get used to it because things are about to get real nasty. The fuckin' games are over.

"Carissa, wake the fuck up!" I say, smacking her in the face. She rubs her skin and looks into my eyes. "I said, tell the lieutenants we have a meeting in two hours. I need you wit me, so man the fuck up!"

"Oh . . . okay. I'll call everybody now."

"We ready to take her to Faye's," the men say, holding Mercedes in their arms.

"Cool, I'll be down to check on you later, Mercedes."

"Okay."

After my orders are given, I turn around to see Chris standing there.

"You okay?" she asks in a concerned tone.

I want to lie and say no, thinking she'd stay then. I look around to see who's watching. There's so much going on, and everyone is so preoccupied with Mercedes, that they don't notice Chris is in my face for the second time that day.

"I'm fine," I say softly, keeping my voice down. "You sure you wanna do this?"

"I'm sure I gotta do this. Bye, Yvette," she responds, walking down the stairs.

"Mercedes!" I hear Derrick screaming as he runs up the stairs toward us, mad as hell.

There's commotion everywhere; but for the moment, all I see is Chris walking away. Even Derrick's distraught voice disappears as he rushes past me. I want to beg Chris not to take another step away, but I can't. She's gone, and my soul misses her already.

Black Water

"If we gonna move, we gotta move now."

The room is almost completely dark, with the exception of the light illuminating from the clock and bathroom light. The fan above the huge brass bed cools Black Water's body. Half asleep, he grips his wife's slender leg when she places it over his. After the sexcapade they had the night before, they are beat.

Shade Holman has been married to Jesse Holman, aka Black Water, since she was seventeen. And now that she is thirty-four, she's borne him twelve children, including his favorite son, sixteen-year-old Tamir. Her body shows no signs of giving birth. Her beautiful dark skin and long, silky hair transferred to all of her children.

Black was careful about picking the right women to bear his kids. He wanted his offspring as beautiful as their mothers. And had he not bought out Dreyfus for 20 million to own Ty-land, the women he picked would've been unattainable to such an unattractive man. But his power and swag made him appealing.

When the phone rings at seven in the morning, it startles Shade a little. "Mmm, baby, you expectin' any calls?" she purrs, gripping him. Her hair falls down her back and her fingers are covered in diamonds.

"Naw," he says groggily. "Answer it."

"Hey, Shannon . . . get the phone," Shade tells her sister, who's also in the bed, on the other side of Black.

Although Shannon is also Black's wife, their marriage is not legal. Shade managed to convince Shannon to participate in the marriage, because Black wanted her the moment he saw her. At first, Shannon refused, cursing the idea of sleeping with the same man as her sister. But when she was presented with a custom-colored pink Rolls-Royce on her nineteenth birthday, it sealed the deal.

Shannon is two years younger than her older sister, Shade. And just like Shade, she possesses the same silky hair, which she keeps neatly locked. The sisters' body frames are totally different. Shade is tall, with large breasts, and Shannon is short, with a fat ass and beautiful brown eyes. Shannon has given him ten children.

Black doesn't lie to his wives, and he always makes his plan clear. He wants to "wife" as many women as possible so they can birth his children. And for their participation, he lavishes them with anything they desire. He wants an army, which he calls the Black Water Clan. His quest for power consumes him.

Shannon complies, rolling over to answer the phone. "Hello?"

"Is Black there?" Cameron asks.

"Who's calling?"

"Tell him it's Cameron. I need to talk to him right now."

"Baby, it's Cameron," she says, holding the cordless phone. "He says it's important."

Black sits up in the bed and angrily accepts the phone. Shade and Shannon rub and kiss his chest. The diamonds on their hands stand out against his dark skin.

"This betta be good," Black says as his wives' caresses cause him to grow hard. His chest is his hot spot, and they know it.

"What the fuck is goin' on in Emerald?"

"I don't know what the fuck you talkin' about, but I ain't one of your bitches! Now I think you better calm down a little, partner, and explain. 'Cause this sounds like a misunderstandin', and that shouldn't be when we 'bout to make money together."

Cameron takes a deep breath and says, "Mercedes was shot last night."

"I don't know shit about that. Sounds to me like you callin' the wrong dude."

"Well, who was it, then?"

"Look . . . niggas get shot all the time in this game. Just 'cause they got pussies don't make them immune. But whateva happened to her was not by my hands. Give me some time, I might be able to find out what went down later."

"Yeah, well, I need to know quick."

"Like I said, I'll check on that and get back wit you." Black is desperately trying to maintain his composure. For now, he still needs Cameron. "Did you get things together wit your peoples in Emerald? If we gonna move, we gotta move now."

"What peoples?"

"Cam, you a'ight? 'Cause you actin' irrational right now."

"I'm fine, nigga!" Cameron barks.

"Good. Now what's up wit your crew in Emerald? Are they ready?"

Still mad that Mercedes got shot, Cameron says, "Yeah. They waitin' on my word."

"So when you gonna give it? Or are you gonna let bullshit get in the way of business?"

"When you tell me what went down last night, I'll place the call. Not till then," Cameron says, hanging up the phone.

As Black lies in the bed, he is trying to avoid having Cameron killed. He doesn't feel like receiving calls over a bitch the nigga said he wanted dead.

"Don't worry 'bout that dumb shit, baby," Shade coos.

"Yeah, big daddy. You still the man, and that nigga betta be glad you even let him in your world," Shannon adds, feeding his already-large ego.

Black knows his wives are right, but he is still heated. Cameron is accusing him of something he didn't do, and is threatening his plans.

The night before

"Get the tires too!" Cristal said to one of Black's men.

"This shit can't get more fucked up than this." Jam J laughed, looking at the ruined black Dodge Magnum. One of the rearview mirrors was hanging off the car, and scratches and dents were everywhere. "Call Ed and tell him we done."

" 'Bout time!" Cristal said, dialing his number. "We almost got caught twice."

It took Ed two minutes to drive his black Honda from the guard's station to the back of Unit B. Ed parked his car, opened his door, and walked toward Carson.

"Carson, I think somebody fucked up your car, man," Ed told him while smoking a blunt. "You betta check that shit out. It don't look too good."

"What?" Carson answered, leaning on the wall next to the back door. "Ain't nobody crazy enough to fuck wit my shit round here."

"Apparently, we got niggas in Emerald who ain't from round here."

Carson wiped his hand over his face in frustration and said, "So you serious?"

"Dead serious, homie. I was drivin' to my crib when I saw that shit."

"Fuck!" Carson said, rubbing his hands over the top of his head. "So you just drivin' around the city and saw my shit, huh?" Ed nodded. "I thought you and Harold was s'pose to stay on post." Carson didn't trust Ed. "The bosses said everyone works."

"Look, man, I was makin' a run to my crib to get some smoke. The bosses wouldn't even miss me, unless somebody told 'em. You not gonna tell 'em, are you?"

"I ain't no snitch, nigga."

"Okay, then. I'm lookin' out for you, but if you don't want me to, that's cool." Ed was preparing to leave, hoping Carson would stop him, and he did.

"Hold on!" Carson yelled. "Can you watch my post while I check on my shit?"

"I'll watch it for you, but you gotta hurry up back."

Carson thought about it for a moment and jogged to the location where he left his car. Ed waited for him to be completely out of view before calling Black Water.

"You can come out, Black. The post is clear."

When Black came out, he hurried to Ed's car and dove in the backseat. Without altercation, Ed drove past Harold at the gate. Since Tyland was only a few blocks up, when he dropped Black off, no one noticed he'd left. When he came back, he discovered Mercedes had been shot. Turns out he could not have gotten Black out of Emerald at a better time.

The present

"Don't worry about that shit, baby," Shannon says. "Worry about this pussy and charge the rest to the game." She continues to stroke his thickness.

"Handle it," he tells her.

Without complaining, she throws back the covers so he can see her putting in work. He loves to watch getting his dick sucked. Shannon always could suck his dick better than her sister—or any of his wives, for that matter. That's why she is favored.

"Shade, tell Energy to make me some breakfast," he says, referring to his third wife, who is in the other bedroom asleep.

"No problem," she says, smacking her sister on the ass. She exits the bedroom, wearing only her royal blue panties.

Energy is Black's third of ten wives. Although Energy is beautiful, she isn't as sexy as his nine other wives. Energy is so light-skinned, she could pass for white; the five children she bore all look like wither—with silky, long hair and light green eyes. But because she could cook her ass off, Black allows her to stay in his apartment with the sisters. His other wives live in the same building, and on the same floor.

Since they all have their duties, things run smooth amongst them. Black doesn't allow bickering, fussing, and fighting amongst his wives. Shade, Shannon, and Energy tend to his immediate needs; the other seven take care of the children. No children are allowed to stay in the apartment with him.

Energy never says it out loud, but she is jealous of the attention he gives the sisters. However, she knows if she raises a dispute, she might lose her position as the third favorite. Because her sex skills are average, she rarely has the honor of sleeping with Black. It hurts hearing the lovemaking sessions at night by the three of them while she lies alone, playing with her own pussy until she goes to sleep. Secretly, she is building her children up to become the strongest, thereby securing her future.

Amongst all of his wives, Black Water has thirty-five kids. And if Kenyetta acts right, he has plans to make her his eleventh. She is stronger than the others, so it is harder breaking her down. He can't win her with promises of riches, because she has her own. In order to get her, he is sure he has to strip her of Emerald. And if things go his way, that would be happening soon enough.

As Energy prepares his meal, Black Water palms the back of Shannon's head in the bedroom.

"Don't forget to hold my balls, baby," he coaches.

"Sorry, daddy," she says, bobbing on his dick and stroking his nuts softly.

As she goes to work, he thinks about what he is going to do about Cameron. He always thinks better during sex; and with the work Shannon is putting in, he feels like Albert Einstein. If Cameron wants to play games, he is going to write the rules—one playbook at a time.

Lil C

"I don't pay a bitch shit but attention."

"We moved that shit already?" Nicholas says, looking like Snoop Dogg did in his prime, with his hair braided. He counts his share of the weed profits from school.

Lil C met Nicholas at Sidwell Friends, a prestigious private school in Washington, D.C. It is the same school Sachi, Lani, and Jona attend. The criterion is tough, and the tuition is heavy, but both Lil C's and Nicholas's families can afford the fee.

Nicholas's mother is a district court judge in D.C. And before meeting Lil C, Nicholas fantasized about the gangsta lifestyle he saw on TV. But with Lil C, he gets to live out his fantasies firsthand. His privileged life was boring and he wanted a release. Lil C used him at first because he had a car. He would've had one himself, if he hadn't failed the knowledge test repeatedly. But after a while, C liked Nicholas for his loyalty.

"We knew that shit would be easy! I think we need to ask Heath for more."

"We gettin' more?"

"Yeah. I'm talking about ten thousand dollars' worth."

"We ain't got enough," Nicholas says, raising his eyebrows.

"We gonna ask him to front us. If he give it to us, we'll get about twenty off it. You saw how quick we moved this shit."

"Damn . . . if we move that, I'ma buy some pussy wit my cut!"

"Nigga, why is you buyin' pussy? That shit don't make no sense to me!" Lil C says, tucking some of his money under the bed, while putting the rest in his pocket. "I don't pay a bitch shit but attention."

"Come on, man. You mean to tell me you wouldn't pay fat Charlotte to fuck?"

"White-girl Charlotte? Wit the Buffie-the-Body ass?"

Nicholas nods and smiles.

"Nigga, I already fucked that bitch!"

"No, you didn't!" he responds, with eyes wide open.

"You don't believe me?" Lil C says, picking up his cell phone.

"Naw! You woulda told me that shit already."

"First off, I don't tell niggas *every time* I fuck a bitch. I leave that shit to y'all fools. But for the sake of clarification, listen to this."

Lil C dials Charlotte's number and waits. He places the call on speaker.

"Cameron? Is that you?"

"Yeah, shortie. How you know it was me?"

"I recognize the number." Lil C winks at Nicholas, already feeling he's won. "Why haven't you called me? It's like you hit and ran. Did I do something wrong?"

"Naw, shortie," he says, looking at Nicholas. "I just been busy. You know I couldn't forget a badass bitch like you. But when you gonna let me feel that again?"

"You can get this anytime you want. Just say the word."

"*Word,*" Cameron says coolly.

Charlotte giggles.

"A'ight, mami. I just wanted to hit you to let you know I've been thinkin' 'bout you. I'ma rap to you lada." When he hangs up, he looks at Nicholas. "Now what, nigga?"

"Yo, you the man . . . for real!" Nicholas responds.

"I told you, I ain't gotta do shit to impress these bitches but say my name."

"If that's true . . . why you bein' faithful to Lani?"

" 'Cause that's my Bonnie. And I know when it comes down to it, she got my back."

"She seems like she don't take shit. She reminds me of your moms."

Lil C laces up his new Gucci sneakers and thinks about what Nicholas said.

"Damn, you may be right. But I ain't tryin' to fuck my moms, nigga!"

"What?" He laughs. "You takin' shit too far. I'm just sayin', Lani spunky as shit."

"Yeah . . . but I fucks wit her. Sometimes I just have to shake her up, 'cause she be violatin' my privacy. But I'ma keep her round, though."

"You tell your peoples 'bout the baby yet?"

"Naw . . . I'ma rap to my pops when he scoop me up later today. And I'ma tell my mother when I get back."

"How you think they gonna take it?"

"All I know is I need to stack more paper, since I got a kid on the way."

"What is you talkin' 'bout, son? Your moms and pops *both* paid!"

"That's they money. That ain't got shit to do wit me."

"Yeah, whatever," Nicholas says, picking up one of Lil C's diamond watches, which his mother bought for him. "All I know is . . . you livin' way betta than a nigga like me."

"You lookin' at bullshit," Lil C responds, taking his watch from his hands and putting it on. "But on everything, I want in the *game* for real. I'm not tryin' to be peddlin' no bullshit at school forever. I'm tryin' to be like my pops. I want the money, power, and respect. Not to mention, my mother gettin' shot fucked me up. She needs me more than she thinks she does."

"We gonna have the money, power, and respect," Nicholas says, squeezing his money stack.

"If we keep fuckin' wit them niggas from Unit B, we gonna have everything."

"That shit gonna do us good right now, but I want big money. And when it's my time . . . I want Emerald."

"You think your moms would let that shit happen?"

"I know she will, but only when I'm ready. And I'ma prove to her that I am."

Cameron

"That nigga just don't know how to handle you."

Cameron hands the keys to his blue Mercedes CLS 500 to the valet attendant at Mercedes' luxurious high-rise at the National Harbor. Taking the elevator up to her floor, he battles with his feelings for his ex. Now that he's unleashed the beast in Black Water, he knows there is no backing out. Although years have passed since he and Mercedes ended their relationship, he still feels like she is his. He is having second thoughts about killing her. When he learned she was shot, he almost lost his mind.

Once he arrives at her apartment's door, he hesitates and quietly listens.

"Please stop fussin' over me, Derrick," Mercedes says. "I'm not dying!"

Suck-ass nigga, Cameron thinks.

"Mercedes, just sit back and let me take care

of you while I can. You know I have to head back to Emerald in a minute, anyway."

"Well, I'll be glad when you get outta here." She laughs. "You actin' like I have cancer. Is Lil C ready yet? Cameron gonna be here in a minute to pick him back up."

"I hear you, Ma. I was just kickin' it wit Nicholas," Lil C says, entering the living room with his friend. "Should I wear my diamond watch or my Movado?"

"You already iced out wit the chain. You should rock the Movado," Derrick says.

"You right, Pops," Lil C responds. "How you feelin', Ma?"

"I'm good, son. Don't worry. It was just a flesh wound."

"I'ma fuck somebody up if they hurt you again."

"Lil C! Don't curse around me."

"I'm a man, Ma. You gotta remember that."

"Well, start by learning to respect your mother, son," Derrick says.

"I know, Pops, but I'm serious. What I look like—lettin' somebody hurt her?"

"Lil C, not right now. You have company," Mercedes replies.

Hearing Lil C refer to Derrick as "Pops" enrages Cameron, so he bangs at the door.

"What the fuck?" Derrick responds as he reaches for his Glock. Walking up to the in-home security monitor, he sees Cameron on the screen. There's an irritated look on his face. "It's

Cameron," he says, putting his weapon in the back of his jeans.

Derrick wants to say something negative about Cameron, but decides against it, because Lil C is present. Instead, he opens the door and walks away.

"What's up, Dad!" Lil C yells, giving him a manly handshake. "Check out my Movado joint! Pops bought it for me."

The room gets silent as Lil C brings to attention what got Cameron angry.

"Did this nigga tell you to call him 'Pops'?" Although he's talking to his son, his eyes remain on Derrick.

"Naw, Dad. It ain't even like that."

"Well, listen. . . . This nigga not your pops," he says, pointing at Derrick. "You got one pops, and that's me. I don't ever wanna hear you call another nigga 'Pops' again."

Embarrassed, Lil C looks at his friend Nicholas and then at Derrick.

"I got you, Dad," he says.

"Cameron, don't act ignorant. You actin' like some jealous-ass lover!"

"Aye, Cameron, I'm out," Nicholas says. "I'ma get up wit you lada, man."

"A'ight, man. I'ma hit you," Lil C responds, giving him a dap.

"Lada, Big C," Nicholas says to Cameron.

"Lada, slim," he replies as he waits for him to leave. The moment he does, Cameron relives the issue. "A jealous-ass lover? Fuck is you talkin' 'bout, Mercedes? I don't want my kid callin' another nigga 'Pops.' Just 'cause you suckin' this nigga's dick don't mean he can take my family too. Whether you believe it or not, some shit *is* off limits."

"Baby, I'ma check on things back at Emerald. If you need me, call me." Derrick ignores Cameron. He is calm and poised, and his brush-off angers Cameron further.

"Don't worry, dude. She gone be fine," Cameron affirms.

"I'm talkin' to my peoples, Cameron. I ain't got no beef with you, and I understand that Lil C is your responsibility, even though I love him like my own. But when it comes to this woman, her welfare is all mines."

Cameron smirks and says, "You can have her."

"I'll take that." Derrick nods. Whenever he wanted to unleash on Cameron in the past, he placed himself in his shoes. It would be tough for anybody to lose a dime like Mercedes.

"Okay, pops," Mercedes says to Derrick as she places a juicy, wet kiss on his lips. She is trying to get Cameron livid, and it is working. "Keep me posted on Emerald."

"You got that." Derrick winks. "Just rest up and don't worry. Lil C, I'ma get up wit you later, homie."

Cameron watches him until Derrick disappears out the door.

"Lil C, go wait in the car. Let me talk to your mother for a minute."

"A'ight, Dad."

When Lil C is gone, Cameron follows Mercedes to her bedroom. She wants to rest, and she wants him to leave. She hopes he'll get the message.

"How you feelin'?" he utters.

"Cameron, please," she retorts, lying down and gripping the covers tightly over her body. "Like you give a fuck."

"You know I give a fuck. And why I have to hear from somebody else that you got shot? You still my kids' mother."

Mercedes looks at him and rolls her eyes. As much as she can't stand Cameron, she still has *some* feelings for him. And at one point, she was going to marry him.

"Where my daughters?"

"At my mother's."

"Good. Now stop ignorin' the question."

"I don't know why I ain't tell you." She shrugs.

"Is Emerald under control?"

"Yeah. I know you heard that some niggas ran up, but we met wit everybody last night and changed the game up a little. A lot of shit is changin'."

"Like what?" he asks, sitting next to her on the bed.

"You know I can't tell you that, Cameron."

The scent of his I Am King cologne by Sean Combs is driving her mad. He has cut his curly hair down a little, but it still does wonders against his chocolate skin.

"I'm your kids' father. You can tell me anything. You know I'd never betray you. I don't care what we going through."

"But you did betray me, Cameron. Remember? You let Thick convince you to dump me after you promised nothing could break our bond." Her voice shakes a little as she relives the pain of his betrayal.

"You trust your fiancé?"

"Wit my life."

"Don't make me hurt you." The room grows quiet. "How you gonna marry a nigga when you still in love wit me?"

"W-what? Where did that come from?" She looks away briefly.

"Stop playin' games. You want me, and I want you. The quicker you realize it, the better off you'll be. You need me to protect you."

"How come lately you been actin' like bein' wit you will save my life? What are you . . . my savior?"

"You can say that."

"Well, save yourself, because Derrick is the only man for me."

He is about to dispute Derrick's love, when she yells in pain.

"Ouuuch!" she says, holding the arm that the bullet entered.

"What's wrong?" he asks, touching her leg lightly.

"Nothin'. . . . Just hand me my medicine right there, and some water out the fridge." When he returns, she takes the Vicodin she got from Old Lady Faye and says, "Thank you, Nurse Betty."

"I'll be that." He winks.

Cameron can feel the sexual tension between them, and her seductive glance encourages him. So he kisses her softly on the lips, suckling her bottom one. Her stomach flutters, and he runs his tongue in and out of her mouth before licking the side of her neck.

"Cameron, don't make me do this. Please. Let me be happy," she begs.

"I'm gonna make you happy right now. Worry 'bout the other shit later."

"But Lil C is waiting outside."

He knew he had her when her argument was no longer whether or not they should do it, but that they take care in not getting caught.

"He fine. Now let me taste that pussy again. That's all I wanna do." She tries to resist. "On everything, I just want to taste you again. After that, I'll leave," he says, palming her breasts.

Before she can refuse, he moves the covers, lifts her nightgown, and drops to his knees. He stares at her pink, wet pussy. To his surprise, she isn't wearing panties.

"Damn . . . she still pretty," he affirms, licking his lips. He is about to lick her, when Derrick enters his mind. Frowning, he looks up at her and asks, "You been wit him today?"

"No. He didn't wanna hurt me," she says as her legs shake in anticipation of his warm tongue.

"That nigga just don't know how to handle

you." He runs his warm tongue in and around her pussy, and her familiar juices arouse him. "Damn, I miss this pussy!"

As he licks her wetness, his mind wanders to their past. He remembers the look on her face when she told him she was pregnant and that it was a boy. He reflects on how she told him while making love that she would rather die than live without him. He even thinks about her smile when he bought her first Mercedes for her, a candy apple–colored car. He misses their life together and he wants her back.

"This shit feels so good, Cameron!" she says as she selfishly enjoys his affection.

Grabbing the back of his head, she grinds into his face. Cameron remembers that Mercedes never could say no to getting her pussy ate. If she had it her way, she'd choose it over fucking every time.

"*Mmmmmmmmm!* Damn, Cameron, you eatin' this pussy good as shit!" she cheers.

Suddenly he realizes tasting her isn't enough. In his mind, he'd be a fool not to try to go further. If she gives him the pussy, he knows he'd have her forever. Cameron carefully lays her down, to avoid hurting her arm, and removes his pants and boxers. And when she's flat on her back, he eases into her slowly. A light smile spreads across his face when he notices her pussy still grips his dick. Apparently, Derrick isn't beating the pussy as hard as she claims. Cameron is stroking her box like a first-class massage therapist. And before he knows it, the look on her face shows him she's about to cum.

"*Awwwwww* . . . I'm cummin', Cameron," she moans. "Don't stop. I'm about to cum."

When she does, Cameron releases himself into her, to spite Derrick.

Her eyes widen. "Why didn't you pull out?"

" 'Cause that pussy still mine," he says.

Now guilt overcomes Mercedes, and the sense of winning lifts Cameron. Silence stays between them as he returns from the bathroom with a wet cloth.

"Open up, baby," he says.

She complies and allows him to wipe his semen from her body before using the same cloth to clean himself. When he's done, he puts the washcloth on the nightstand.

Taking a deep breath, he says, "Look . . . I know you're fucked up right now, but you not supposed to be wit that nigga, anyway. It's been two years, and you love me—just like I love you. If it wasn't true, we would not have fucked. So I'ma give you some time to break shit off wit him before somebody gets hurt, Mercedes, 'cause I don't know how much longer I'ma let this shit go on. Hear me, and hear me good. . . . End the relationship wit him. And I'ma call you later. A'ight?"

Mercedes nods in agreement, just so he will leave. She wants and needs to be alone.

Cameron, on the other hand, glides to his car. He knows, if nothing else, that her and Derrick's relationship is permanently damaged.

Kenyetta

"You feelin' that liquor too much today!"

Yvette and I decide to walk around Emerald to see if everything is in order a week after our city was raided. And although we know they are still hiding behind our walls, we make it virtually impossible for them to make another move.

With five buildings in Emerald City, and twelve floors in each of them, we create a vicious plan. There are now two armed soldiers on each floor on the opposite ends in every building. They act as security and monitor the comings and goings of everyone. If something seems out of line, they deal with it immediately.

We don't stop there, though. We also make sure we have two men in the front and back of every unit. Even the guard's station has two men manning the post at all times. In total, there are 150 armed men in Emerald at all times. Yeah, we have shit on lock.

"So what's up wit you, Yvette? You seem different," I ask as we walk back to Unit C.

Yvette's hair hangs down her back in a tight ponytail and she isn't wearing earrings or makeup. She is also sporting a heavy black ski coat and baggy blue sweatpants. She looks down and drops her head.

When I look closer, I see tears streaming down her face. In all my years of knowing Yvette, I have seen her cry twice: once at Stacia's and Dex's funeral, and the other time when Thick broke her heart.

"Yeah . . . somethin's on my mind and I don't know how you'll take it."

"You know you can say anything to me."

Before Yvette says anything, Carissa walks up the steps and sits down next to us.

"Everything at the gate's cool. I don't care what y'all say, though. I can't stand Harold's and Ed's asses," Carissa details, gabbing.

I look at her funny, hoping she'll get the clue and leave, but it doesn't work.

"What? Is this a private conversation or somethin'? What, we keepin' secrets now?" She sips from her blue Dallas Cowboys cup filled with vodka.

Yvette sighs and says, "I was just tellin' Kenyetta that somethin' has been on my mind lately. I'm seein' somebody who's different than anyone I've ever seen before."

"Anybody you'd be with would be different. You been with Thick all your life," Carissa responds. Lately she has been drinking too much.

"Is he white?" I ask.

"No." She laughs. "I wish it was that simple, though."

"Then what's up? Is he short? Fat? What?" I persist.

"He . . . is a she."

If I could describe the looks on my face and Carissa's, you still couldn't imagine our reactions. Carissa's cup tilts as the liquor pours out. And my mouth opens so wide, you can see my ovaries.

"Say somethin'!" Yvette yells, breaking the unbearable silence.

"Y-Yvette . . . what you talkin' 'bout?" I stutter. "You not gay."

"Yeah, Yvette. What the fuck you sayin'?" Carissa finally says.

"You think if I had a choice I'd be in love wit her? This shit is stressin' me out!"

"You in love?" Carissa asks, with her eyes wide open.

"Yes. We been together for two years now. And since I hid her from y'all, she cut me off. She's getting a new apartment, and everything."

"Y'all lived together too? I mean . . . how did you hide this from us for so long?"

"It's easy, Kenyetta. We all don't see each other when we leave Emerald."

"Damn . . . that's why you been dodgin' us lately?" Carissa points out.

"Maybe you should put the cup down," I reply.

"Why? I'm just sayin' this explains everything to me. Your bitch ass over there lickin' pussy! Damn, Yvette! I can't believe you like women!" Carissa continues.

"I don't like *women*. I like Chris."

"So what's it like, in the bedroom?"

"Damn, Car! You feelin' that liquor too much today!" I shout.

"Don't act like you don't wanna know too. We over the shock of her being wit a woman. Now let's get down to the details. So start talkin', Yvette. What's it like?"

Yvette smiles a little and says, "You don't really wanna hear that shit."

"Yes, we do!" I blurt out. I cover my mouth, realizing I was now acting nosey.

"Now who's feelin' themselves?" Carissa laughs.

"Well, it's tender, sweet, and soft."

"Girl, stop bullshitin' and get to the details! Is the sex good or not?"

"*Fuck yeah!* And don't let her strap up! Last time she fucked me wit that rubber-dick thingy, I called her 'daddy' for weeks."

"Wow! You makin' my pussy wet! She got a brother?" Carissa questions.

"Girl, stop trippin'!" I laugh, hitting her on the arm. "Lavelle would fuck you up!"

"That's after I get mine!"

"It's the girl who walked to you the other day? Wit the Mohawk?" I ask.

"Yes."

"She's a cutie. I see why you like her," Carissa interjects.

"What's wrong, Yvette?" I pry, noticing she's crying.

"I can't believe I let her leave me! I was so happy, and now she's gone!"

"You mean you let a good fuck walk out your life because of us?" Carissa adds. "Even if we didn't approve, that's your life, Yvette. You don't let someone you care about leave over some bull-shit."

"Yeah, Yvette. If that's your only problem, you ain't got one."

"You sayin' that now, but you called her a 'bitch' and Carissa called her a 'carpet muncher'!"

We all laugh again.

"We were nervous," I respond. "Look at all the shit that happened that night. And this strange person walks up to you? We were on guard."

"I know . . . but y'all still said it."

"We still want you to be happy, Vette," Carissa adds. "Real talk."

"Well, what about Mercedes? You heard the comments she made when she first saw Chris's face. She called her a 'dyke'!"

"You gotta ask her, Yvette. But I think she'll recognize that real *love* is hard to find. We gonna get used to you bein' a lesbian . . . over time."

"I'm not a lesbian."

"If you lickin' pussy, you a lesbian. Fuck what you heard," Carissa clarifies.

"Anyway, Yvette," I interject. "If you love her, get her back. For real."

"Yeah, and when you get her back, ask her to lick your ass again for me. You been in a bad mood all week. Shiiittt . . . if I'da known that's all you needed . . . I'da licked your ass a long time ago!" Carissa giggles.

Silence fills the air until we all burst into laughter.

"You know you went too far, right?" I tell her, holding my stomach due to laughing so hard. I snatch the cup from her hands. "Let me take this shit before you say somethin' else dumb tonight." I am still teasing Carissa when Yvette grows silent.

"What now, Yvette?"

"I really hope Mercedes is as cool wit this as you guys are. Somethin' tells me she won't be."

Mercedes

"I can be a stone-cold killer if you fuck wit what's mine."

I'm scheduled for duty this week in Emerald, but I can't focus. Guilt has consumed most of my waking thoughts as I replay in my mind what happened between me and Cameron. I shoulda never had sex with him. And then he had the nerve to be acting like we were back together, or somethin'! Calling my house all hours of the night!

I decide tonight, before going to Emerald, to deal with Cameron personally. When I knock on his door, I hear my daughters playing in the background. I smile.

"Who is it?" a woman's voice calls from inside.

"Mercedes. Is Cameron here?"

She opens the door and grins at me. She's tall and busty; her skin is honey brown. She has a shoulder-length haircut with a Chinese bang.

"Hi, Mercedes. Come on in. Cameron's downstairs."

I walk in and she closes the door.

"You are?" I say.

"I'm . . . so silly." She laughs. "Your beautiful babies been keepin' me busy today. I'm Toi, Cameron's new girlfriend."

She extends her hand and I shake it. For some reason, I'm not jealous that she's Cameron's new girl. Maybe it's her kindness or the fact that I want his attention taken off me, which prevents me from feeling negative.

"It's nice to meet you, Toi. Can you get him? It's kinda important."

"Girl, please! You gave that man three kids, so that makes you family. Go on downstairs. He ain't doin' nothin' but runnin' his mouth with his friends. They been yappin' nonstop. Sometimes they worse than little girls." She laughs.

I chuckle and say, "Okay, I'll go downstairs."

"Let me know if you want somethin' to eat. I made spaghetti."

After hugging my baby girls, I make my way to Cameron's basement. I have to give him credit; his crib in Largo, Maryland, is fly. And I wonder how things would have been if we made it together. But when I think of my luxurious apartment in D.C., I smile. I have it all with Derrick.

When I reach the bottom of the stairs, I stop short when I hear two extra voices. One of the voices belongs to Lavelle, but the other voice I don't recognize. Wanting to hear more, I stand behind the wall that separates me from view.

"This is crazy, Cameron. They not goin' for that shit. Trust me," Lavelle says.

"They already went for it," the unfamiliar voice interjects. "That's what you don't get. Maybe y'all handled things the wrong way last time."

"Cam, we not hurtin' for money," Lavelle responds. "We ain't gotta do this shit."

"I'm tired of this shit. Look, Cameron, if you want this dude involved, you give him a cut of your money after everything is done," the other man says, obviously irritated. "I'm not fuckin' wit no scared niggas."

"Who the fuck you callin' 'scared'?" Lavelle counters.

"Cameron, you initiated this shit, not me." The stranger ignores Lavelle. "What we gonna do?"

Something about their conversation scares me and I involuntarily make a sound.

"Hold up. Who that?" Cameron asks.

I walk around the wall and make myself seen. Giving a nervous smile, I now know who the other voice belongs to. He's Black Water from Tyland. So why is he here?

"Uh . . . look, man. I'm 'bout to roll. I gotta take care of some things back at the crib," Lavelle says. He walks up to me and kisses my cheek. "It was nice seein' you again, Mercedes. Bye."

"Bye, Lavelle," I reply, looking at Cameron. Lavelle seems scared.

"I'm out too, man," Black responds, standing

up. He looks so much like Biggie Smalls, it's scary. "Is it cool to leave Tamir here?"

"Yeah, man . . . it's cool."

Black exits, without so much as looking at or speaking to me.

"What was that about, Cameron?"

"Business. It don't have nothin' to do wit you," he tells me, walking up to me.

"So you fuckin' wit Tyland Towers niggas? You couldn't stand them at first."

"I don't fuck wit Tyland niggas now. I fuck wit money."

"You know what? I don't even know why I came."

"I do. You miss me, like I miss you."

"Actually, I came by to tell you, it won't happen again."

"Yeah, okay, Mercedes."

"I'm serious! And didn't you move on with your new girlfriend upstairs?"

"What, you jealous?" He laughs.

"Nigga, I have a man!" I say, placing my hand on my hip.

His face frowns and he says, "She not my girl, Mercedes. You are."

"That's not what she said. I'm surprised she would even fuck wit you."

"Why? Because she's attractive?"

"No . . . because she knows how to treat people. Stay the fuck outta my life, Cameron. Outside of the kids, I don't want to deal wit you no more. I'm serious."

I have one foot on the step when he says, "You want me to murder that nigga, don't you?"

Turning around, I face him and say, "Don't fuck wit my life. I'm not the dumb bitch you left in Emerald. I can be a stone-cold killer if you fuck wit what's mine. Remember that."

I walk away before he can say anything else. Heading to Emerald, my mind remains on what I saw. What is Cameron doing dealing with Black Water? We used to hate his guts, and now they in business together? I smell larceny. I press my Gucci boot to the gas pedal. I gotta tell my girls that I think somethin's up.

Cameron

"I don't give a fuck who it is!"

"Toi, get down here!" Cameron yells upstairs after Mercedes leaves.

"Hold on, baby. Let me put the plates in front of the girls."

Cameron paces the floor, ready to give her a piece of his mind. He can't believe she's not smart enough to let him know Mercedes was in his house before she came downstairs. Most of all, he wonders what Mercedes heard.

"Sorry, Cameron. I fed the kids. You hungry?"

"Naw," he replies grumpily.

"Okay . . . what's up?"

"How long was Mercedes in my house?" he questions with an attitude.

"Not long before she left. . . . Why?"

"Why would you let her downstairs, Toi?"

" 'Cause that's your kids' mother." She shrugs. "What's the problem?"

"Look . . . don't let nobody in my fuckin' house witout lettin' me know. I don't give a fuck who it is! She came in on a private conversation, Toi! Use your fuckin' head!" he screams.

Toi takes two steps toward him, places her right hand on her hip, and smacks him in the face with her left. Turning around to leave, she doubles back and says, "Take care of your own fuckin' kids! I'm outta here!"

Stomping up the stairs, she slams his front door in a little bit. Shortly after, he hears her tires peeling out of his driveway. Cameron stands in silence, thinking about what just occurred. He had been feeling Toi, but her aggressiveness and no-nonsense attitude made him hesitate. He desires a girl like Mercedes used to be before he changed her.

Sure, he could've rushed upstairs and chased Toi down for placing her hands on him, but he'd let it pass because, at least, she is gone. Right now, he has one thing on his mind: finding out how much Mercedes heard of his conversation with Black Water. Because he knew firsthand what happened if pit bulls attacked.

Lil C

"You heard my word."

"So what you gonna do, man?" Tamir asks, sitting on a chair at Lil C's computer station. "You not gonna be able to slide out here tonight. Your pops home."

Tamir is tall, has brown skin, and is slender, with long, silky hair like his mother's. He keeps it in a ponytail, not wanting to braid or cut it. Everybody jokes about how he looks just like the singer Lloyd.

Although Lil C has only known Tamir for a few months, they have hung out a few times, mainly whenever Black comes over. Although Lil C doesn't know Tamir's father as Black Water—a secret Cameron hid from him on purpose—he does know Tamir comes from drug money. His pockets are as deep as his whenever they hang out. What Cameron and Lil C don't know is that Tamir is a spy more than anything else.

"Nigga, I'm leavin' outta here tonight. I got money to make. You comin'?"

"Naw . . . I know this shortie a few blocks over. I'ma check her out."

"A'ight, playa . . . playa," Lil C says as his phone rings for the tenth time.

"You hot as shit tonight. Tell them bitches, stop callin'," Tamir says, examining Lil C's new Gucci green leather jacket on the bed. "I might have to get you for this."

"You must be 'bout to leave six stacks on the table," he responds, turning his attention to the caller. "Who this?"

"It's me . . . Jona. You busy, C?"

He looks at Tamir, shakes his head, and frowns. He told him earlier how she has been pressing to be with him.

"Kinda. . . . What's up wit you, though? I heard you out the hospital."

"I am, but how come you didn't come see me? It's all your girlfriend's fault," she coos in her usual high-pitch baby voice.

"I know, and on everything, I got into my peoples' shit for stabbing you. She got into my Facebook account and saw your messages. But I gave your moms some cash for when you came back. She give it to you?"

"Yeah . . . thanks. I appreciate that."

As she's talking, he laces up his Nike boots and looks in his full-length mirror. Wearing an

Ed Hardy black T-shirt, he can't help but smile at how good he looks.

"You wish you look like me," he says, seeing Tamir placing his jacket on. Shaking his head, Lil C decides to let him live in the jacket a few more seconds. After all, most of his friends admire his fashion sense.

"This me all day long," Tamir says. The smell of leather fills the room.

"You wish, partna."

The moment Tamir removes the jacket, his T-shirt lifts up, revealing what looks like whip wounds on his back.

"You there, C? 'Cause you bein' rude," Jona says.

"Hold up, J."

C pauses, and then asks, "Tamir . . . what's up wit your back, son?"

Uncomfortable, Tamir releases Lil C's coat, pulls his shirt down, and turns around. "What you talkin' 'bout?"

Not wanting to kick his business while on the phone, C says to Tamir, "I'ma holla at you in a minute." He focuses back on the call. "Look . . . Jona, I'm 'bout to go. Nick on his way to scoop me 'cause we got business in Emerald tonight."

"If you in Emerald, I know you gonna stop by and see me."

"Can't do it. . . . My girl on to us now. I ain't tryin' to hear no shit from her."

"So you gonna let her stop us from doin' what we do?"

"Like I said . . . I can't fuck wit you no more. Trust me, I'm fucked up 'cause your head game not to be fucked wit."

"So you gonna just dump me like that?"

"You heard my word. I gotta go. Lata."

When he hangs up, C questions Tamir about what he saw. "Dog . . . who the fuck ripped your back?"

Tamir is embarrassed. "Those battle wounds. My pops makes sure we stay tough! It don't hurt no more."

He raises his T-shirt and exposes all of the scars on his back. Lil C has never seen anything so horrifying in all his life. There are about twenty or thirty deep scars on Tamir's back that have risen and turned to keloids.

"I don't know about all that shit . . . but if your folks puttin' in work like that on you, your pops is fucked up, man."

"No, he not! 'The man makes the body what the body needs to be.' "

"What?" Lil C laughs.

"I said, 'the man makes the body what the body needs to be.' It's not the other way around. People of the world worry too much about flesh and material bullshit. I can survive under any kind of pressure. My family too. We preparing for the bigger picture . . . war."

"Nigga, I don't know what you talkin' about, but that's some abusive-ass shit right there!" Lil C laughs. "I'ma have to get you one of them 800 numbers before your pops kills you." Lil C eases

into his Gucci jacket when he sees the head-
lights to Nick's Jaguar. "But on some other shit . . .
Nick here, so I'm 'bout to hit it."

Tamir grabs his black-and-white letterman
jacket.

"I'll get up wit you lada."

As they sneak out through the garage, Tamir
is consumed with jealousy as Lil C jumps into
Nick's car. Although he'll never say it out loud,
what Tamir really wants is to be like him, but Lil
C's swag is tailor-made.

*Months earlier, about a week after Tamir first met
Lil C, he found out from a few people in Emerald City
that C was keeping time with Jona. Once he got word
and a picture of her, he made sure he met Jona in a
mall.*

*"Aye . . . can I holla at you for a second?" he said
after walking up on her in the shopping center.*

"You sure can, cutie," she said.

*By the end of that day, he had her in his bed. They
had sex every day for two weeks, and Tamir bragged to
everybody that he was fucking the prince of Emerald's
girl.*

*"You know, Lil C only fuck wit that shortie on the
side, right?" one of Tamir's friends said to him at a
bowling party. This was seconds after he bragged how
she sucked his dick moments earlier.*

*"Naw, that's his girlfriend," he said, looking at her
while she bowled.*

"It ain't, man. Trust me."

Humiliated, he cut Jona off without notice and never called her again. It took weeks and a death threat from Tamir's girl cousins to finally get her to stop calling.

"I found out who he really be wit," the same dude said a few days later. "She a twin. My cousin hang out wit her sometimes in Emerald. I'll find out more info for you."

Tamir learned where Lani got her hair done and arranged for one of his sisters to get her hair done that same day.

"Damn . . . you fine as shit," he told Lani as she sat in a chair waiting to get her hair styled. Even with her hair undone, she ran rings around everybody in there. "Can we exchange—"

"Let me stop you there. My boyfriend's a boss, and I don't fuck around wit nothin' less. You cute, and everything . . . but I'm taken."

The entire beauty salon laughed at the way she shut him down. What she didn't know was that Tamir was relentless, and he didn't have plans to stop until he got what he wanted.

And at that time, what he wanted was Lani.

Carissa

"I just don't know how to tell them."

I am on my fourth cup of liquor, and trust me when I say, I haven't drunk this much in years. I don't feel safe in Emerald anymore. And I can't wait till it is my time to go home for a week.

We are sitting on the steps at night, looking at our surroundings, when Mercedes runs upstairs. I am surprised because she isn't due back until tomorrow. And then I remember, Yvette is on the phone, trying to see if Chris will come out and officially meet us tonight. It would be a mess if Mercedes ran into her.

"Hey! We all gotta talk. Now!" she says the moment she reaches the top.

"Can it wait for a minute, Mercedes?" Yvette says, holding the phone. "I was about to end this call, anyway."

"No, you gotta hear this shit *now*."

"Just give me a second to get off this call. I'll make it quick," Yvette continues.

"What's up?" I ask, my voice slurring out of my control.

"Carissa, I think you need to take it easy on the liquor. You drinking nonstop. And you need to be sober for what I'm 'bout to say, 'cause it involves you too."

"Go ahead, Mercedes," Kenyetta adds. "You making me nervous. We'll brief Yvette later when she gets off the phone."

"I think Cameron and Lavelle planning to take back Emerald wit Black Water from Tyland Towers."

"Damn! It's my phone again," Yvette says after the phone rings a second time.

They ignore her.

"My Lavelle?" I ask.

"Yes . . . your Lavelle, my ex, Cameron, and Black Water's ugly ass from Tyland."

When she says that, I notice the look on Kenyetta's face turns to horror, while Yvette steps farther away to finish her call.

"Why you say that? Lavelle wouldn't do anything to hurt me!"

"I was just at Cameron's, tellin' him it was over, when I walked downstairs and saw Lavelle and Black Water in his basement. This not a joke, Carissa! They up to something. All of them."

"Wait a minute! I don't know where to start. The fact that you had to tell Cameron it was over, or that Black was in his house. He hate that nigga's guts," I respond.

"Hold on, Mercedes. I think Yvette on the phone wit—" Kenyetta is interrupted before she can finish.

"Let me get it out in the open. A day after I got shot, Cameron came to my house and licked my pussy and fucked me. So now that that's outta the way, can I please finish what I really came up here about?"

"Mercedes!" Yvette grips the phone and places it behind her back.

"What? This is serious, Yvette! It can't wait."

"It's Derrick," she responds. "He on the phone."

I am so drunk . . . I had forgotten he called moments earlier to update Yvette about the unit. Yvette, Kenyetta, and Mercedes shoot me an evil glare. This is not good. It can't be.

"Lavelle, what's goin' on?" I ask him on my cell phone in the hallway. I watch my friends and know they're still mad at me. "Why you dealin' wit Black?"

"I knew Mercedes' ass was gonna start some shit. First off . . . you know I can't stand that nigga. That's Cam's man."

"So why were you there, then?"

"Because Cam invited me on some other shit."

"I don't believe you."

"Well, you should. I love you, Carissa. And I think it's time you left Emerald, 'cause things ain't the same, baby. You got enough cash stashed away to be good, and you know I got stacks. Just walk away. I'm beggin' you."

"Why, though? Is somethin' 'bout to happen?"

"Baby, I been screamin' at you to leave Emerald. So don't act like what I'm sayin' to you is new."

My head drops and I say, "I *have* been thinkin' about leaving, Lavelle. I just don't know how to tell them." I look through the glass door at my friends. Mercedes is crying on Kenyetta's shoulder, while Yvette rubs her back.

"For real, Carissa?" he says excitedly. "You serious about leaving?"

"Yeah . . . I don't think I'm wanted around here no more, anyway."

"Well, you wanted here. I got you, Car. Come home."

"Okay. I'm ready."

"You don't know how good it feels to hear you say that shit. Don't worry about the girls. We'll think of somethin' together to tell them. I'ma call you later. I love you."

"I love you too. Bye."

I feel like a phony, but I can't deny how I feel inside. I just want to be home with my man and raise our little girls, even if it means losing friends.

Yvette

I would need more than her strength to get me through.

I hate leaving Mercedes while she's going through a breakup; but when I called my house to invite Chris to Emerald to meet the girls, my maid told me she was busy getting the last of her things. I have to catch her before she leaves.

"*Hola,* Yvette. I didn't know you'd be here so early. Would you like me to prepare a meal?" Rosa, my maid, asks.

"I'm fine, Rosa. Where's Chris?"

"She's in the bedroom."

Rosa takes my purse and I walk briskly down the hallway to our bedroom. Her cologne freshens the hall and makes me light-headed, because I miss her so much. I slowly open the door and notice everything on the left side of the room is gone. And in our walk in-closet, Chris is collecting her clothes.

"Chris," I say softly, interrupting her busy body motion. She's wearing a new black Gucci sweat suit, with a pair of Gucci sneaks. Damn, she looks good.

She turns around and smiles. "Hey . . . I was just gettin' the rest of my things. I'll be out your way in a minute."

"Chris . . . can we talk?"

"Not right now, Yvette. I'm meetin' somebody later to let me in my apartment."

My heart drops when she says "my," because it no longer means "ours."

"Please. It'll only take a minute."

"There's not a lot to say," she says, setting a blue duffel bag on the bed. "I can't be who you want me to, so I gotta bounce."

"I don't want us to move on without each other, Chris. I made a mistake. People make mistakes," I say, walking up to her. "But you were right about me being ashamed of you, and I was wrong to hide you from my friends."

"You say that, but it's always the same shit." The sun hits her eyes and turns them hazel. "I'm just tired of it." She continues throwing her clothes in the bag on the bed.

"I told them about us."

She doesn't stop moving.

"I said, I told them about us. They know everything, Chris. I told them that we live to-gether, and that you're my world. There's no need in me hidin' you anymore. I love you." My expression turns serious.

"Don't play wit me, shortie. That shit ain't cool."

"I'm serious. They know."

"All of 'em?" she asks.

"Yes," I lie.

"Damn." She sits down. "I never thought you'd tell them."

"I did. I was a fool, but not anymore."

"What changed?"

"You left. And I'm askin' you to please stay wit me. Don't leave me, Chris."

She pushes her bag out of the way and sits all the way on the edge of the bed. I sit next to her, needing her strength right now.

Placing her hand on my knee, she softly says, "A'ight. I'ma give this thing another try. But if you deny me again, I'm done, Yvette."

"It'll never happen again. I'm mad it happened the first time. I love you."

We make love until the morning. With her by my side, I can conquer the world. Little did I know, the next day I would need more than her strength to get me through.

Kenyetta

I'm gonna ruin his life for a change.

Entering Tyland Towers, I locate Black's building and walk upstairs to his door without altercation. Little did he know, many of his men would kill to work for us at Emerald. Black would never be able to come into Emerald City without problems, but I could enter his territory without meeting resistance.

"Who is it?" a female calls from behind the other side of his door.

I hesitate, back up, and double-check the apartment number. It says 316.

"Is Black here?"

A light-skinned female, with green eyes, opens the door and looks me up and down. Although pretty, she seems homely for what I imagine Black's tastes are, and she doesn't look anything like the exotic types of women that Black is said to go for. Then again, I really don't know Black.

"How can I help you?"

"You can't help me. Does Black live here or not?"

"Yes, he lives here. Is that all you wanna know?"

Frowning, I say, "Who are you?"

"I'm his wife."

Did she just say "his wife"? I can't believe he's married! She slams the door shut before I can say another word. Angry, I decide that Black has played so many games, I'm gonna ruin his life for a change.

I bang on the door; seconds pass before she flings it open again.

"What!" she screams.

"Just so you know, your husband has been with other women. I just want you to know, in case you think you livin' happily ever after. If I was you, I'd leave his bum ass while you still can."

She laughs like she's crazy. "Shade and Shannon, come here for a minute." She holds the door open. I reach in my Gucci purse and place my hand on my Glock.

When the door widens, I see clearly inside. Although they live in the projects, from what I can see, the inside of his apartment is laid out with expensive furniture.

"Yeah, what's up?" a girl with dreads asks.

The other girl stands next to her; her hair is

as long and silky as mine. I have to admit, they are both beautiful.

"This chick says Black been fuckin' other women," the light-skinned girl says.

"Now, is that so?" the one with dreads says. "By 'other women,' do you mean you?"

I remain as calm as they are and say, "Yes, I mean me."

"You must be Kenyetta," the one with the long, silky hair remarks. "He told me you were a sexy little thing, and I must agree with him."

She tries to touch me and I smack her hand. "You know about me?"

They laugh.

"Honey, we know *everything*," the other one says. "Black has ten wives."

"Are you bitches crazy?"

"We taken care of," the light-skinned girl remarks. "Every bitch has a cheatin' man. Ours just tells us up front. It's all good."

The hallway seems to spin. I never heard anything like this in all my life. In my confusion, I'm not surprised when Black appears from behind the women.

"I got it from here," he says, taking the time to kiss all three on the mouth before they leave without another word. "Come in, Kenyetta. I've been expecting you. We got a lot to discuss."

The Setup for the "Finale"

Cameron

"I just want a piece of the pie when it's cut."

In the VIP section at Lux Lounge in Washington, D.C., Black Water, Lavelle, and Cameron sat on large, plush burgundy sofas. Opened bottles of Ace of Spades and Cîroc sat on the table in front of them as women danced sexily, hoping to gain their attention.

"Cameron, my men been in that apartment, going on two weeks now." Black sips on vodka. "They got two niggas guardin' every floor, makin' it hard for us to move. I keep tellin' you, we gotta push on this shit now."

"I'm ready," Cameron says confidently. "But you never got back with me on the info about the shootin'. I tried to find out somethin' myself, but came up blank."

"One of my niggas told me them dudes were from Clifton Terrace, uptown."

Lavelle shakes his head, then clears his throat at the mention of Clifton Terrace.

" 'Clifton'?" Cameron repeats, looking at Lavelle. "That's your territory, ain't it?"

Lavelle takes a deep breath and says, "Yeah. But what happened was not my plan. Shit got fucked up."

"Damn! I gotta give you credit, after all," Black Water responds with a smirk on his face. "Here I thought you was a bitch-ass nigga all this time."

"I'm five seconds from breakin' your jaw," Lavelle promises.

"Whenever you get ready . . . I am too, lil man." Black raises his cup.

"What you mean your plan 'got fucked up'?" Cameron presses.

"I was tryin' to scare Carissa outta Emerald. I need her home wit our daughters. So I paid these dumb-ass niggas to scare her, but they started shootin' for survival."

"You know they vicious wit their aim, Lavelle. Fuck was you thinkin' 'bout by instructin' them niggas to go into Emerald? You led your soldiers astray."

"I know. It was stupid on my part."

"You know they shot my baby mother, right?" Cameron holds an evil glare.

"I'm sorry, Cam. That shit fucked me up when I heard Mercedes got hit."

"Ain't you gonna have Mercedes killed, anyway?" Black slyly asks Cameron.

"Naw, I just want a piece of the pie when it's cut."

"You wanted Mercedes killed?" Lavelle interrogates.

"Yeah. . . . I mean no. . . . I realize I was trippin'."

"Look . . . I don't care who lives and who dies, at this point. Right now, I have a vested interest in Emerald. And I need to know what we gonna do."

"I got at least twenty men who waitin' for me to take back Emerald. We ready," Cameron says.

"What 'bout you, Lavelle? How many men you got?" Black asks.

" 'Bout ten."

"Well, wit the twenty men I have, it brings us to about fifty."

"Okay, so what's this plan?" Cameron queries as Young Jeezy's "Vacation" blasts on the club's speakers.

"I say that we take over Unit B first. That'll be easy, because my men are already there. When I run operation 'Finale,' your men will leave their posts, wherever they are—even if they in Unit C. When we call, they will head to Unit B. When everybody gets there, my men will come out and flood the building. I'm not gonna lie. There's gonna be some bloodshed. But after it's all said and done, we'll have what we want."

"What about the girls?" Lavelle asks.

"I suggest you find a reason to keep them away that night," Black advises. "I can't be responsible for what might happen." Although he is advising the men to get the women out, he has plans to kill them, anyway. Alive he knows they are more trouble than they are worth.

"I'll deal wit Mercedes. She won't be there, even if I have to kidnap her myself."

"And I think I got Carissa."

"I'ma give Kenyetta a warning, but she might get caught up in this shit," Black reveals.

"Kenyetta? What you mean?" Cameron asks.

"Oh . . . you ain't know? I been fuckin' shortie for a minute." He laughs.

Cameron and Lavelle can't believe what they're hearing. To think that their man Dyson's ex-girl was fucking with Black, this is sick.

"She didn't know who I was when we first got together. But when she found out, by that time it was too late."

"Damn . . . I bet the girls don't know that shit." Cameron chuckles.

"Prolly not, we might be able to use that shit to our advantage too," Black offers.

"You got this all worked out, don't you?" Cameron says.

"I planned it the moment you told me what you wanted done."

"I bet," Cameron says.

"This was your idea, not mine," Black reminds him.

"Once we get the building, then what?" Lavelle jumps back on topic.

"When everyone takes over Unit B, Harold and Ed will let four vans inside, which'll be holding twenty niggas each. They'll raid the stronger Units C and A. I hear that's where they hold the cash and product. Once we got the main units, it's a wrap."

"Unit C's security is tight. You not gonna be able to get in easy," Lavelle adds.

"I got a plan before the vans come that will help us get in. I guarantee it. Two weeks from now, we move. That'll give us enough time to brief everybody."

"What about Dreyfus?" Lavelle brings up. "I know he let you buy out Tyland, but the girls turned Emerald into a gold mine. He not lettin' that shit go so easy."

"Dreyfus thinks money. If we present him with enough, he'll be fine."

"You sure about that?" Lavelle responds.

"Positive," Black says. "So get ready, 'cause y'all about to be two of the richest niggas on earth!"

Mercedes

I just need to get away now!

"You want some of this?" Carissa asks, holding her cup out filled with liquor.

I ignore her ass, like I have the past few days.

"Mercedes, how long you gonna be mad at me?"

"This *has* gone on too long. You should at least hear her out," Kenyetta advises.

"There's nothin' to hear out. My life is some shit now, and it's all her fault."

"Carissa ain't have shit to do with you fuckin' Cameron. That was all you, Mercedes."

"Oh, so what? Now y'all takin' each other's side?"

"No. I love both y'all, but the blame needs to be placed in the right place."

"And where's that?"

"On Cameron, for bringing his big dick

146

–swingin' ass round your house when Derrick was gone. And you, for being vulnerable."

I laugh for the first time since the breakup. "And how do you know it's big?"

"Don't play," Kenyetta retorts. "Have you forgotten when we made a pact to take camera phone pics of Dex's, Dyson's, Cameron's, Lavelle's, and Thick's dicks? Cameron won!"

"He do have a fat-ass dick," I agree.

Carissa laughs, and I prevent myself from laughing and roll my eyes, instead.

"Come on, Mercedes," Kenyetta persists. "Let's not fall apart now. Not at a time like this. We need each other now, and you need us while you going through this shit."

The moment I think of forgiveness, Derrick walks upstairs.

"Everything is in order. I'ma check on Unit B and I'll hit y'all back if I find anything outta place." He looks right over my head and addresses Kenyetta and Carissa.

"Derrick, can I—"

"Is my boss talkin' or my ex-girl?" he asks, interrupting my sentence.

"Your girl."

"In that case, fuck you, bitch!" He walks away, and I cry uncontrollably.

"Ugh . . . ," Carissa says out of the blue.

"Ugh what?" Kenyetta asks, rubbing my back.

"He sounded like a lil girl. Talkin' 'bout, 'In that case, fuck you, bitch!' Don't no man roll they head and eyes like that."

I giggle softly and wipe my tears.

"Carissa, you trippin'!" I tell her, and she runs up to me and wraps her arms around my neck, reeking of alcohol.

"Oh, my Gawd, you talked to me!" she cheers, rocking me like a baby.

"Yes, but you have to get yourself together, Car. You're drinkin' too much!"

"I know . . . I know, but I have a lot of shit on my mind. Y'all stronger than me!"

"No, we just deal with what we have to deal with."

Carissa smiles and sits down.

"I'm so glad y'all made up. Too much shit happenin' wit us lately. We need each other," Kenyetta observes.

"You right," I say. "So how's Yvette? Do we know what's goin' on wit her?"

Kenyetta looks at Carissa with the should-I-tell-her-or-not look.

"What? Tell me somethin' to help get my mind off Derrick."

"She dealin' wit a female," Kenyetta says.

I'm so disgusted that I almost don't respond. "Come again?"

"Yvette's been datin' this girl for two years," she continues.

"Two years! What the fuck is she thinkin' 'bout? Yvette ain't gay!"

"She is, Mercedes," Carissa says softly. "And she didn't wanna tell you 'cause she thought you wouldn't love her the same."

"That's some gross-ass shit, y'all . . . and I hope y'all told her 'bout herself." They remain

quiet. "What did y'all tell her?" I ask, looking between them.

"We told her as long as she happy, we fine wit
it," Kenyetta tells me. "And you should be too."

"That's some bullshit, Kenyetta. Yvette ain't
no fuckin' dyke! She probably needed us to set
her straight, and y'all run and tell her lies.
Don't forget she was wit Thick all her life. This
girl probably got up in her head because she
was lonely."

"Mercedes, this ain't no fly-by-night bullshit.
They serious 'bout each other," Carissa mutters,
despite being drunk. "Her feelings are real, and
she's in love."

"*What the fuck is goin' on around here?* I feel like
I'm losin' my mind! Niggas tryin' to take Emerald, I get shot, Carissa turnin' into a drunk, and
you fuckin' wit Gawd knows who!" I yell, pointing at Kenyetta. "Now I'm hearin' that Yvette's a
lesbian and Derrick dumps me because I fucked
my kid's father! I need to get outta here before I
go the fuck off!" I scream, running away.

Don't ask me where I'm going, because I
won't be able to tell you. I just need to get away,
and I need to get away now!

Jona

"You wanna make some money?"

Jona sits on the floor, in the corner of her bedroom, with a cream-colored phone in her hand. Every day since she's returned home from the hospital, she's called Lil C, except today. She's convinced herself she'll leave him alone, but she can't. Blocking her number, she decides to call him again, to see if he'll pick up. After two rings, he answers.

"Who this?" Loud voices play in the background.

"It's Jona. You busy?"

He breathes heavily into the phone and says, "What's wrong wit you, shortie? Up until now, I never pegged you for no stalker-type bitch."

"I'm not a stalker. I just wanna talk." Still sitting, she pulls her knees toward her chest and rests her head on top of them. "Why can't we at least be friends?"

"I told you what it is, Jona. So why you buggin'?"

"Just come see me one time, and I'll leave you alone. I know you in Emerald. My friends say they saw you."

"Jona . . . don't call me again, young. It's not a request no more."

Lil C hangs up.

She cries softly, hoping her mother doesn't hear her. But unlike the other days, now she is angry. Wiping her tears, she decides to call her crazy cousin, who is staying with her uncle Hawk in Unit B. It is the same building she knows Lil C is in.

"What's up, cuzo?" His Southern accent is as heavy as usual.

"Nothin'. I'ma stop by tomorrow, before y'all leave."

"Cool . . . 'cause you know we goin' back to Texas in two days, right?"

"Yeah, Uncle Hawk told me. Where he at?"

"Out runnin' the streets as usual. He said he was gonna bring back some grub."

"Look, Beatz, you wanna make some money?"

"You know I do. Just give me names and info."

Jona gets excited.

"My brothers, Yuri and Gamal, wit me and they gonna want in on it too. We were just sayin', we broke as shit. Uncle Hawk gives us what he can, but, for real, it ain't shit. Is the pie large enough for all of us?"

"Yeah, but the dude you hittin' up is major. His father used to run Emerald, and his mother still does."

"If he human, that mean he bleed like me. So tell me where to find him."

They spend a few more moments on the phone, going over the details. She tells them everything she knows about the dude Lil C cops his weed from. She tells them to move quickly, because he probably would be going to Lani's after he leaves Unit B. It would be harder to catch him then, and she makes it clear that she wants him dead.

When Lil C rejected her, Jona decided that if he was going to cut her off, she didn't want him with Lani either.

Without another word, Beatz wakes up his brothers and gets down to business.

Lil C

"I'm about this paper, and if you ain't wit it, we can just split ways."

"Yo, we made out like shit! I told you that last package wasn't gonna take us no time to move." Lil C holds a blue bag firmly packed with weed.

"Yeah . . . but I don't like him frontin' us this much weight," Nick warns as they walk to the elevator. "We got enough money. . . . So how come we don't buy what we can afford?"

" 'Cause that ain't enough for what I'm tryin' to do. This our last time, because I should have enough saved for when my baby is born. I wanted this one to be big."

"What's up, Lil C?" one of the Emerald City men asks as they reach the elevator. Even though they all know he is sneaking into the city, they never tell Mercedes. They just look out for him when he is there. "You out?"

153

"Yeah, I'ma get up wit my girl and then I'm gone," he says, entering the elevator. The soldier watches him as he waits on the elevator. He wants to make sure C gets in safely.

"I hear what you sayin', but I don't like it," Nick continues. "It don't feel smart."

"What?" C asks with a grin on his face. "You just started playin' gangsta since you been rollin' wit me. So what you know about this shit? Everything you learned, I taught you."

He hesitates and says, "This reckless, man."

"You can think what you want," Lil C tells him. "I'm about this paper, and if you ain't wit it, we can just split ways."

The elevator knocks around a little.

"Why it gotta be a problem when I say somethin' 'bout business?" he replies, putting his hat back on. "I'm watchin' out for both of our backs."

"Don't worry. I got this. Just worry 'bout—" His statement is cut short.

The moment the elevator door opens and they step our, Beatz hits Lil C in the face so hard, he's temporarily blinded and stumbles back. Nick rushes from behind him and does his best to help his friend. He lands a few blows on Beatz's jaw, but his brothers, Yuri and Gamal, punish him with repeat blows to the gut. Nick's wreck game is no match for two Southern brothers from the Deep.

"Yo, Gamal," Beatz calls to his younger brother. "Take the package and bounce!"

Gamal rubs his knuckles and snatches the blue duffel bag.

"Do you know what you doin'?" Lil C questions, standing halfway on his two feet.

Beatz laughs and says, "I know who you are, and that don't mean shit to me, nigga. But you keep talkin' and I might let them pretty lips suck my dick."

Lil C is furious and rushes Beatz with his body weight. Once he has him up against the wall, he steals him multiple times in the face. With his focus on Beatz, he doesn't see Yuri take out a knife and plunge it into Nick's gut. Suddenly he hears Nick yell out in pain.

The three of them stop momentarily and look at Nick as he drops to his knees. Touching his stomach, Nick feels his own silky blood and falls face-first onto the grungy floor.

Lil C is just about to go after Yuri, until Beatz says, "Don't move, nigga." Beatz laughs, cocking the nine-millimeter piece in his hand. "The fun and games are over."

"Fuck y'all want wit me?" C yells. "You killed my man and took my work!"

"We want your life, partna. 'Parently, you got somebody real fucked up wit you."

"Fuck you talkin' 'bout, nigga?"

"Since you gonna die, anyway, it don't even matter. What did you do to my cousin Jona, nigga?"

Lil C's entire body trembles. Silently he prays he'll get out of the situation alive, because if he does, he'll pay her a visit.

"I hope you had a nice life." Beatz raises his hand, preparing to fire, when four men enter the basement doorway. Three of them are carrying guns and they quickly aim at Beatz and Yuri. Lil C knows all of them.

"Lil C, bounce. We got it from here," Paul says, with his eyes glued on Beatz. Fear washes over Yuri and Beatz as they realize they are outnumbered.

"How did you know I was here?"

"Cameron called me to come get you. Rap to him about all that when you get to the crib. We got work to do, and there's a car waiting to take you home."

"What about Nick?" he asks, pointing at his friend's body.

Paul looks down and says, "We'll take care of everything. Go."

Before leaving, Lil C walks up to Beatz and steals him in the face so hard his right thumb jams. C doesn't acknowledge the pain, because the agony he's in is a small price to pay.

"You fucked wit the wrong nigga," Lil C warns. "I hope it was worth it."

With that, he dodges out the door.

"Don't take too long," Tony, one of Cameron's friends, says to Lil C in the car. Although he works in Emerald, he remains loyal to him. "Cameron wants me to get you out of Emerald as soon as possible. He says a lot of shit been goin' on lately."

"Just give me five minutes. I'll be right back," he promises.

Tony agrees and Lil C jogs up the stairs and knocks on Jona's door. She unlocks and opens it.

"What's up? I thought you couldn't come," she says nervously, opening the door wider.

"I changed my mind. You not happy to see me, or somethin'?"

"Yes." Although she's frightened, she hopes he doesn't know about her betrayal.

"Well, are you gonna let me in?"

"Uh . . . sure." Jona opens the door wider for him to enter. Lil C walks in without noticing that Lani sees him entering her place.

"You by yourself?" he asks. There's an evil glower on his face as he stares around the apartment.

"Is everything okay, Cameron?"

"Are . . . you . . . by . . . yourself?" he asks, locking the door behind him.

"Y-yes," she stutters. "My moms on her way back, though."

Not wasting time, he grips her neck and pushes her against the wall. Her feet are no longer on the floor as she claws at his hands and face. His right thumb is throbbing, but he doesn't release.

"They . . . killed my friend!" He squeezes her neck more tightly. Spit escapes his mouth, and tears run down his face. "They killed my fuckin' friend!"

Jona continues to fight until she can't fight anymore. Small sounds escape her mouth, but these are not audible. Her eyes roll to the back of her head. He squeezes a little more tightly, releases her, and watches her body fall to the floor.

"Fuckin' slut!"

With his first kill under his belt, he wipes his face with his good hand and leaves.

Ed

"It will work out, and if it doesn't, no one will ever know!"

Between each unit in Emerald City, there is a ramp. It was built for handicap access and leads to the elevator. But most times, the dopeheads utilize it to shoot up in private. Tonight the ramp between Unit A and Unit B will be used for a different purpose.

"There she is," Ed says as he stoops down within the ramp. "When I say 'go,' we gotta grab her quick before somebody see us."

Kit is shaking so hard that his teeth can be heard rattling.

Kit had abandoned his post earlier to run this caper. Had he not, Nick would've never gotten killed.

"I don't see her," Kit whispers.

"Just wait."

Harold called Ed the moment he saw Mer-

159

cedes walk away from Unit C. She is making their job easier, because they have orders to kidnap her later. Black Water wants to keep her as collateral, in case Cameron reneges on their deal. And to get Harold and Ed to betray Cameron, Black has paid them five hundred dollars each. A small price to pay for honor.

"Go!" Ed yells as they run toward her. Mercedes recognizes his voice.

They grab her when she's not looking and forcefully pull the hood of her coat over her head. She's caught off guard because her mind is on Derrick.

"Ed? What the fuck are you doin'?"

"Say my name again and watch what I'll do!" he promises.

"Get the fuck off me, Ed!" she screams, clawing at Ed's face.

"What I tell you, bitch?" He hits her with a closed fist.

Although his duty is for Black, jealousy is his real motive right now. He hates having to report to women, so he strikes her so hard in the face that her tooth falls down her throat.

"Help me bring her inside," Ed tells Kit. His cohort is so overwhelmed by how Ed is treating her, he doesn't move. "Did you hear what I said? Help me get her inside!"

"I don't know 'bout this, man," Kit finally replies, grabbing her arm. "This the boss. We gonna get killed if this shit don't work out."

"It will work out, and if it doesn't, no one will ever know!"

"How you know?"

" 'Cause I'll kill this bitch myself first. Now help me get her in the elevator before somebody comes lookin' for her." Ed opens the basement door and they walk past the small puddle of blood in the hallway from where Nick's body was.

"Fuck happened in here?" Ed talks to himself.

"Ed, please . . . please don't do this," Mercedes whimpers.

He doesn't answer. She wishes she had enough strength to fight, but she doesn't. She's in so much pain that her head throbs uncontrollably. When the elevator opens, they rush her inside. When it moves, Ed grabs his phone and calls the person assisting him on the fourth floor. Like the other units, there are two soldiers on each post, so they have to get rid of the other one.

"Yodi, we on our way up," Ed says as he eyes Mercedes lustfully. He can't wait to be inside her. "Get rid of that nigga."

"Got it," he tells him.

"Yo, Peanut," Yodi says after placing his phone in his pocket. "Somebody just called and said they need you downstairs. They said Kenyetta wants you."

"Why Kenyetta ain't call me?"

"I don't know 'bout all that, but you betta check it out."

"I'm not supposed to leave post."

"Let me call him back and tell him you said, 'Fuck Kenyetta.' " Yodi pretends to be dialing out.

"I'm goin'!" Peanut yells, stopping him.

Against his instinct, Peanut leaves his post and heads for the elevator on his side of the floor. It is the opposite end from the direction where Ed and Kit are coming.

"He gone," Yodi says, calling Ed back. "But hurry up before he comes back."

"We comin' now." He lifts Mercedes up, who is helplessly lying against the railing. "We got to get this bitch in Harold's crib quick. And I don't know 'bout you, but I'ma hit this shit before I go back on post. I wanna see what boss pussy be like."

Mercedes

When I was younger, I didn't believe in hell.

I can't believe this is happening to me. I'm actually being kidnapped by Ed and taken into Harold's apartment. Carissa told me she never trusted them, and I wish I would've listened. And the way I left, saying I just needed to get away, I doubt if they will try to find me anytime soon.

"Is that who I think it is?" someone says when we enter.

"Yeah . . . ," Ed boasts, closing and locking the door. "This one of them."

A bunch of men I don't know circle me and feel my body. I fight back tears.

"Back up, niggas." Ed laughs. "I know y'all been stuck in here forever, but whatever y'all plannin' gotta wait. Me and Kit caught the fish, so we get to eat it first."

"I'm fine, man," Kit says, shaking his head. "You go 'head."

"Suit yourself." He removes the gun from his coat and strikes the back of my head with the handle for no reason. He follows up with another blow across my face, which slits my eye. Blood rushes inside it. "I'm fuckin' this bitch, until I can't fuck her no more."

I fall to my knees and he drags me by my hair to the bathroom. My body brushes up against empty pizza boxes, beer cans, and trash all over the floor.

"This nigga actin' like a caveman! Don't bash her up too bad, and shit!" someone says. "I want her pretty, when I get to her."

"Fuck you, nigga, before I make her off-limits to y'all funky bastards."

They laugh, and Ed opens the door and throws my body across the edge of the tub. The porcelain presses against my stomach. He roughly removes my coat and pulls my jeans to my ankles. He tugs at my panties until they tear apart. I am naked from the waist down and feel completely exposed.

"Ed, we been good to you," I say softly. "And if you let me go, I won't tell anyone about this. I'm the mother of Cameron's kids."

The moment I say Cameron's name, he pushes his dick inside me hard. "Please!" I beg, sobbing. "You're hurting me!" He violently grabs my hair, pulls it backward, and licks my face.

"Bitch, all this was Cameron's idea, anyway. You callin' that nigga's name ain't doin' shit but making me hard. So shut the fuck up before I get *real* violent."

He slams my head forward and it bounces off the inside of the tub. More of my blood exits my body and goes down the drain. For twenty minutes, he rapes me, until he can't rape me no more.

Then, one after another, men enter the bathroom and then my body. I count about twenty men after Ed left me. Some are gentle, while others are rough, nasty, and rude. But after the third one, I become numb. There is no more crying, and no more begging them to stop. I need to preserve my energy.

After they are done . . . hours pass, and the rapes stop. They carry on conversations, like I'm not there. In between shitting and pissing in the bathroom, they talk to me like I am trash. One of them makes me open my mouth while he pisses inside it. I throw up for an hour, until he gets tired of hearing me gag and threatens to kill me.

When I was younger, I didn't believe in hell. I thought it was a place old people talked about to keep you in line. I was wrong. Because there's no way you can't tell me that I'm not in hell . . . on earth . . . right now.

Lil C

"I shoulda known you was foul!"

Lying on his bed in the dark, Lil C is still battling with the loss of his closest friend, Nick. To make matters worse, his father won't tell him what was done with Nick's body or his car. The moment Lil C got home that night, Cameron stopped him from telling anybody he was the last one with him.

The first day, Lil C hated his father for making him lie to Nick's mother. It was difficult to hear her cry, begging him for any details. Just when he thought things can't get any worse, he discovered his mother has been missing for days. Lil C is taking things hard.

"You ready to talk now?" Cameron asks. He turns on the lights in his son's room and plops down on the edge of his bed.

Lil C, lying flat on his back with his hands behind his head and his legs crossed, briefly acknowledges his father. "Not really."

"Well, we gotta talk, anyway, C. Now I know you're hurtin', but what's done is done. You wanted in the life. Now here it is."

Lil C nods.

"So how does it feel?"

"How does what feel?" Lil C turns to look at him.

"Your first kill."

Lil C is shocked by his father's statement.

"I know everything. One of the soldiers saw you enter that youngin's apartment on the night her mother found her murdered. Don't worry 'bout it. They told me, so we took care of everything."

"I don't know how it feels. I mean . . . the first night, I kept seeing her face. So I stayed up that whole night. Now I'm fine. I just can't get over Nick. He was tryin' to protect me, and they killed him. They had what they wanted, so why didn't they just let us go?"

"That's the game, son. You wanted to be a man, and this is how it is. The rules are heavy, and if you gonna be in this lifestyle, get ready. Everybody's a target."

"You know 'bout the drugs too?"

"I know everything you do, C. I sent my man to scoop you up from Unit D the moment I found out you snuck out of here. Usually, I let you be, because I know you growin' up and wanna be with your friends . . . but not this time. I'ma tell you the truth. I ain't know shit 'bout them niggas 'bout to rob you. They out-of-towners. Right now, anybody not from the city got the spotlight on 'em. So when they passed one of the soldiers at the elevator and said your name in conversation, my man called me right away. I called Paul and had him shoot over there. Sounds like he got there just in time."

"Not really. . . . They still got Nick," Lil C says in a low voice.

"I know, but they ain't got my son. But look, C, you gotta stay away from Emerald. Shit is heavy."

"I ain't scared of no niggas! I go hard!"

"I'm not askin'," Cameron says, scowling. "You gotta stay the *fuck* out of Emerald. And wit your moms gone, I wanna keep an eye on you to make sure you're safe. She don't need to be stressin', when she come back. Understood?"

"Yes."

"Good. Don't make me catch a body for somebody hurtin' my only son."

"Where you think Ma go?"

"I don't know. People sayin' she needed to be alone."

"You think she gonna come back?"

"I think she will. Everybody need to escape sometimes."

Lil C takes a deep breath and says, "Dad . . . I gotta rap to you 'bout somethin'."

Cameron nods for him to proceed.

"Lani pregnant."

"How, man?" Cameron is upset. "I get you a pack of rubbers every time I get mine."

"I know, but she my main shortie. It just happened."

Cameron shakes his head. "How you know it's yours, C? These young bitches be runnin' game out here."

"I can't really explain it. . . . I just know."

"Well, you know what that mean, don't you? You gotta do right by your seed."

"I plan to. That's what I been grindin' for."

"You ain't gotta grind, C. You know we got you."

"I'm a man, Dad. I gotta take care of my own seed. How I look like, gettin' money from my peoples for my kid?"

Cameron smiles at his son and says, "You're right. How come she hasn't called?"

"I don't know. We ain't talked since Nick died. I just wanted to be alone."

It wasn't until then that Lil C realizes that Lani hasn't called him.

"A'ight . . . but look, I settled your bill on that package you copped from the kid in Unit B. And we caught up wit Hawk, broke a few legs, and made him tell us where his nephews rest in Texas. I'ma send somebody there to take care of him next week. He sold it for half of what it was worth to some niggas on Kennedy Street before he left."

"Thanks, Dad. I got you later on that."

"I know, next week you work for me. This way, I can keep an eye on you."

Lil C nods and Cameron leaves the room. Picking up the phone, C calls Lani.

"What's up, Cameron?" she says dryly.

"Look . . . before you get started, I know you mad at me for not calling you. I been goin' through some shit and needed to be alone." He pauses. "So I been—"

"What do you want, Cameron? I got company, so right now I'm busy."

"Company? What you talkin' 'bout?"

"I understand you been gone awhile, but it sounds like you still know English," she says sarcastically. "So let me spell it out. I have *C.O.M.P.A.N.Y.* And since you like to fuck my friends, I decided to try yours." She giggles and Lil C feels his blood boil.

"So you fuckin' other niggas now? That's how you carryin' it?"

"We *done*, C. So get over it, 'cause I'm already over you."

Lil C pumps himself up to unleash on her and says, "You know what? It don't even matter to me. Just as long as that nigga, whoever he is, stays away from my baby when he's born."

Lani laughs and says, "Boy, I had an abortion yesterday. Trust when I say you free to go on with your life, boo-boo."

She gets off the phone, and someone says, "I'ma need you to stop callin' here. I wasn't tryin' to get in y'all's business, but you still on the phone, dude."

Tamir's voice enrages C.

"I shoulda known you was foul!"

Tamir laughs.

"So you fuckin' my girl?" C barks.

"Naw . . . I'm fuckin' *my* girl."

Lil C tries to understand how Tamir even knows her. Although he rapped to him about Jona, he never talked about Lani, because he respected their relationship around his friends. Taking two deep breaths, he decides not to let any more of his feelings show.

"You can have that slut, but don't let me catch you on the streets, playa."

"Don't worry, homie. Our time will come."

"Indeed."

Tamir hangs up the phone, and Lil C decides to make another call.

"Is Monie Blow home?" he asks the woman who answers.

"Who the fuck is this?"

"Lil C. A friend of hers."

The phone drops and the woman yells, "Monie, get this fuckin' phone! I told you I don't want nobody callin' my house!"

"Ma, shut the fuck up!" she says, picking up the phone. "Who dis?"

"It's C, from Emerald."

"Oh, hey, C," she says in a nice voice. "I'm glad you called, 'cause I ain't think you liked me. You know, wit you bein' from Emerald, and all."

"I fucks wit you. That's why I'm callin'. You know Lani and Sachi jumped your cousin, right?" he says, hating how petty he sounds.

"I know. That bitch betta neva let me catch her."

"She said she waitin' on you. I just wanted you to know. Be careful."

"Waitin' on me! I'm from Tyland T all day!

We don't play that shit! Wait till I tell my girls! It's gonna be on!"

C gets off the phone with her and lies back in his bed. He knows Monie and her girls will handle Lani, and he has plans for Tamir. He can't predict how many men he'll kill in the future, nor does he know their names. But C is certain that before he leaves this earth, Tamir will be put to rest by C's own hands.

Yvette

"You and me together would've burned this city down."

"Kick that muthafucka in!" I tell one of the four men with me.

Boom! Crash! Crash! When the door comes down, a lady feeding her infant jumps up quickly and hides her breasts.

"Run through this muthafucka and tell me if Mercedes in here." I look at the frightened mother. "Don't worry. If she ain't in here, we'll be out in a second."

As I await their word, my hand remains on my weapon. I'll kill this bitch if I have to. Ever since I heard the way Mercedes left, I felt uneasy. Upset or not, she wouldn't leave us like this.

"She ain't in here, boss," Carson says, walking out.

"Fuck!" I look at the woman and her child. "Look, I'm sorry."

"I—I understand," she stutters. "I really hope you find her."

"For a lot of people's sake, I hope we do too."

Carson gives her some money for the repairs, and we move to the next apartment. We must've kicked down twenty doors with no signs of Mercedes yet. I'm losin' it!

"Kick it in," I instruct them at the next apartment.

When the door swings open, inside the apartment, I see a man I always talk to. I used to give him his props for taking care of his daughter alone. And here this nasty muthafucka is, sittin' on the couch and making his ten-year-old daughter suck his dick!

"What the fuck!" I scream.

"Fuck is this dude doin'?" Carson asks, enraged at the sight.

I don't have to tell them what to do next, because all four of my men stomp him until he's motionless. I hold his daughter back with my hands so she won't get hurt.

"You okay, baby?" I ask.

"Yes . . . yes," she says, shaking.

"Where's your mother?"

"Locked up."

"Why?"

"She stabbed him for hurting me."

Dirty bastard. "Look, put some clothes on. I'ma take you to the lady next door."

She trots in the room and gets dressed; we take her to the next-door neighbor.

"Don't worry. I'll take care of her." The neighbor lady smiles. "Go find your friend."

We were just about to knock down another door, when Carson says, "Boss, I don't think she in this building. I think we should try Unit B."

"Why? Somebody said the last time they saw her, she was over here."

"Somethin' seems weird about Unit B lately. I remember walkin' up on two dudes the other day, and when they saw me comin', they stopped talkin'."

"And?"

"Well . . . the night Mercedes was shot, Harold came round back when I was on post. He was actin' funny and seemed weird. It always stuck wit me. He said he was on his way to his crib when he *happened* to see my ride fucked up. I'm tellin' you, boss, I think he got me to leave my post on purpose. I know it wasn't the same night Mercedes left, but I think them niggas in that buildin' up to somethin'!"

"Harold, huh? Carissa said repeatedly that she didn't trust them."

"Yeah . . . I *really* don't trust him or Ed. And somebody said the night Mercedes left, Ed wasn't on post. Said he was gone for 'bout thirty minutes."

My breaths are quick, and I try to slow them down. I'm on the verge of a panic attack. I had to plan a better raid. We could go over to Unit B to kick down doors, but that could backfire. I'm gonna have to play it smart.

"Look, when I tell you to, I want you to bring Ed to me tonight."

"What you want me to say?"

"Tell 'em we tryin' to find Mercedes and we havin' a meetin' with only the people we trust. I'll take care of the rest."

"Got it."

"Gimme an hour. I have to set a few things up and I'll call you."

"Okay. And I'm sorry I ain't tell you earlier, boss. I guess I thought he was just slackin' and it wasn't a big deal."

"Never wait to tell me somethin' again, Carson. Trust your instincts. Always."

"I will from now on. It'll never happen again."

"Why you leave without me?" Kenyetta asks when I run up the stairs. "You can't be on a mission alone. What if somethin' would've happened to you?"

"I wasn't alone, Kenyetta. But I gotta find Mercedes." I look at her worried face. "Okay, Kenyetta, I'll be more careful, but I got a plan to find her, which I think will work."

"What is it?"

"I think she's here. In Emerald. So we're gonna hold a meeting with our most trusted men. Somethin' in my blood tellin' me some shit is goin' on, especially after Mercedes said Cameron and Black were together. I think Mercedes going missing and that meeting with Cameron and Black are all tied together."

"Damn . . . so what you want me to do?" Kenyetta asks.

"I want you to invite twenty people you trust, and, Carissa, you invite twenty too." Carissa has been so quiet that I almost forgot she is here. Her face is in her cup. "If you can't trust them fully, don't invite them. You wit me, Carissa?"

"I can't do this," she says under her breath. "I'm tired of being afraid."

"So you wanna abandon us? At a time like this?" Kenyetta responds.

"I just wanna raise my kids wit Velle. I don't want any of the money."

"Money? Fuck you talkin' about?"

"This not me no more, Kenyetta."

"I can't believe this shit!" Kenyetta screams.

"Please don't be mad at me." Carissa is crying. "I'm still your friend. Please!"

"A friend? Who abandons?" Kenyetta responds. "No such thing."

"Let her go," I say, gently touching Kenyetta's arm. "Just let her go."

Kenyetta looks at me and shakes her head. "Whateva happened to the pact we made? Right after Thick dumped you? We said nobody could break our bond. So why are you leavin' at a time like this? What about Mercedes, Carissa? She needs us!"

"It's over, Kenyetta. If she wants out, we have to let her go."

Kenyetta walks away and down the stairs. I grab my phone and call Carson. "Look, keep an eye on Kenyetta. She just left Unit C, upset. Make sure nobody hurts her."

"I got it, boss."

After the call, I think about Carissa. I saw the breakdown in her eyes a while ago.

"You free to leave, Carissa." I smile. She gets up and hugs me, and I hug her back.

Before leaving, she tells me, "I love you. I love all of you."

"I know you do. Now go take care of yourself."

When she leaves, I see Derrick rushing up the stairs. His eyes are bloodshot red.

"Why you ain't tell me, Yvette?" he yells. "Why you ain't tell me Mercedes been missin' all this time?"

"Calm down!" I say, with my arms out in front of me so he can't approach me. "I didn't tell you 'cause you and me together would've burned this city down. But don't worry. I got another plan. We gonna find her, Derrick. Trust me."

Carson

"Must be nice to be so relaxed."

The weather is cold, but the stars shine brightly on the field of Emerald City. Carson found Kenyetta, and Yvette was thankful. She then had him go get Ed.

Carson walks toward the guard's station, where Harold and Ed are standing post. But before reaching them, he approaches two soldiers, who are a few feet from the gate. He considers them cool, because the girls hired them all and they got their chances together. Most of the other soldiers were hired on Cameron's watch.

"What up, B?" Carson says to one of them before giving him a manly handshake.

"Ain't shit, shawty," Dipbug says. "The city on high alert! Niggas 'noid as shit around here!"

"I feel you," Carson confirms. "What 'bout you, Kit? You holdin' up?"

Carson isn't saying it, but what he is trying to do is feel them out.

"I'm good. I just be glad when shit gets back to normal around here."

Carson takes note of how fidgety he is.

"No doubt. You a'ight, though?" Carson asks Kit. "You lookin' kinda nervous."

"I'm good. It's just cold as shit out here."

"I feel you. Look . . . I gotta holla at Ed right quick. I'll get up wit y'all later."

"Everything cool?" Kit asks.

"I don't know. . . . Is it?"

Kit doesn't respond.

"I'm just fuckin' wit you. Like I said, I'll get up wit you later." Carson makes mental notes to tell Yvette that something is up with Kit too.

"A'ight, man," Dipbug says.

Carson walks toward Ed and Harold, who are playing cards in the booth. "Must be nice to be so relaxed, considering the city is on high alert."

"It is nice," Harold replies. "So why you not on post?"

" 'Cause I'm on some otha shit tonight." Carson smirks. "Ed, let me holla at you."

"What up?" Ed asks before looking at Harold. "I was 'bout to crush this nigga in this game."

"I gotta rap to you *now*, homie . . . and we got to do it alone."

"A'ight," Ed relents. When they are alone, he says, "What's up?"

"Look, man, Yvette holdin' a private meetin' wit the people she trust. So everybody ain't invited on this one."

"She trusts me?" Ed points to himself.

"Why? She shouldn't?"

"Fuck no!" Ed says cockily. "Yvette know I got her back."

"Cool, we need you to come right now. We tryin' to find Mercedes."

"Oh, a'ight. Let me tell Harold."

"Man, we have to leave now. If she wanted Harold to be in on it, I would've told him myself. We gotta roll now," Carson demands. "Harold gonna be a'ight. Dipbug and Kit got him."

Carson can tell Ed is guilty. Not only were they too lax at the gate to be in the middle of a war, but his vibe is foul. Both of them. And if the opportunity presents itself, he'll be the first to take them out.

Ed

"If I can do anything to help, count me in."

Ed and Carson walk to the community center. There are ten rooms inside, and Ed is led to the one on the far end of the building. Ed's instincts tell him something isn't right, but what can he do? Once inside the room, he sees Derrick sitting behind a desk.

"What's goin' on, man?" Ed asks him. "Where's Yvette?"

"She comin'. For now, you need to sit back." Ed sits. "You a'ight?"

Ed swallows hard. "I'm cool. I just wanna do my part to find Mercedes."

"Is that so? Tell me, if you were gonna find her, where would be the first place you'd look?" Derrick gets up and sits on the edge of a table across from him.

"I don't know. But I'm fucked up about her missin', like you."

"Fucked up about her missin', like me?" Derrick points to himself. "Naw, my dude. You could never be as fucked up about it as me. Neva."

"You know what I mean. If I can do anything to help, count me in."

"Oh, I know you will help me find her." Derrick smirks at Ed. "I'm sure of it."

Ed's phone vibrates, indicating he has a text message. The message says: **In twenty minutes we movin'. Be ready.** It was from Harold.

Looking up at Derrick, Ed's expression shows guilt. "That was my man," he says, trying to erase the message.

Carson snatches the phone and reads it. "Fuck does this mean?" he asks Ed. He doesn't respond. "Derrick, look at this shit!"

Derrick takes the phone, reads the message, and looks at Ed with an inquisitive stare.

"You got two minutes to tell me somethin' before I start pushin' your teeth down your throat."

He stands over him.

Ed spends the next hour explaining what he can about the message, softening his involvement in everything. He hopes what he is willing to say will be enough.

It isn't.

Yvette

"Years ago, we fought to keep Emerald. And we won."

I look around the conference room in the community center and see fifty-six men we feel we can trust. They all wait on my word.

"As you all know, Mercedes is missin'. And we think whoever came through our gates had something to do with it. We also think they're still here. We called you all here because we need your help finding her, and we know all of you are loyal to Emerald. We have to look out for one another during these times. Things are about to get serious," I say.

"Can I say somethin'?" Kenyetta asks, walking up to the front.

"Sure," I respond, backing away so she can take the floor.

"This is war, fellas. Years ago, we fought to keep Emerald. And we won. We are fighting a new war today, and we'll win again. There will be bloodshed and lives may be lost. But we promise, if you ride wit us, you'll all benefit for your sacrifices. Can we—"

Before Kenyetta can finish, Derrick bursts through the community center door.

"I gotta talk to you," he says, interrupting the meeting.

"Excuse us for a minute," Derrick says. We all take a few steps back, and the men in the meeting talk quietly amongst themselves as they wait.

"We got Ed," he whispers. "And he told us they plannin' to take down the city tonight." Derrick is anxious. "Black Water and Cameron are involved."

I see Kenyetta stumble a bit and I help her keep her balance. "You a'ight?"

"Yeah. Yeah, I'm good." She stands on her own two feet. "Go 'head, Derrick."

"They're sendin' texts to everybody involved in their plan. Whoever with them will receive a text and walk off, no matter where they are, to meet in Unit B. I ain't sure, Vette, but I got a strong feelin' my shortie in there too. That nigga stuck to his guns 'bout not knowin' shit 'bout where she at, but I know he lyin'. Cameron involved."

"I just can't see Cameron bein' involved in kidnappin' her," I say.

"If he ain't involved, it sure looks like it," Derricks responds.

"The boy Cameron never learns," Kenyetta says. "He fucked up! He needs to move on!"

"I know," Derrick adds. "Looks like he's gonna need my help."

While we are talking, one of the men in the front row looks at his phone and walks toward the door. Derrick, Kenyetta, and I look at each other.

"What's goin' on, Vick?" Keneytta says to the man *she* invited to the meeting.

"I just gotta check on my post right quick. I'll be back."

"Well, *we* tellin' you it's fine. So they can wait," Kenyetta tells him. "Nothin's more important than finding Mercedes."

"It can't wait." He continues moving toward the door. "I'll get up wit y'all later."

He is almost at the door, when I yell, "Drop his ass!"

A few men move to do it, but Doctanian, one of our oldest friends, enters the door and knocks Vick out. He had been coming in as Vick was going out. I called him earlier to tell him what was happening, but I couldn't reach him, so I left a message. Apparently, he came straight over after hearing it. And although he owns a sports bar outside of Emerald City now, and is no longer in the drug game, he's still considered family.

Rubbing his knuckles from laying Vick out, he says, "Who is this nigga?"

"Somebody who got exactly what he deserved! Dropped!" I tell him.

Doctanian laughs and walks up to us. We embrace, and I already feel safer with him around.

"I heard about what happened, so I dropped everything and came through. Whateva you need me to do, I'm in!"

Derrick gives him a handshake and pulls him into a one-arm hug. "Thanks, man, for comin'!"

"Please. You was there for me when Erick killed my shortie and dumped her."

The thought of the same fate happening to Mercedes sickens our stomachs.

"And I'm here for y'all. I don't give a fuck who we gotta murder! We fam!" Doctanian continues to say.

We talk a few more seconds privately, and then reconvene our meeting. Shit is about to get real serious in Emerald. Guaranteed.

Black Water

"By the time they make a move, it'll be too late."

Black is watching his sons fire at empty beer bottles in the back of Tyland Towers' parking lot. These sons, ranging from ages sixteen to nineteen, crash each bottle with a single shot. Although young, they are marksmen. And at present, no man or woman in their age range or older can fuck with their firing skills. Black Water has been training them since they were old enough to hold a weapon. His other sons who range from ten to thirteen are waiting to fire at the targets next. Because tonight it will be them, not their older brothers, who get a chance to show their skills. In the entire world, there is not a group of children more vicious or cold-blooded than the children of the Black Water Clan.

"What you mean, you can't find Ed?" Black

asks as his younger sons finally step up to practice. He's on his cell phone. "When was the last time you saw him?"

"When Carson came to get him. I don't know what was said, because they stepped off. But the way Carson looked at me, it made me feel like somethin' was up," Harold says. "They may know something."

"You could tell all that by a look?"

"That—and, one by one, dudes started leavin' their post, and shit. I asked a few of 'em what was up, but they ignored me. They knew something I didn't."

"It don't matter. By the time they make a move, it'll be too late."

When Black's call ends, he watches his wives Shade and Shannon walk toward him with their guns in hand.

"Y'all ready?" he asks, kissing them on their lips.

"We were born ready, daddy," Shade says, wrapping her arm around his waist. "So don't worry, we got you. Everything gonna go smooth."

"It better," he says.

The War Has Begun

Harold

People have chosen their sides, and now it is time for battle.

"Okay, it's 'bout to be on," Harold says when he enters his apartment. The men had recently got off the phone with Black and knew now was the time to move. "I just spoke to Black, and our troops are movin' toward this building as we speak. I doubt very seriously all of us gonna make it outta this shit alive, though. So if you wanna get some pussy from that slut in the bathroom, you betta do it now, 'cause it might be your last fuck in life."

A few of the men line up next to the bathroom door, preparing to rape Mercedes again. Harold raped her earlier that day and isn't interested anymore.

As he looks out the window, he wonders what is to become of him. He is frightened.

There is not a soul in the field. People have chosen their sides, and now it is time for battle. He wonders if the women they called "pit bulls" are as vicious as he's heard, or if it was just a rumor. Either way, he realizes it is too late to turn back now.

Mercedes

If I'm gonna die, I'm gonna die fighting!

I don't know what happened, but I *snapped*. I grew tired of the sexual abuse. Fifteen men raped me today, and I was raw and in pain. No longer could I just bend over and *take it*, like they told me over and over again.

Don't ask me where the strength came from, 'cause I can't be sure. Maybe it was the food Kit snuck me every day when everyone else was asleep. Or maybe it was thinkin' about my children being left with Cameron. Whatever it was, it caused me to grab the last man, who was about to climb on top of me, and choke him until the life left his body.

"Fuccccccck youuuuuuu!" I scream. My shoes and my jeans have been removed. My panties had been shredded during the first rape. I'm completely nude from the waist down.

Spit escapes my mouth and drops on his face. I'm in a murderous rage. If I'm gonna die, it'll be fighting. I squeeze his throat so hard, my entire body trembles. When he stops fighting, I place my head on his chest, but my hands remain on his throat.

"Muthafucka!" I say out loud, squeezing his throat one last time.

When I'm sure he's dead, I take his weapon and remove his jeans. They're too big for me, but they will do for now. Once dressed, I grab the 9mm and open the bathroom door. The weapon shakes. I tell myself if someone tries to stop me, I'm pushing his wig back.

I heard them earlier saying a war was getting ready to take place in Emerald, and I need to be there for my friends. For my family. Easing out of the bathroom, I notice everyone is gone. I hate the apartment, which held me hostage for so long.

Barefoot, I tiptoe past the living room and to the front door. I stop myself from opening the door right away. I hear their voices . . . in the hallway. Suddenly I'm scared. What if they catch me? Fuck it! If I'm gonna die, I'm gonna die fighting! There was just no way I could give up. Pressing my ear against the door, I listen attentively.

"That nigga betta hurry up and come on," someone says.

"He probably in there makin' love, and shit," another one says.

They laugh.

Judging on how they sound, I gauge they're a few feet from the door. Taking one deep breath, I open it and run into the hallway. The gun in my hands shakes as I aim at them in whipping motions from side to side. My hair's all over my head and I'm nervous. The oversized jeans I'm wearing fall down a little, exposing my vagina. And I focus on Kit, the man who nursed me through the toughest experience in my life.

"Get your hands up!"

They slowly comply as I pull up my pants.

"K-Kit . . . get the fuck outta here!"

He looks at me.

"Go, Kit! Now!"

He carefully runs down the stairwell.

"I knew I ain't trust that nigga!" Harold says.

"Shut the fuck up!" I yell. "Don't make me shoot one of you muthafuckas!" I scream, backing up slowly. I caught them off guard so they couldn't pull their weapons when I first entered the hallway. "Stay still, or I'll shoot anybody who makes the slightest move! I'm not fuckin' playin'!"

They remain still and I continue to back up toward the elevator. I press the button with my free hand. Someone moves and I fire, hitting him in the chest.

"I'm not fuckin' playin'! Don't make a fuckin' move, or I'll shoot all of you niggas one by one! Keep your hands in the air!"

They remain like toy soldiers. And the moment the elevator door opens, I jump inside. When the door closes, someone says, "Get that bitch!" My heart races.

Sweat runs down my forehead as I nervously stand in the elevator, my bare feet stuck to the filthy elevator floor. If they run down the stairs before this door opens, I'm dead. I hit the basement button several more times, trying to hurry it along.

"God, please help me. Please," I say, trembling.

Once the door opens, I run out of it and away from the building. I hear their voices behind me. Their footsteps pressing against the grainy dirt grow closer, but I'm barefoot and fighting for my life. I can't let them catch me. I won't let them catch me.

"I'ma kill you, bitch!"

"Fuucckk you!" I shout.

They are many, but the gap between us grows larger. I'm too fast! I am fighting for my life. It's hard to catch a person who's running for her life. My feet appear to grow wheels as I run faster and faster.

"Yvette! Help me!" I scream into the field.

I wonder where everyone is, but I'm relieved I don't hear anyone behind me anymore. They're all gone! Thank God! They're all *gone!*

I run to the community center, because we made a pact a long time ago. If one of us ever got in trouble, someone would always be at the community center to receive him or her if they could just get there. The plan was made when Dex and Stacia were alive, and we prayed we'd never have to use it. But I needed this plan to work for me right now.

Once there, I push open the double doors. My bare feet make a squishy sound. I walk quietly toward the door where we hold our meetings and twist the knob. It's dim inside, but I see someone on his knees, praying. I walk closer, aiming my gun, and the person stands.

"Derrick?" I ask, shaking terribly. I smell his cologne and know it's him.

"Baby!" He walks up to me and takes my weapon. Placing it on the table, he says, "Is that really you?"

He examines my bruised face, messy hair, and oversized jeans. "You so beautiful. You're alive, and you're so beautiful!"

I fall into his arms and he holds me tightly. For the first time in days, I'm home. In his arms, I'm really home.

Carissa

For the moment, I need to be comforted.

I can't believe I'm free from Emerald. And up until a few weeks ago, I never realized I wanted to leave. Luckily for me, I have a man who loves me, no matter what.

"What you thinkin' 'bout, baby?" Lavelle asks as he runs his fingers through my hair. We're stretched out on the couch, watching Keyshia Cole's TV show, which I recorded.

"I'm just happy to be here wit you. That's all."

"You just sayin' that," he jokes. "You ain't tryin' to be wit a nigga, for real."

"I *am* happy." I look up at him. "Had it not been for you, I probably would've gotten killed in Emerald. I'm tired of having to look over my shoulders all the time."

"I don't know what I would've done if somethin' happened to you. But you ain't gotta worry 'bout shit now. I got you. . . . I got us."

"I know. . . . I just don't wanna lose my friends. They like my sisters."

"They should love you, no matter what. And didn't you say Yvette understood?"

"She did, but Kenyetta didn't, and Mercedes still hasn't come back yet."

"You can't worry 'bout them. Your focus should be on me and our family."

"That's easy for you to say. You and Cameron still cool. You have your friends. I don't."

"We are cool, but, for real, we not."

"What's that supposed to mean?"

"Nothin'," he says, rubbing my face. "Shit just not the same wit me and Cam. For real, shit ain't been the same since we left Emerald. Don't get me wrong. Cam gonna always be my nigga. We just don't see eye-to-eye on every-thing anymore."

"Me and my friends are like that too." I laugh remembering our beefs. "But I got you, so, for real, I don't care."

"Yeah, well, if that's true, how come it don't seem like it?"

"I'm sorry, baby. It's just that a lot of shit kicked off in the past few weeks."

"There you go worryin' about that Emerald City bullshit again. You a woman, not a man. So stop trying to do man's work."

"Lavelle, you sound selfish. I mean . . . why wouldn't I care about my friends?"

"It ain't selfish!" he yells. "I'm tired of you worryin' 'bout shit that don't concern you. To be honest, you might as well get used to the idea that as long as they stay in Emerald, somethin' *will* happen. Be grateful you got out in time."

I sit up and look into his eyes. I feel he's trying to tell me something, but I don't know what. So I scoot next to him and say, "What you mean?"

He takes a deep breath and briefly looks away from me. I pause Keyshia's show and can feel my heart racing.

"I'ma be real wit you. Emerald about to fall, and that's why I wanted you out."

" 'Emerald about to fall?' You act like you know somethin'."

"I do," he says seriously. "Cameron plannin' to take it back."

" 'Take it back'?" I remember Mercedes talking about Cameron, Lavelle, and Black being together. But when I asked him if something was up, he said no. He even threatened to end our relationship if I asked him again. "Fuck you talkin' about, Lavelle?"

"In the next few days, Black from Tyland and Cameron runnin' up in Emerald. And when they do, they not plannin' on leavin' without the money and the city."

"La-La-Lavelle!" I can't catch my breath, and I feel betrayed. "When I asked about this shit, you told me no. I trusted you. Why did you lie to me?"

"Because I did what I had to do to get you out. That's why."

"Please explain to me what you're talking about." I stand and place my hands on my hips.

He looks down at the floor, stands up, and walks up to me. "I'ma tell you this 'cause I don't want you to hear it from nobody else," he says, placing his hands on my shoulders. "I had somethin' to do wit them dudes who ran up in Emerald, blastin'."

"The ones who killed the guard?"

"Naw, the ones who shot Mercedes."

I smack Lavelle and his mouth bleeds.

"I deserved that, but you know I never meant to hurt you. And if I had to, I'd do it all again. I love you."

"You love me? You don't love me! It's 'cause of you that Mercedes got shot. What if she would've gotten killed?"

"I know I fucked up, Car. But they wasn't supposed to shoot y'all. I paid them to scare you a little, and that was it. I guess they got nervous and felt like they lives were on the line. But just so you know, your girl Kenyetta guilty too. She been fuckin' around wit Black behind y'all's back."

"Stop lyin', bastard!" I yell.

"I'm serious! He got a thing for black women with that Indian look, and Kenyetta is it."

"Why should I believe you?"

"Because I'm your man. Now, I'm sorry, baby." He pulls me into his arms. "But I was worried about you. Can't you understand that? Come here. Let's not do this. Okay?"

I don't respond and fall into his embrace. For the moment, I need to be comforted. And had he walked away, I'm not certain that my limp body wouldn't have dropped to the floor. I know it's wrong—and I may even seem disloyal—but for the moment, I need him.

Lavelle

"So what she plannin' to do wit me?"

Lavelle sleeps hard after making love to Carissa for two hours straight. When he wakes, he can't get over the sensation of feeling drugged. A smile creeps across his face when Carissa tells him that despite his lies, she'll still stay by his side.

He dozes off again. Waking up, he turns around, preparing to go another round. But when he touches the sheets, he notices her side is cold, and she's gone.

"Carissa!" he yells, thinking she is preparing breakfast. "Get back in the bed. I'm tryin' to get some mornin' pussy."

"She gone, man," a soldier from Emerald says.

When he looks in the direction of the voice, he sees two men inside his bedroom. They are sitting in chairs. He recognizes both of them.

"But she asked us to be here when you woke up," the soldier continues.

Lavelle reaches for his weapon under his pillow. It's gone. He reaches for it on the nightstand. It's not there either.

"It's not there, dude," one of them says. "And if you get outta line, we got orders to slump you."

Lavelle sits up and leans against the bedpost. His bare back is cold against the wood. With everything going on, he laughs to himself. He hadn't seen this move coming along. Carissa is smarter than he thought.

"She went to Emerald?" he asks.

"Yeah . . . man."

"So what she plannin' to do wit me?"

"We don't know yet. But the moment we find out, we'll show you."

Yvette

"Then let's get ready for war!"

After the meeting, we exit through the back door. The sight of fifty men outside temporarily stops my heart. We didn't invite them, so what do they want? Are they with the others?

"I know y'all not tryin' to do this shit right here." I look at the men. " 'Cause I can guarantee you if it goes down like this, a lot of bodies droppin'. So what y'all wanna do?"

"We not here for that, Yvette. The city is divided. Some went to Unit B, and we're here to fight wit you. Everybody talkin' about a war, and we wanna make sure we on the right side," Smiths says. His young face is sliced in six different directions.

"Yeah, we ain't 'bout to let them niggas just run up in here and take our shit!" another one rallies.

I'm not too sure I can trust them. But when I look into their eyes, I feel they're being true, and we need their help. The more, the better.

I smile, walk up to them, and say, "Then let's get ready for war!"

We tell them as quickly as possible what they need to know about our plan. Leaders are picked. After our session is over, we split up in groups to cover various parts of the city.

"Y'all ready for this shit?" I yell at my twenty men.

"Fuck yeah!" they cheer.

"Then let's drop these niggas and show them the mistake they made for violatin' our city!"

Weapons clank in the air.

As we walk toward Unit B, I notice everything is quiet. Not one soul is outside in the field, not even tenants. Word travels fast, so I'm sure they're staying clear of drama. They know what's getting ready to happen.

"Yvette, I think it's finally happenin'," Kenyetta says, looking around. "We really going to war. We really have to fight for what's ours."

"You think," I say playfully. "I've never seen the city like this before. It's a ghost town."

"I'm so ready for this shit, though," she says excitedly.

"Good, 'cause they not gettin' Emerald unless they take my life with it."

"They betta take mine too," she responds, touching my hand.

As we walk toward the back of Unit B, I hear a

voice calling my name. My men immediately cover us.

"Yvette, it's me! Mercedes!" She runs toward us, and the men part.

She moves toward us, and my body shivers. My friend—my best friend—is here. And I thank God for answering my prayers.

"Oh, my God . . . she's alive, Vette!" Kenyetta screams.

We run toward her, meet in the middle, and embrace. She's alive!

"You don't know how good it feels to see you," I say, holding her face in my hands. "Do you know what I was about to do?"

" 'Bout to do?" She laughs. Her face is bruised and she limps. "I heard you were in Unit C kickin' down doors!" We all laugh. "I'm just happy to be back."

"Where were you?"

"Let's talk about it later," she says as sadness washes over her face. "But thanks for remembering the plan to have someone waiting in the community center."

"You know I would never forget something like that."

She smiles and squeezes my hand. "Thank you. Hey . . . where's Carissa?"

"It's a long story," Kenyetta tells her.

"So what's the plan now?" Derrick asks, bringing us back to the present and our reality that the war is far from over.

Kenyetta, Mercedes, Derrick, and I continue our walk toward Unit B. Our men walk behind us.

"Most of our men are guarding Unit C, because the cash and product is there. But we're hitting Unit B first, because we know they're inside. Two men will guard each of the eight floors, and two will guard the back—in case anybody tries to get in or out. Two more men will also watch the front and they'll also keep watch on the yard. The setup will be pretty much the same for all units.

"We have to break down their inside crew first and then prepare for the takeover later tonight. Now, on one of the floors in Unit B, we already have two men inside. They reached out to us earlier and told us they were going undercover. Black doesn't know about them and thinks they're with him. But on our command, they'll do what's necessary. Once we're in position, we're gonna take over two apartments on each floor that'll allow us to see the yard clearly. That way, we can cover all bases in case someone tries to come on the grounds."

"What about the gate?" Mercedes asks.

"It ain't safe, so our men on the roof will kill anybody who tries to enter."

"It sounds solid," Kenyetta says, nodding her head. "I think it'll work."

The look on Derrick's face tells me he thinks otherwise.

"What's up, Derrick? Are we missin' somethin'?"

"I'm not sure, but somethin' not right. I mean, why would they flood Emerald and stay in Unit B? The money and shit in C."

"It's hard to get in Unit C. They had to get into the weakest unit."

"Naw," he disagrees. "Somethin's up. Somethin's not right."

"We got to do somethin', D. We have to move."

Derrick takes a deep breath, still visibly uneasy, and says, "Then let's do it."

In a Unit B apartment

"They're here. Tell Black," Harold says to Tamir on the phone.

"Why you ain't call him?"

"I did . . . but he ain't answerin' his phone. So he told me whenever I couldn't reach him, hit you."

"A'ight . . . I'll get him the message."

"There's somethin' else. The girl Mercedes got away."

Tamir laughs. "He not gonna be happy wit that, but I'll let him know. Just hit me back if anything changes," Tamir stresses.

Harold doesn't like taking orders from a kid, but something tells him if he works for Black, eventually he'll have to deal with him, anyway.

"And, Harold, don't fuck up again, 'cause in our family, *losers die.*"

Mercedes

I hope my judgment isn't clouded.

My body's sore, but I don't tell them. I want the focus to be on Emerald City, not on me. I focus on the field in front of me. When my phone vibrates with a blocked number, I decide to answer.

"Who is this?"

"Ms. Mercedes, it's me. Lani."

"Lani, why are you calling me? And why are you blocking your number?"

"Because I thought you wouldn't answer."

"What do you want?"

"To speak to C. He won't talk to me. And I need to talk to him."

"Lani, I spoke to C earlier today and he told me you got with his friend, so your problem is your own."

"Please, Ms. Mercedes, his friend beat me, and I broke up with him."

"Lani, now is not the time. Lil C's got a lot going on, and so do I. So don't call me anymore."

After I end the call, I try to reach Cameron again, but he doesn't answer. He's avoiding me, but eventually we'll speak—whether he wants to or not. I know he has everything to do with the rapes, and that hurts me.

Thoughts of what I did to Ed run through my mind and make me smile. Derrick gave me the pleasure of killing him, and I did it slowly. I wrapped my hands around his throat and squeezed as tightly as possible . . . until he was gone. I didn't take my eyes off him until the Vanishers removed his body.

Now, standing at the bottom of Unit B's steps, I watch the gate and the yard. Kenyetta is at the top of the stairs, watching me. And I am growing sick of her asking if I am okay.

"You okay, Mercedes?"

I turn around, look up at her, and say, "I'm cool."

"Who was on the phone earlier? You look angry."

"It was Lil C. He been at it since I been gone. When I talked to him earlier, he said he got somebody pregnant. She aborted the baby and then got with his friend."

"Lil C having sex?"

"I know. It's gross, right?"

"I don't want to think about it anymore."

It is silent until light gunfire sounds off in Unit B. I worry about Yvette and my squad. I look up at Kenyetta, who says, "Yvette and Derrick gonna be fine. Trust me."

"I know, it's just that . . ."

Before I finish, five kids come running from the gate, through the yard.

"Help! Help!" the children cry, fanning their arms. "They gonna kill us! Please!"

They are carrying backpacks and are barefoot. From where I stand, they look to be between the ages of ten and thirteen. Loud and hysterical, their pleas for help are the only sounds in the quiet field.

"What you want us to do, boss?" one of the soldiers asks from one of the apartment windows in Unit A. His gun is aimed in their direction. After his question, I hear multiple weapons *clicking*, although hidden from view.

"Hold fast!" I tell everyone, speaking with my hands up. "Don't do nothin' yet. They just kids." Turning around, I say, "Stay there, Kenyetta. I'ma check this shit out."

"Don't go by yourself," she says worriedly. "I can't see you clearly over there."

"I'ma take Keith from Unit A with me," I say, jogging toward the gate. "You just stay here in case Yvette calls. And watch my back."

"You know I got you! Be careful!"

"Keith, come with me," I holler.

"I'm on it!" he says, running behind me.

On the way there, I see the children are followed by two women. The women look scared, and both have complexions like Kenyetta's. To be honest, the three of them look like they could be sisters. I notice one of the two women is carrying a gray hobo-style purse and her feet are bare. The other is wearing slippers.

"Fuck are y'all doing in Emerald?" I ask them.

Keith's weapon is drawn.

"Please . . . you gotta help us," the woman with the dreads says.

"I ain't gotta do shit, bitch! But you betta tell me somethin' I wanna hear—and quick—before you have a situation to deal wit right here!" When I see her holding a purse tightly, I say, "Take her purse, Keith, and look through that shit." While he's looking, I say, "Now, what's goin' on?"

"Someone wants us dead. And we're responsible for these kids. Trust me when I say we had nowhere else to run. This was the quickest place we could get to on foot."

"Where do you live?"

"In Tyland Towers," she says softly.

Keith looks at me. His eyes say what I'm thinking: *This is a setup.* But the children are confusing me. Either they are good actors, or they are really scared.

"I know this looks crazy, but we run a day- and night-care center. Their mothers had *just* dropped them off, when my boyfriend, who works for Black, told me he was goin' to have anybody who had family in Emerald City murdered. My cousin lives here, and he knows it. You don't

know it, but Black . . . he's crazy." She is sobbing.

As we speak, the children continue to cry, re-
maining huddled against the women.

"When we found out," the other woman, who
has long, silky hair like Kenyetta's, says, "we
came runnin' over here."

"Y'all don't have a car?" Keith asks.

"We do, but we don't have enough space for
all the kids," she replies.

"What about the parents?" I question.

"We didn't have time to call," the one in the
dreads says. "When my boyfriend called and
said Black had some people on the way up, we
had to move."

"Please help us," one of the kids says, grabbing my leg. "I want my mommy."

"Get off of her," Keith tells the child.

"It's fine," I tell him. "They just babies."

"Boss, I'm not tryin' to disrespect you, but
this don't feel right."

"I got it," I assure him. "I got it."

I look down at one of the boys and he reminds me of Lil C when he was younger. Suddenly I feel bad for them. After all, I'd just
escaped a near-death situation and would've
wanted someone to help me. I hope my judg-
ment isn't clouded because of it.

"Can you help us?" the woman with the dreads
repeats. She looks behind her once more, in
fear. "I'm worried if we stay out in the open,
they'll kills us. I'm beggin' you."

"Which unit does your family live in?" I ask.

"Unit C. I have her number, if you want me to call her," she continues.

Reaching in my pocket, I pull out my phone. She gives me the number; and the moment I hear a squeaky voice, I know who it is. A trouble-maker.

"Keri, it's me, Mercedes. Somebody's out here for you. What's your name?"

"Whitney," the one with the dreads replies. "I'm her cousin, and this is LeLe."

"She says she your cousin Whitney, and some chick name LeLe wit her too. You know them?"

"Yeah," she says without hesitation. "Are they okay?"

Still not sure if this is real or not, I say, "Describe her."

"She's real pretty and she wears dreads."

I know even if Keri was looking out the window, she couldn't see them clearly because of where we are. Anyway, her window faces the back side of the building. I quickly make up my mind to save the children.

"She on her way up. This betta not be no bull-shit, Keri, or I'm comin' for you," I say, hanging up on her. "What's up with the bag?" I ask Keith.

"It's clean. The only thing she got in here is a tampon and a bag of M&M's," he continues, tearing the edge of the bag and eating the candy.

"A'ight," I say, looking the women up and down. "You can take the kids upstairs."

Something in my spirit tells me I'm making a bad decision. All of them are about to walk away, when I say, "One of y'all stayin' wit me."

"O-okay," the one with the dreads stutters.

"You with the dreads, stay with me. I wanna keep y'all separated."

"But Keri's my cousin," she complains.

"Stay wit me or get the fuck outta Emerald. It don't make me no never mind," I lie.

If she didn't take my offer, and I found out later something happened to these children, I'd feel some kind of way. But true to my word, if she didn't listen, all of these muthafuckas would have to get off our grounds.

"Okay," she says, putting her head down. "I'll go with you."

"I'm stayin' wit you too," the shortest child says, holding on to her leg.

"Is it okay?" she asks, looking down at him and then up at me.

"Whatever. Just come on before I change my mind."

"Boss, you want me to look in them backpacks before they go inside?" Keith asks.

"Hold up!" I yell, stopping everyone from walking toward the building. "What they got in them bags?"

"We don't know. Their parents bring them every day when they drop them off. We told them to grab what they could before we left. You're welcome to look inside," LeLe replies.

I look at the kids and remember how Lil C was when he was little. I made a point that whenever I needed a sitter, she would have to stay at my house just so my kids could be around their things.

"Let 'em go." I turn to the men in front of Unit C. "They goin' up to Keri's! Let 'em inside and tell whoever's guarding the floor to call me when they get there!"

"Got it!" one of them responds.

As we walk up the stairs to Unit B, a nagging voice in my head yells, *"You're making a mistake!"*

The only thing is, it is too late.

Kenyetta

The Lost File

When Mercedes walks up the steps with some-one from the gate, for a moment I think she's lost her mind. At first, the night sky conceals the person from view, but I soon recognize her. She's one of Black's wives. I met her at his place, but what is she doing here?

"What the fuck is she doin' here?" I ask Mercedes when they reach the top.

"Don't worry. I got it. Black was on some bull-shit in Tyland and they had to hide out here. I'll figure things out later."

As Mercedes speaks, Black's bitch smirks at me. She knows I didn't tell Mercedes about Black, and she's using it against me.

"Let me take them inside," Mercedes says, "and then we'll talk."

The moment they attempt to pass me to walk

to the door, I lose all sense of reason. Taking out my gun, I aim . . . pull the trigger . . . and hit her in the head. Guts and blood from her body hit the dirty glass window and my face.

"Oh, my Gawd, Kenyetta!" Mercedes screams, holding her mouth. She is bloody too.

When I'm sure she's dead, I aim at the child, but Mercedes jumps in front of him.

"Fuck are you doin'?" Mercedes asks, placing the child behind her. "Whatever's goin' on, you know I got you, but I can't let you shoot no kid!"

"Are y'all okay over there?" one of our men yells from another unit.

"You need us?" another one calls.

"Uh . . . yeah, everything's cool!" I reply.

I look at Unit B, hoping Yvette will be out soon. I just want this over with, and I never thought I'd have to do what I am about to do: tell one of my closest friends that I betrayed her.

"Kenyetta, what the fuck is up?" she screams again. The child is looking around her and up at me. I'm not sure, but something tells me he has deadly plans.

"Please don't hurt me, miss lady! I'm just a kid," the child cries.

When I *really* look at the boy's face, I feel sad. What have I become?

"I'm sorry, Mercedes. I'm losin' my mind right now, but I got to talk to you," I tell her, putting my weapon up. The dead body is still at our feet. "Jones, can you keep him in the hallway with you?" I ask one of our soldiers inside the building. He is guarding the first floor.

"I'ma have somebody take him up to Fat Nay-Nay's later."

"No problem, Kenyetta," he says nervously. "I got lil man."

When the child steps over the dead body, my heart breaks. It feels like we are living in Afghanistan, instead of in our nation's capital. We are becoming so used to murder that it isn't fazing us anymore. We place a quick call to the Vanishers, and I prepare myself to be honest with my friend.

I take a deep breath. "Mercedes, I got to talk to you."

"Go 'head," she responds anxiously. " 'Cause you got me fucked up right now."

"I . . . um . . . used to date Black."

"Black who?"

"Black Water, from Tyland."

"I'm not understanding what you're tellin' me."

"You know Dyson never used to let me leave the house. When he was alive, it was like I was his slave. If I wasn't with y'all, I couldn't go anywhere else. I was his little Indian girl." I laugh, realizing how stupid I was back then. "I felt like I was in hell sometimes. He would leave for days, and when he came back, he did not want to be with me. It was just me and my worrisome-ass grandmother all day in that apartment by ourselves. I was bored and hated life." I look at Mercedes and pause.

She says, "Go 'head, Kenyetta. I'm listening."

I exhale. "Well, because I never got out, I never

saw Black's face. I had heard of him, but I never saw him. And when we finally met, he didn't tell me who he was at first. A year passed before he finally told me. By that time, I knew I should've dumped him, but I didn't. I was in love."

"Damn, Kenyetta," she says, shaking her head. "That's some heavy shit."

"I know!" I cry, wiping a tear from my face. "I know it's fucked up, but that's not all. He wanted me to have a baby, and I was so wrapped up in having a man that I brought him on Emerald City's grounds to have sex. He was testing my loyalty to him and I fell for it."

"What?"

"I'm sorry. I violated our bond and our sisterhood and I was wrong."

"The Vanishers here!" a man calls, breaking our conversation. "Let them in?"

We look at the beaten black van coming through the gate and I say, "Let 'em come through."

Although no one is guarding the gate from the station, our men still have intentions of shooting to kill. Our conversation pauses as the Vanishers walk up the stairs, pick up the body, and remove it from the grounds. As usual, they never ask us questions and we never volunteer answers. Just as long as their direct deposit is sent to an offshore account monthly, all is good. Ng did a good job of keeping our secret.

When they are gone just as quickly as they came, I look at Mercedes. "I'm sorry about this shit. I really am."

"Did you help them niggas come in here? The ones who killed Jake?"

"No! I swear! I knew nothing about that! I let Black Water in once. I felt bad and never saw him again."

Mercedes exhales and says, "I'm not gonna lie. This shit is fucked up, Kenyetta. But—but . . . I know you love us, and I understand how it is to be wrapped up in some bullshit. I just fucked a man who didn't deserve me, and almost lost a man who did. So who is she? That girl you killed."

"His wife," I say, shaking my head. "That nigga got ten of them. I can't believe the shit this nigga's on. He had the nerve to ask me if I wanted to be his eleventh wife. He's crazy!"

"You didn't know he was into that shit?"

"Fuck no! You know we never really talked about Black. The only time we mentioned his name was when we heard that they were tryin' to steal our customers some years back. It was when Critter was alive. I never knew he was a bigamist!"

"Yeah . . . he been wivin' chicks for years! Damn, Kenyetta, I never realized how clueless you really were."

"I know." I smile. "Dyson was my life."

"You got any other secrets I should know about?"

I take a deep breath and say, "Yes. I had sex with Dex before he and Stacia were killed. I was at my lowest. I know it was wrong, but I had to tell somebody, because it's been eating me up alive."

Mercedes looks away and says, "I already knew."

I gasp. "You knew?"

"Yeah, she told us. She said he told her what happened between you two. He said you were about to take your life. She was hurt, but she loved you enough to keep the friendship and not cause you any pain by bringing it up."

"Dex told Stacia we made love?"

"Yeah. I didn't think you'd ever tell us, especially after they died because the secret went with them. But Stacia cried for days after Dex told her, and when she was done, she put it out of her mind. I don't know if you remember her sitting with us one day when we were on the steps at Unit C."

"She sat with us all the time."

"I know, but this time she sat close to you and told you she loved you. She told you that nothing could ever break y'all's bond. Stacia knew you weren't trying to steal him from her. And she never held it against you."

"I can't believe it," I say.

"I know. But in her mind, it was *us* before them. If she had to choose between you and Dex, it would've been you. Trust me, if Dex didn't get her out of Emerald, like our no-good–ass niggas back then, she would've rode with us to the death."

Wow. I would've never thought Stacia would've

handled it the way she did. She was a real solider! And I would forever look up to her after hearing this. Had one of my friends fucked my man, I don't know how I would've reacted. On second thought, I probably would've handled it like she did. I guess it speaks to our friendship. We had a bond that was unbreakable.

We were still talking, when Yvette came running out the front door.

"We found some of 'em," she says, breathing heavily. "Most of them were in apartments spread out on the second floor. We killed eight of them already. They weren't in Harold's crib, though, Mercedes."

"I figured," she says.

"Doctanian and Derrick are watching the floor right now. We gonna have the men knock on a few more doors, so we can get the rest of 'em. And then we goin' in, blazing."

"We only have twenty-somethin' men here. If we all go upstairs, the front and back doors won't be secured."

"I know. But we still got the men guarding the yard in the other units. They'll let us know if anybody comes in or out of here. But we got to move. This shit got to stop tonight. We need to reclaim what's ours."

Cameron

"It ain't about how many goons you got, it's how you use 'em."

"You comin' or what?" Black asks as he sits in the back of his chauffeured stretch silver Hummer. "Tonight's the night. We movin' on Emerald."

He and Cameron meet in the parking lot of Eastover Shopping Center, on the borderline of D.C. and Maryland.

Cameron takes a look at the limo and says, "This a bit much, ain't it?" He places his hands in his pockets and steps back to get a better view.

"If you got it, it ain't. This how ballers roll."

Cameron laughs and says, "I bet. Look, there's been a change of plans."

"You sure it's not a change of heart?"

"You can call it what you want," he says, stepping closer. "I tried to call you to tell you I ain't

227

fuckin' wit it, but you ain't answer your phone," Cameron says nonchalantly.

Black pats his pants, realizing he left his phone on the bed at his house. He'd taken it off right before making love to his three wives.

"A'ight . . . well, I missed the call. So what that mean . . . you bailin' out now?"

"First off, get out of the car and talk to me like a man. I ain't some bitch you tryin' to hook up wit."

Black laughs and exits the car. His height, size, and build make him seem more powerful than Cameron believes he really is. But one look in Cameron's eyes, you know that he is more powerful.

"Now what?" Black barks.

"Like I said, I'm not fuckin' wit it. It's done. Shit has gone too far already."

Black Water shakes his head in disgust and breathes out heavily. "I knew you was gonna pull some shit like this." He laughs. "That's why I had that whore baby mother of yours kidnapped for collateral. Don't you get it, Cameron? Shit ain't over till I say it is."

"I think you missin' an update," Cameron replies in a sinister tone. "And you betta be glad I don't smoke your bitch ass right now."

" 'An update'?"

"Yeah, she got away. I taught her good."

The smile is wiped from Black's face and his lips press tightly together. He's in a furor. "You know you betta never step foot on Emerald City grounds again, right?"

"You just betta hope I don't find a reason to," Cameron retorts.

"Is that so?"

"That's so . . . and you can forget about my niggas helpin' you in Emerald. They behind the girls now. You on your own, partna. Good luck." He chuckles.

"Do you really think I'ma let Mercedes live, once Emerald is mine?" Black counters.

"I don't think about it either which way. All I know is what's done is done, and at this point, I'm sure she could hold her own."

Black looks toward Cameron's car parked a few feet over from his. A girl is inside. "I see why you not trippin'."

Cameron looks back at Toi, who is impatiently waiting. He smiles. "Naw. I ain't trippin', 'cause I don't give a fuck."

"Well . . . I guess we said all we need to. For your sake, I hope our paths don't cross again. I got niggas everywhere," Black says, pointing behind him. There are five vans parked behind Black's car. "Remember that."

"It ain't about how many goons you got, it's how you use 'em," Big C replies. He points at Black's jacket.

Black follows his stare and sees a red dot on his leather coat. "You got it," he says nervously, not knowing where Cameron's gunman was located. "For now, anyway."

"I got it always," Cameron replies.

Black gets in his car and it drives off.

When Cameron steps back in the car, he

braces himself to deal with Toi. He knows she is mad after sitting in the car for thirty minutes, waiting on him.

"Are we goin' to the Lux or not? I'm ready to get a drink and party."

"Give me a kiss first," he says. "And stop being so damn mean. You gonna make your face ugly."

Toi laughs and their lips meet.

"You betta watch the people you hang around. Everyone not in your corner, Cameron."

"Toi, mind your business. It's over, anyway. I got it."

"We'll see."

Emerald City Soldier

"I'm two seconds from takin' care of that attitude problem for you."

Twenty-year-old Wallace is leaning against the wall, watching the first floor. In the game for only two years, Wallace has visions of moving up the ladder and becoming a lieutenant. He works tirelessly around the clock and often gets by with less than three hours of sleep. He lives and breathes Emerald, and the girls have noticed. He is well on his way.

The kid who is left with him is sitting on the bottom step after Yvette and the others go upstairs. The little boy spends most of the time in his book bag and seems to be preoccupied with its contents.

"What you got in that bag, man?" Wallace asks playfully. "You been in that muthafucka for five minutes straight."

"Why?" the kid questions in a smart tone. He

231

looks Wallace dead in his eyes as he waits for his response. "I didn't ask you what you got in that wack-ass coat you wearin', so why you all in mine?"

Wallace is caught off guard by the boy's attitude. Earlier, he seemed timid and scared. Now something in his eyes tells Wallace that everything he did was an act.

"You got a smart-ass mouth to be a lil youngin'," Wallace tells him, standing up straight. "You betta watch that shit, though. You might find yourself in a situation you can't get out of."

"Nigga, fuck you. I ain't gotta watch shit! If somebody got a problem wit me, they can suck my dick."

Wallace is about to break on him, until he takes into consideration the murder the boy witnessed earlier. He figured seeing the death is causing his brash tone.

"Was that your moms who got hit earlier?"

"No. She was my aunt. Why?"

"Hey, shawty, I'm two seconds from takin' care of that attitude problem for you. So how 'bout we do this—don't talk to me until it's time to roll, and I won't say shit to you."

"How 'bout I just shut you up permanently," the child says, standing up, his arms behind his back.

"Lil nigga, you trippin'—"

Wallace's statement is cut short by a bullet entering his body.

The sound of the gunfire was quieted by a silencer. But Wallace was hit in the shoulder. Had he not moved a little when he saw the gun, it would've entered his heart instead. His body falls against the bronze mailboxes as he slides to the floor.

"What the fuck," he says, touching the wound. His fingers are wet with his own blood. He needs access to his weapon in his coat; but Wallace knows that if he moves, the kid will fire again.

"I see you ain't sayin' shit now," the kid gloats, walking up to him. "You should learn not to talk so much, 'cause you never know who you talkin' to."

The boy is preparing to shoot again, when Chris opens the building door, knocking the little boy to the floor with a blow to his face.

"What the fuck is goin' on?" she says, rubbing her knuckles and staring down at the child. "Kids killin' niggas, and shit!"

"I don't know who you are," Wallace says to her, "but I'm sure glad you came through when you did. That lil muthafucka was about to smoke my ass."

"It looks like he already did."

Chris is only there because she is looking for Yvette and heard she was in Unit B. When she saw the little boy holding a gun and approaching Wallace, she thought her eyes were playing tricks on her. But the closer she got to them, the surer she became. A child was definitely about to kill a man.

"I sure hope you on the right side of this shit

round here," she says, stooping down to look at his bullet wound. " 'Cause I might have to finish you off myself."

"I should be askin' you the same thing," he responds, trying to avoid showing his pain.

"Is there somebody I can call for you? You losin' a lot of blood."

"Yeah . . . my phone in my pocket. Just redial the last number."

Chris grabs his phone and makes the call. Both of them keep their eyes on the unconscious boy.

"What's up, Wallace? Everything cool?" a female asks.

"This ain't Wallace," she says, standing up. "This Chris. He been shot."

"Who the fuck are you, and what you talkin' 'bout?"

"Your man is lying on the floor and he losin' a lot of blood. He needs help."

Mercedes gets silent for a minute before saying, "How do I know this ain't a setup?"

"Hold on." Chris stoops back down and places the phone to Wallace's ear. "She wanna talk to you."

"Mercedes, I don't know who this is, but she just saved my life," he says as the phone rests on his shoulder. "But I'm real fucked up right now. I need some help."

"A'ight, I'll be down in a moment. Just hold tight."

It takes Mercedes two minutes to get downstairs. She brings her soldiers Lando and Neo with her.

"What happened?" she asks Wallace as the men help him up.

"I don't know. I was about to check the lil nigga for his attitude, and the next thing I know, he starts shootin'. I think it had somethin' to do wit Kenyetta smokin' his peoples."

"Damn," Mercedes says, briefly assessing the situation. "Keith said lettin' them fuckin' kids in without checkin' they bags was a mistake." She pauses and grabs her phone. Calling Keri, who she believes is involved, she's disgusted when she doesn't answer. "Look, Neo, take my man to Old Lady Faye's to get him fixed up. Then find out where them kids in Unit C at. I think somethin's up."

Neo helps Wallace up.

"What about the kid?" Lando asks.

"Take him to the community center after y'all drop Wallace off. Don't let this lil nigga out of your sight. Guard him wit your life."

"Got it, boss!" they say as Lando lifts the child from the floor.

"Now, what the fuck are you doing here? And how did you get past my men?" Mercedes asks Chris.

"I was here before everything went down. I been stayin' at my friend Davida's and her man's crib in Unit A."

"So how you find us?"

"Somebody told me she saw her outside a little while ago. Look . . . I ain't tryin' to start no shit, 'cause I can see a lot goin' on around here right now. But if my girl's involved, I am too." Chris taps the bulge in her jacket, which conceals her weapon.

Mercedes rolls her eyes. "We don't need your help, dyke! It's gonna take more than lickin' pussy to get us out of this shit."

Chris takes two steps to her and says, "You know, they say women who are afraid of other women's sexuality have secret tendencies. So what's up? You want me to hit that shit?"

Mercedes walks up to her and steals her in the face. "Bitch, you got me fucked up! *I'm strictly dickly!*"

Chris rubs the side of her cheek and says, "You got that, but I promise . . . you *won't* get another one. Now, I felt exactly like you did when you called me a dyke. Don't disrespect me, and I won't disrespect you. I love Yvette, and if you can't see it, that's your fuckin' problem. I'm not leavin' here witout her!"

Mercedes grabs the child's gun off the ground and puts it in the back of her jeans. Then she says, "You know what? It don't even matter to me." She walks away from her and toward the hallway steps. " 'Cause once Yvette finds out you here, she goin' off, anyway. I just hope you ready for it."

"I guess I'ma have to take my chances."

Emerald City Soldier

"We'll try, but we can't make no promises."

"I think they in one of the last eight apartments on the east side of the hall," Yvette whispers. "Nassir just texted me and told me he inside one of the apartments wit one of Black's niggas, and he saw the rest going in apartments down there too. Nassir got an orange Northface jacket on, so don't hurt him if you see him."

"We got it," somebody says. "We won't hit Nas."

"Cool. Nassir said they know we comin', but they don't know when." Yvette continues to whisper as everyone huddles at the west side of the hall. "We goin' in twos and kickin' doors down. If you can help it, try not to hit up no kids."

"We'll try, but we can't make no promises," another soldier says.

"How we splittin' up?" Doctanian asks.

"Grab a man, everybody," she says, watching them pick partners.

When Kenyetta notices how Derrick and Doctanian have chosen each other, she says, "I want you guys to pick somebody else. The plan will work better if we have you two paired up wit one of the newer soldiers."

"She right," Yvette responds. "So, Doc, you take Adriel. And, Derrick, you go wit Paul. Everybody else can stay where they at."

As they are preparing to move toward the end of the hall, Mercedes and Chris walk up the stairs behind them and into the hallway. Everyone turns around and aims in their direction, until they see who it is.

"Damn, Mercedes! We almost blazed you," Kenyetta says. "What's Chris doin' here?"

"Y'all go 'head," Yvette says to everyone, attempting to keep her privacy. Everyone walks away, except Mercedes and Chris. And Yvette's knees grow weak the moment she sees Chris's face.

"What-what you doin' here?" Yvette asks, looking at her and Mercedes.

"I told her not to come, Vette, but she wouldn't listen."

"If you here"—Chris points at Yvette—"then so am I. And it don't look like you got a lotta time to make a decision, so we betta move." Chris takes out her Glock and cocks it back, making sure it is ready to fire.

Chris is right. There is no time for disputing, because Yvette's men are already on their way to deal with the violators. She needs to be with them too.

"If this is what you want," Yvette says, pulling out her weapon. "Then let's hit it." She walks toward her men. "Everybody, move slowly and quietly," she whispers. "Shoot to kill."

As Derrick walks with Paul, Doc notices how Paul looks at Derrick. It's as if he has ill will in his heart toward him.

"You a'ight, man?" Doctanian asks Paul.

"Wh-why you say that?" he stutters.

"Just checkin'," Doc responds, sizing him up.

"A'ight . . . on three, we knockin' down doors," Yvette directs as they all take their positions in front of an apartment.

With her hand in the air, she counts down with her fingers: one . . . two . . . and on three, they kick in the doors.

"Don't move, or I'ma shoot!" one soldier yells.

"If a nigga so much as wink, I'm burnin' this bitch down!" someone else screams after kicking in a door.

Some men come up empty-handed, while others locate their marks and fire. Tenants who are uninvolved are running everywhere for cover. They pour out of the doors like water.

"Go to the community center, you'll be safe there!" Yvette tells the people after seeing them run for safety. To ensure her safety, Chris remains by her side, watching her every move. She isn't used to seeing Yvette in *boss action*, but Chris can tell she is in her element.

When Yvette and Chris kick in another door, they see a lady sitting on the couch, with a man on each side of her. All three of them have their eyes glued to the TV, and the men's arms are resting on the couch behind her.

"What's goin' on here?" Yvette asks.

"Nothin'," the woman nervously says, shaking her head. Her eyes don't leave the television. "Just watching TV with my boyfriend."

"Oh really? Which one?"

A tear streams down the woman's face, alerting Yvette instantly. Before she answers, one of them reaches into the side of the couch and fires in their direction. Yvette ducks the bullet, which misses her head by inches. Chris drops to the floor and shoots the dude who fired at them. He takes a bullet in the kneecap. The other man grabs the lady's head and holds a gun to her temple.

"I'ma shoot this bitch!" he promises, standing up with her. "Now I'm gettin' the fuck outta here, and ain't shit you goin' to do 'bout it."

"We can't let you do that," Yvette tells him. "So you betta let her go."

"Don't fuck wit me, Yvette! I'll shoot her!"

"I'm sorry," Yvette tells the lady, who is shaking nervously, pleading for her life. "But we can't let him leave."

"P-please, Yvette. I—I want to live. Please don't let him kill me."

"If you let us leave, I promise I won't kill her. I don't want nothin' to do wit this no more," he bargains. His gun is shaking inside his hand. If he shook any harder, he'd fire by mistake, anyway. "I just wanna go home."

"It's too late for that, nigga," Chris says from the floor, hitting him in the middle of the head. His body drops and his weight pulls the woman down with him.

Yvette's finger was on the trigger, preparing to shoot him herself, but Chris beat her to the punch. The woman gets up, looks down at her assailant, and runs out the door, screaming.

"Damn," Yvette says, looking at the body and then at Chris. "You ain't no joke."

"You fuckin' wit a heavyweight." She winks. "Now let's finish what we started."

They enter the hallway to continue on their mission: to kill anyone who didn't belong. They have already lost three men in the war, but the violators have lost many more.

When Derrick is about to kick in the last door, Doctanian grows increasingly uneasy with the way Paul is acting. He doesn't trust him and decides to go with his instinct. So the moment Derrick kicks in the door, Doc sees Paul point the gun to the back of Derrick's head, preparing to squeeze the trigger. Doc walks up behind Paul and blows his brains out.

"What the fuck!" Derrick responds, moving out of the way.

"That nigga was 'bout to kill you, man," Doc says, looking down at the lifeless body before him. He smiles and says, "You lucky I'm—"

Before Doc finishes his sentence, he is hit twice in the back by someone behind him.

He was so concerned with Derrick, he didn't assess his surroundings. Derrick fires multiple times into the chest of the man who shot Doc. It isn't until he hits the floor that he recognizes the man as one of his own. He actually answered to him in Emerald. All this time, the man had larceny in his heart and Derrick never knew it. After Derrick makes sure his own life isn't in danger, he bends down and lifts Doc's head.

"Damn, Doc. Why you let 'em catch you, huh?" Derrick continues trying to hold back his tears. Blood oozes out of Doc's body.

Although Doctanian left Emerald City, the two are very close. It hurts Derrick to see him like this. They held secrets about one another—the kinds no one else knew but them. It was Derrick whom Doctanian first chose to tell that he killed Dex and Stacia because Thick had blackmailed him. And it was Derrick who prevented Doc from taking his own life. Now Doctanian had repaid him with his life.

"I—I . . ." Doc's words are gargled by the blood escaping his nose and mouth.

As the other Emerald City soldiers claim victory, they grow silent when they look for Derrick. When they spot him, holding Doc in the doorway, Kenyetta, Mercedes, Yvette, and Chris walk toward them.

"Fuck!" Yvette yells, punching at the wall, after seeing Doc's body.

Chris grips her and holds her tightly as she cries on her shoulder.

"Who got him?" Mercedes asks, holding back her tears.

"The nigga lying at your feet," Derrick answers. They look at him.

"Coney? Damn!" Mercedes says.

"Damn, Doc," Kenyetta adds, looking at his face. He looks terrified. "I'm sorry we let you come back, man. We shoulda told you to stay away from Emerald. You did good to get away. Fuck!"

Yvette pushes away from Chris and says, "They gonna pay for this shit, Doc. On my life, niggas is gonna pay for this shit!" She is taking it the hardest because she is the one who called him.

"We got all of them niggas," Nassir says, walking up to Yvette. "Everybody that was wit Black gone." He glances down and sees Doc. "They hit Doc?" Nobody responds to the obvious.

Doc opens his mouth and grips Derrick's shirt. "I—I de-de . . ." His words don't exit.

"Don't talk, man."

Doc grips him again and softly says, "I . . . d-deserve . . . this . . . for . . . k-killin' . . . D-D-Dex and . . . Stacia. I—I'm . . . sorry."

"What did he say?" Mercedes asks.

Doc takes his last breath and closes his eyes.

"Nothin'," Derrick lies, deciding to let Doc take his secret to his grave. "It was between us."

The air is immediately filled with remorse and fear that Doc's been murdered. Quiet chatter fills the hallway, but Yvette remains silent and walks away from the crowd. She has a moment of clarity; suddenly things begin to make sense.

"They were pawns," she says to herself. "They were fuckin' pawns. They were never s'posed to make it outta here alive."

She knows then that Black sacrificed his own men for the bigger picture. He wanted Emerald to be preoccupied with the men in Unit B so that they'd overlook what was really happening—a takeover. But the moment the thought enters her mind, Black's real warriors come through their gate, armed and ready for war.

Black Water

Operation Takeover

Black Water sits in his Rolls-Royce a few blocks down from Emerald. He is speaking to his men on the phone before they rush the gate.

"A'ight, this it! Y'all better go in there and wrap that shit up in an hour. It's twelve now, and that's more than enough time. We got the best weapons in D.C., so your jobs should be easy. If you feel like shit is too rough, remember bitches run this city, and then imagine what I'll do to you if shit don't go my way. Make it happen."

Six vans filled to capacity with his crew members roll past him. He smiles and says to his driver, "Take me to that strip club off of New York Avenue in D.C."

"The Rogue?" the driver asks in his deep, heavy voice.

"Yeah. I wanna see some pussy before I turn into the richest man in the city."

"You got it, boss."

As his driver pulls off, the first van enters Emerald and parks in a location where it can avoid bullets. They had been given the layout by their inside man, who is now dead within the walls.

The moment that the van parks, the Emerald City members who were assigned to guard the yard start to fire at the van with all they have. They are shooting from the windows and the rooftops. The bullets bounce off the bulletproof vehicle with ease. Covered in bulletproof vests, the men swing the door open and run out. The sixth man remains inside, along with the driver. His duty will come later.

Once outside the van, the men holding M240 machine guns lay into the buildings with extreme firepower. Pieces of bricks from the units fall off the buildings like clay. Windows shatter and many of the Emerald City men who are on the front side of the building are instantly killed. The bottom line is this: their weapons can't be fucked with.

Not expecting to face this type of artillery, most of the Emerald City men desert their posts and run for cover, away from the front of the building. When enough damage is done, the sixth man exits the vehicle, carrying a bullhorn. Before saying anything, he brushes his suit off with his hand.

"By now, you know we not fuckin' around,"

the tall, light-skinned man says. He looks more like a lawyer than a killer. "The next move is up to you."

Each of Black's men remains in front of a unit, waiting to fire again if need be. They all survey the grounds, looking for anything or anyone out of place.

"Black Water is fair . . . so this is what we gonna do. We gonna give anybody who wants to live a chance to leave." The loudness of the bullhorn echoes throughout Emerald. "I'm gonna count to five, and if you walk out before I count down, we'll let you pass without fail. But if you don't leave *our* city, you gonna die. The choice is yours, and it will be given only once. One . . . two . . . three . . ."

When he says "three," the next five vans enter Emerald City and park in front of each of the units in Emerald. The men already outside, who are holding their machine-gun weapons, keep their aim in case someone fires. Once each van parks, the eight men inside each of the vans get out and stand on the steps of each unit.

"I guess no one wants to live." The bullhorn man chuckles. "I'll give you credit for having heart, while it still beats. You made a major mistake by not taking Black up on his kind offer. Five!" he counts, before getting safely back into the van.

The first group of men holding the weapons unleashes into the side of the buildings, while the others jump out and run inside the units. A full-fledged war has begun.

Emerald City Squad

"We all dropped the ball on this shit."

Yvette and her ten crew members are standing in the hallway in Unit B when they hear *tat . . . tat . . . tat* multiple times. The sounds, followed by light crashing noises, resemble rocks falling off mountains.

"What was that?" Nassir yells. "Sounds like Mac-10's!"

"What the fuck?" Derrick responds, standing up in the hallway. Doc's lifeless body is still lying on the floor.

"It sounds like a whole rack of 'em too" is the last thing Nassir says before his head is blown clean off his body.

After Nassir is killed, bullets fly over their heads and against the hallway walls like rain going in the opposite direction. The force of the bullets causes the walls to crumble with extreme ease.

"Run!" Yvette screams as they take off toward

the far end of the hallway. "Go to the last apartment on the left!"

All of them run for cover as the guns continue to do major damage to the building. When they get to the apartment, they rush inside and the men move a heavy china cabinet, placing it in front of the door. The door had been open already, and no one is inside but them.

"Move to the bedroom in the back! They must be firin' from the field." They do as she says, closing the bedroom door behind them. Once inside, everyone sits on the floor.

"What's goin' on?" Mercedes asks. She is out of breath and is ducking as low as possible. "It sounds like the National Guard out there."

"It's gotta be Black," Yvette replies, shaking her head. "I knew this was a setup. What was I thinkin'?"

"Don't blame yourself, Yvette. We all dropped the ball on this shit," Kenyetta consoles.

"Y'all must've pissed the wrong nigga off," Chris adds, still not believing what is happening.

Tat . . . tat . . . tat . . . tat continues to sound off in the background.

"I knew that nigga was plannin' somethin' else," Derrick adds. "I shoulda hit him in Tyland, like I planned!"

"Don't beat yourself up, baby. We didn't have time to plan. Everything happened so quickly," Mercedes assures him.

"Did y'all see Nassir's head get blown off?" one of the young soldiers asks. He is visibly shaken and in shock. "One minute he was talkin', and the next minute his head was gone."

"Don't think about that," Mercedes tells him. "We have to focus."

"I—I gotta tell y'all somethin'," Kenyetta says, preparing to tell them about Black. "I—"

"Kenyetta, this don't have nothin' to do wit you," Mercedes cuts her off. "So leave it alone. A'ight?"

Kenyetta is surprised that Mercedes doesn't want her to reveal her secret about dealing with Black and sneaking him inside. She decides not to speak about it and nods in agreement.

"I'm not tryin' to give 'em Emerald," Yvette says plainly. "I can't give these niggas our home."

And then they hear a voice that says, *"By now, you know we not fuckin' around. The next move is up to you."*

After they listen to what the stranger is saying on the bullhorn, fear washes over them.

"You think they really gonna let us go?" the young soldier says hopefully.

"No . . . this may be it. I don't care what he says, but they never gonna let us leave outta here alive," Yvette advises softly.

"Baby, don't say that shit," Chris tells her. "We gettin' the fuck outta here!"

"Chris, even if me and the girls do walk out, they gonna murder us the moment our feet hit the concrete. They can't let us leave here alive. Trust me. Black knows the only way to keep Emerald, if he takes it, is to murder us. Otherwise, we comin' back, fightin'."

Kenyetta and Mercedes look at one another and drop their heads.

"Why don't y'all go 'head," Yvette tells the soldiers and Chris. "We gonna stay. It's us they want, not y'all."

"Have you lost your fuckin' mind?" Chris asks her.

"Yeah, you must be trippin' if you think I'm leavin' my shortie and y'all in here alone. If we in it, we in it together!" Derrick tells her.

Silence fills the small room as gunfire gets louder outside the apartment.

"I can't believe it's gonna happen like this. I mean . . . I always knew I'd die in Emerald, but I always thought it would be more peaceful, like in my sleep or somethin'," Mercedes says, looking around at everyone.

"At least you thought about dying," Kenyetta responds. "I figured I'd live forever."

Chris wraps her arm around Yvette and holds her tightly. "If you die, at least you're dyin' wit me."

"You really love her, don't you?" Mercedes asks.

"Wit my life," Chris responds, looking at Yvette.

"I can feel it," Mercedes says. "I'm so sorry, Chris . . . for unleashin' on you. And I apologize for the smack."

"You smacked my baby?" Yvette asks.

"Yeah . . . she got one out on me. But it's cool, though. That shit don't even matter no more."

Mercedes grips Derrick and then hugs

Kenyetta. They all hold one another. The sounds of the enemies' powerful weapons grow closer.

"They in the building, y'all. They lookin' for us. They know we here," Mercedes tells them.

"Well, I hope they ready for a battle, 'cause I'm not givin' up easy," Yvette tells them. "I got five bullets. How many y'all got?"

"Eight . . . six . . . ten . . . two . . . nine," they tally up and report.

"Well . . . that sounds like enough for a hell of a fight," Yvette assures them. All of a sudden, she starts laughing.

"What's so funny?" Mercedes asks.

"I'm just remembering when you and Derrick used to go at it all the time." Yvette is giggling. "I thought y'all were gonna kill one another. And now y'all all bunned up."

"I know, right?" Kenyetta agrees.

"He used to get on my fuckin' nerves!" Mercedes says, looking into his handsome face. "Now I can't live without him."

"I hope so." His tone is soft, but the implication of her infidelity looms. "But I never hated you," he shares publicly, looking at Mercedes' bruised but beautiful face. "I knew from the moment I saw her that she was the one. Everybody else saw it too. That's what was fuckin' me up." He smiles. "You everything to me," he says seriously. "You my soul mate. And if I got any say-so in the next life, I'ma choose you again."

There isn't a dry eye in the room. Yvette stands up and holds out her hand. One by one, everyone gets up and they place their hands on top of hers.

"Emerald City in life and death!" Yvette proclaims.

They repeat after her, " 'Emerald City in life and death!' "

"If I gotta die, I rather die with y'all. I'm goin' out wit some real-ass niggas." Yvette looks around at them.

"We proud to go out wit you too," one of the soldiers says.

As they say their good-byes, Black's men reach their floor with orders to kill them without questions asked.

Unit C

"In war, there are casualties."

In Unit C, Black's kids have already killed ten men and have taken control of the stash houses. Because Wallace, Lando, and Neo didn't get a chance to relay Mercedes' message about the kids being possibly dangerous, the soldiers' guards were down, and they paid with their lives. And now that Black's men have arrived to take the children home, they are free to go, escaping any wrath.

"Everything's clear," one of Black's men, who's holding a machine gun, says to the child. He remains in the doorway of the stash house; his foot props the door open. "I'm ready to take y'all downstairs. Get your mother."

As they speak, men in Black's squad come in and out of the apartment, removing drugs and money.

"I'll get her now," Lance, Black's son, says. "They ready, Ma. We gotta leave. They got the van parked out front."

His brothers push past him and enter the hallway. They've had enough excitement for the day and just want to go home.

"You ready, Ma?" Lance asks his mother, who's in a daze.

"I don't wanna leave your brother," Shade says. "Nathan's still in here somewhere."

"You heard what they said. . . . Auntie Shannon was killed. Nathan might be dead too. We gotta move on, Ma. In war, there are casualties," he says with conviction.

"Lance, I know. You don't have to tell me that," Shade says sternly.

"If I ain't gotta tell you, what's up then?" the kid shouts. "You actin' like you don't get it! Dad would flip if he saw you actin' like this!"

With the mention of Black, she pulls herself together and stands up.

"I'm coming." Shade walks behind her children to the van.

Her heart is broken because her sister is dead and her child is missing. But she knows she can't blame anybody but herself, and that hurts worse. She feels the burning sensation rising in her nose, forcing her to cry. But if she shows emotion, Black would certainly punish her in the worst way. Although he reserves violence for the children, he doesn't spare his women if they show signs of weakness during dire situations.

Instead of crying, she sits quietly in her seat, reciting her son's words: "In war, there are casualties."

She adds her own words: "Even if the casualty is my own son."

The Community Center

"Wake up, young man. Everybody got guns."

The community center is jam-packed with people displaced from their homes in Unit B. Hope is in their hearts that soon the fiasco will be over and they can return home.

Nathan opens his eyes and realizes he's sitting on a hard-plastic orange chair. One of the tenants covered him earlier with her jacket. When he jumps up, he pushes it off.

Happy the child is doing better, the tenants smile at him slightly.

"You a'ight, lil nigga?" Lando asks when they see him standing.

"What happened?" he says, although he remembers.

"You shot my man. That's what happened. And if you try some shit like that in here, you won't be gettin' back up."

"Why you do that, anyway?" Neo questions him.

Nathan thinks for a minute about what he is going to say and remembers his conversation with Wallace.

" 'Cause I was mad," he says, pouting.

"Mad about what?"

"I was mad that—that . . . they killed my auntie," he says sadly. "I wanna go home." He is crying. "Please take me home."

"You ain't goin' home no time soon, so you might as well get used to it," Neo tells him, looking out the window. "None of us leavin' here tonight."

"Where you learn how to shoot, anyway?" Lando interrogates.

"My dad taught me."

"Ain't you too young to be holdin' a gun?"

"I guess . . . but my dad don't think so."

When Lando walks toward the window to look out too, Nathan rushes toward them. He removes the gun from the back of Neo's jeans.

"Put your hands up!" he warns.

Neo and Lando turn around, throwing their hands up in the air. The sad expression on the child's face is replaced with satisfaction.

"Sorry . . . but I gotta go," he tells them.

"Son, why don't you put that gun away," one of the elderly men says. "You're gonna hurt somebody or yourself."

"Fuck you!" Nathan yells. "What you think? I'm playin' or somethin'? I'm not playin' wit y'all! I'm leavin'."

"Son . . . put the gun down," the old man begs him. "I don't want to see you hurt."

Scared that the man will tackle him and take the weapon, he shoots him in the shoulder. Everyone gasps in disbelief.

"I coulda killed him," Nathan says, moving the barrel of the gun around the room. "I coulda killed him, but I didn't. I'm a sure shot. See," he says as he fires into a picture of Stacia and Dex on the community center's wall. The bullet goes straight into her head. "See, if I wanted to, he'd be dead. All I wanna do is go home. That's it."

"A'ight, lil man," Neo says, holding his hands in the air. "You got it."

In the back of the room, a man who'd brought his own weapon sits quietly next to his wife. Not even she knows he is toting.

But when she looks at her husband and sees the handle in his hand, she says, "Don't, honey. He's just a child."

Many thoughts run through the man's mind, including not being able to defend his wife of thirty years. He hates how a disability he gained in the war forced them to live in the worst conditions: Emerald City, a project. His wife, who could barely read and write, took odd jobs cleaning homes for rich people in Maryland just to make a little more money than what the government gave them on his disability checks. He feels worthless.

Despising how his life has turned out, and how the young people have taken over Emerald

City and have turned it into an even worse nightmare, he decides to take it out on someone.

"Pete!" his wife screams when he stands up, fires, and shoots the child in the chest. His body falls to the floor.

"Oh, my God!" someone cries out. Everyone looks at the man and then the slain kid.

Neo and Lando rush the man, taking his weapon. They don't want him unleashing on them next.

"Sorry, old man," Lando says, gaining access to his 9mm, "but I'ma have to get this up off you."

The man sits back down without a fight. Besides, he did what he wanted. He made someone pay for his failures.

"Why, baby? Why?" his wife cries softly. "He was a baby."

"You saw that boy's eyes, Estelle. If he lived, he would've been nothin' but a stone-cold killer."

"Who are you? 'Cause I don't know you no more!" she says before getting up to sit at another seat far away from him.

"Thanks, old man," Neo says to him after taking back his weapon from the dead child. "That lil nigga was crazy, anyway. You did everybody a favor. Don't worry, we didn't see nothing. Right, everybody?"

No one says a word, because they already know the unspoken rule: keep your silence and keep your life.

"He wasn't the only one crazy, you know?" one of the older ladies says. A few people gasp.

"What you talkin' 'bout?" Lando asks.

"I'm talkin' about you. The both of you! All of you Emerald City bangers are just as crazy as that child! Where do you think he got it from?"

"Whateva!" Lando brushes her off.

"Look what y'all helped them killers do to our homes. Look!" She points with her wrinkled finger toward the door. "We livin' like we're in a foreign country. Locked up and afraid of our own people. You young boys don't give a shit about what you're doing to our generation or your own."

"I'm not tryin' to hear that shit." Neo laughs. "If anything, we protectin' you right now. 'Cause if we weren't here, who knows what would happen?"

"Wake up, young man," another man says. "Everybody got guns. Don't you see?"

"You're destroyin' us," another female tenant adds. "You're destroyin' your own people. You better than this. I know you are."

"Look . . . in case y'all didn't fuckin' notice, I'm in here with you. I'm on your side," Neo explains.

"You're selling drugs and killing your own people. You might as well be out there with them. You're on money's side."

The preaching is becoming unbearable to Neo and Lando, and they want out. If things don't end soon, they could honestly see themselves killing somebody else.

"Listen . . . what's done is done! Ain't nobody ever teach me nothin'! I mean, how many of y'all ever did anything for me besides tell me to get away from your front door? When I was a youngin' comin' up in dis fucked-up project, nobody ever did shit for me. I had to go out and make moves to feed my family. And now you wonderin' why we this, and why we that? Take a look around! The blame is just as much yours as it is ours!" Lando tells them.

"So you blamin' us now," an old lady asks.

"I'm blamin' anybody who blamin' me. You think I wanna be livin' like this? Fuck no! But I'll tell you this, I'm willin' to do what I gotta do, and I don't give a fuck who got somethin' to say 'bout it," Lando continues.

"Son . . . we did our work already," she says to him softly. "It's because of us, you ain't got to do this no more, but you choose to. We marched for civil rights. We spoke up for our freedom. You just choose not to take advantage of it. We did what we had to so that you all can have a part of the American dream. So stop blamin' everybody else and start lookin' at yourself."

"You know what? Sit your old ass down and shut the fuck up. I'm through talkin' to y'all." When they don't sit down quick enough, he pulls out Pete's weapon and cocks it back. "Do I gotta ask you again?"

Everyone sits down and Lando looks out the window. What the woman said weighs on him, and he is angry. Sure, he doesn't want to live this lifestyle, but he doesn't see any other alternative. As he stares out the window, he sees ropes dropping down the walls of Emerald. Then he sees one man after another sliding down them. There are many men.

"Cut the lights off!" Lando yells.

"They in the back now!" Neo warns.

Everyone starts making noise.

"Shut the fuck up before they hear us," Lando tells them. "I'm not fuckin' around!"

Everyone grows as silent as possible. When the lights go out, Neo and Lando continue to peek out the blinds. They fear Black has stepped up his operation, and is not letting anyone leave Emerald alive. Now the seriousness of the situation has finally set in . . . for both of them.

District of Columbia Police Department

"You better be careful about the shit you say around here. You just might come up missin'."

"What you want to eat, Jones?" Officer Tath says, standing over his desk with a pen and a pad. "We're about to put our orders in now."

"I'm not hungry," he responds, never looking away from his computer screen.

"We ordering from V-Burgers," Tath persists, hoping he'll change his mind, so they'll get the discount on the delivery charge.

"I said I'm not hungry. I didn't come here to eat no expensive-ass burgers from V's. I came here to uphold the law, but that's not what y'all wanna do around here." This time, he looks at everyone in the station, including Tath.

"What do you mean?" Officer Kerry asks, sitting at the desk next to him.

"Stop acting like you don't know what I mean. . . . We've received ten calls in the last hour from people in Emerald City, but we do nothing about it! Why?"

"It's just the way it is," Tath responds, walking away. "They got their laws, and we got ours."

"Do you hear yourself?" Jones asks.

"No, do you hear yourself? You're worryin' about a couple of drug-dealing niggers, when you should be worryin' about yourself."

Jones is heated because although he is far from a nigger, he is still African American.

"Niggers are people too," Jones replies.

"No. . . ." Tath chuckles. "They're just *nigger* people."

"I bet you won't be laughing if I call the mayor's office," Jones threatens.

The smile is wiped clean off Tath's face.

"You better be careful about the shit you say around here. You just might come up missin'," Kerry advises.

Jones turns around, looks at him, and says, "We'll see about that."

Lone Soldier

He failed to create a backup plan.

Black's men grow lax as they enter each unit, because the search-and-destroy mission has dwindled to finding Yvette and the other women. But just when they think victory is completely theirs, an army more dangerous than their own enters from the back of the city.

One of Black's soldiers arrives at the apartment Yvette is in, his weapon aimed and ready, when the sound of weapons firing outside frightens him. This is odd because he has been given word not too long ago that they won Emerald.

"What the fuck?" he says aloud to himself as he walks away from the apartment and down the hallway toward the staircase door.

The moment he opens it, he's rushed by two men, who unload multiple bullets into his body. He drops to the floor, and his body prevents the door from closing. Once he's murdered, the men push open the door and step over him. The sounds of gunfire rise again. A war ensues—amongst Black Water's men and another crew. But because their guard was down, Black's men drop, one by one.

Black has made a dangerous mistake. He failed to create a backup plan, and that major error is going to cost him the war.

The Fallout

Black Water

"Many bitches would die to be in your shoes right now."

A few hours earlier

Although she wasn't a dancer, Black Water was turned on by her apparent attraction to other women. She threw dollar after dollar on the stage as the dancers fought for her attention.

"Excuse me, my boss wants to meet you," Black's driver said, interrupting her.

She took one look at the driver and then at Black and said, "What are we, in middle school?" She laughed and remarked, "If he wants to meet me, tell him to meet me himself."

With that, she tossed her long hair and turned her focus back on the women. Five minutes later, Black walked up to her.

"You gonna hang out wit me at my table?" he asked.

"Who's asking?"

"Me. And I'm only asking once."

The woman looked him up and down and accepted.

"So what's up?" she inquired, sitting next to him.

"You."

"Me?" She pointed at herself. "How am I up, when you just met me?"

" 'Cause I know what I like."

"And what's that?"

"For one, I fucks wit chicks wit that long, silky black hair. You my type . . . trust me."

She waved him off, as if she's uninterested.

"No joke. I found the finest thing in here, and she's not on the stage."

"Is that right?" She smiled.

He didn't respond.

"You funny," she commented.

"And you bad as shit! So what's your name?"

"Candy," she confessed.

"Candy, huh? I like that. You gonna be mine before the night is out."

They kept each other company for the rest of the evening. And when the club closed, he invited her to breakfast. After enjoying a small meal together, Black instructed his driver to take them to a nearby hotel. He continued to drink excessively, believing there was much to celebrate. After all, in hours, Emerald City would be his.

Once in the hotel room, he asked, "So . . . w-what were you—you doin' in a strip club?" He plopped down on the end of the bed and removed his shoes.

"I guess it was research, since I'm opening my own spot in Virginia in a few months."

"So you stealin' dancers?" he asked, stretching out on the end of the bed.

"Naw, I'm just checking out my competition," she told him, lying next to him in the bed.

"Do you know who I am?"

"No. Who are you?"

"I'm probably the richest nigga you'll ever meet in your life." With that, Black unbuttoned his pants, pulled out his dick, and stroked it to its complete thickness.

"Is that right?" She smiled, looking at it and then at him. "And how do you know you're the richest man *I've* met in *my* life? I been around money longer than I can remember."

" 'Cause I run D.C. And everybody in it," he said as his words began to drag.

"Well, I don't live in D.C.," she said, moving closer to him. "But say you are. . . . What does that have to do with me?"

"It means, for now, I want you to get on your knees and suck my dick 'cause many bitches would die to be in your shoes right now." There was a brief moment of silence. "Fuck you waitin' on?" he asked, scowling.

"You used to getting what you want?" Candy said as she stood, walked toward the table, and poured two more cups of liquor. "I can respect that." She handed him the plastic cup filled with

Rémy and sipped on the other. "But what you gonna do for me?"

"It depends how good you are," he said, downing what was left in the cup before throwing it to the floor. "Now get over here."

"I got you," she responded, seductively taking off her clothes. "But let's do it the right way."

The next morning

Black awakes to a throbbing headache. Candy is next to him, naked, with an empty bottle of liquor between them.

"Get up," he says groggily. "We gotta go."

"Already?" she moans. "I was hoping you'd be up for round two."

"Look . . . get the fuck up or I'm leavin' you here."

"All right . . . all right. . . . I'm movin,'" she says, stretching around a little before finally getting up.

When they are dressed, they walk toward the Rolls-Royce. Black is stumbling the entire way. Candy opens the door and Black slides in, with her right behind him.

"Take me to get some coffee from McDonald's," he tells his driver. "Then take me to Emerald."

When the car doesn't move, Black asks, "Did you hear me?"

"Yeah . . . I heard you."

Black recognizes the voice, despite it not belonging to his driver. He sits up straight and leans toward the privacy window separating them. His thick index finger rolls the control window down and the man is revealed.

Black's urine escapes his body and he stutters, "Wha-what the f-fuck is goin' on? W-where's my driver?"

"He gone. But don't worry, I'ma take you where you need to go."

With those words, the woman he knew as Candy plunges a knife deeply into his stomach. When his flesh covers the entire blade, she pushes again before twisting it once. Black's mouth opens and he succumbs to the pain.

The driver, who is actually Dreyfus, looks at Black, studying him until Black's eyes are closed. Then he says, "I told you not to fuck wit my money. But I ain't gonna have to tell you no more."

Emerald City Squad

"Looks like you all fucked up the city pretty good."

The sounds of weapons firing cease completely in Emerald City. And the smell of gunpowder seeps beneath the apartment doors. There is a gloomy presence throughout the city. Death, destruction, and fear are all realities.

"I'm goin' out," Yvette says. "I can't stay in here without knowing something."

"You sure we should?" Kenyetta asks. "It's too quiet. That usually means something's up."

"We can't stay in here forever," Yvette warns. "We hid long enough."

"I think she right," Derrick says, rising up. The men stand up next to him. "Y'all follow closely behind me."

The men move the china cabinet and they all walk carefully into the hallway. Pieces of the building's structure are scattered everywhere. Emerald City is partially destroyed. When they all reach the stairwell, they see a body stuck in the doorway.

"Hold up," Derrick says, approaching him cautiously. "Let me check him out." He approaches the body with his 9mm drawn. When he reaches it, he bends down and looks at him. The corpse's eyes are wide open, so Derrick knows he's dead. "He gone. Let's move."

Everyone enters the stairwell and runs down the steps to the bottom floor. Pushing the door open and walking outside, they feel their hearts drop at the death and destruction around them. Even the brightness of the sun can't soften the despair.

"Damn, boss," one of the men says. "You think they got scared and left?"

"Naw . . . somethin' else went down," Yvette responds, looking around. "I don't know what."

Just when she says that, Black's Rolls-Royce enters the gate. Everyone heads back toward the building and remains inside. If he exits the car, they will use every bullet they have to kill him.

"Back up," Yvette says, looking through the shattered door. " 'Cause if that nigga gets out that car, I'm blazin' his ass."

"I'm gettin' in on that too," Kenyetta adds.

When the car drives into the middle of the yard and parks, they remain quiet. And all of a sudden, a woman with silky, long hair gets out on the passenger side. Once outside of the car, she removes a long wig and looks up at the units.

"Is that Carissa?" Yvette asks, staring closely through the stained-glass door.

"It damn sure look like her," Mercedes adds. "But what is she doin' here?"

Yvette pushes open the building door and everyone follows her. Now they clearly see that it is her.

"Carissa!" Mercedes yells from the top of Unit B.

They run down the stairs and up to her, in the middle of the yard. She smiles when she sees their faces; they all embrace without saying a word.

"Oh, my God! When I came in and saw the city like this," Carissa says, looking around, "I was so worried that something happened to you-all. I'm so sorry for abandoning you! Trust me when I say that will never happen again."

"We know," Kenyetta replies. "And I'm sorry for how I treated you when you wanted to leave. I really am."

"Shut up, bitch! We together now," she says, hugging her again.

"But what are you doin' here?" Yvette asks. "And what are you doin' in Black's car?"

Derrick and the soldiers allow the women to have their moment as they keep watch over the city.

"It's a long story, so let me make it short. I found out from Lavelle that Black was moving on the city, so I knew we needed help if we wanted to keep what was ours. So I got it."

"Who you get?" Yvette questions.

She walks to the driver's side of the car and opens the door. Everyone waits patiently until Dreyfus, who is on the phone, comes into view.

"I'll see you later," he tells the caller. Focusing his attention on the women, he says, "Looks like you all fucked up the city pretty good." He looks around.

"You don't know the half," Yvette responds.

"Well, look, you got your city back. I'ma get outta here. I got a flight in six hours to Cancun, and I ain't missin' it for anything in the world."

"Thanks, Dreyfus." Yvette smiles. "We'll find some way to repay you."

"Don't worry about it now. You owe me. Just make sure you pick things up around here and get back to business. And next time, call me sooner."

"Got it," Yvette tells him.

When he drives away, Yvette says, "Say what you want, but that nigga always comes through when we need him."

"I feel you, but I wonder what he'll want for repayment?" Kenyetta whispers as they look at the car going out of sight.

"I guess we'll find out," Yvette states. "So what happened to Black?" she inquires.

"He dead, and Dreyfus sending another message that anybody affiliated with Black's business betta get outta Tyland. He's taken it back, and he wants *us* to run it."

"Run Tyland and Emerald?" Kenyetta questions.

"Yeah . . . think we can do it?" Carissa asks Yvette.

"I'm not sure. To be honest, I'll have to think about it. Somethin' tells me we should focus on home and leave the rest alone."

"I feel you," Carissa answers. "Well, he says if we want it, we can have it. And if not, he'll get someone else. They over there right now cleanin' house."

"Hey, what happened to Lavelle?" Mercedes asks.

"Oh . . . hold on." She smiles. "I have to make another phone call."

Lavelle

"So it's just like that, huh?"

Lavelle sits in a chair next to his bed and watches a Katt Williams comedy special on HBO, along with the two guards. They laugh constantly at his uncensored humor. The more time goes by, the more confident Lavelle grows that he'll make it out of the situation alive. After all, if Carissa had wanted him dead, he'd be gone already.

When the phone rings, one of the men says, "Lavelle, can you pause that right quick?"

"No problem," he says, stopping the show. He knows it is Carissa and he isn't worried.

"Hey, boss. What's up?"

There's silence as Lavelle sips his Sprite and places it back on the nightstand. He glances out the window, trying to remember all he has to do today. Life seems to move by him, and the frustration is quickly becoming irritating. In his heart of hearts, all he wants is for Carissa and him to move on with their lives. While looking outside, he smiles at his neighbor. She's taking her trash out, wearing tight jeans and a white shirt with no bra. But just as quickly as he smiles, his grin is removed from his face when he sees the raggedy black van drive up and park in his driveway.

"The Vanishers," Lavelle says out loud. He looks at the soldiers, who stand up after ending the call with Carissa. "So it's just like that, huh?" he asks.

"Looks that way, man," one of them says, aiming his gun.

"She didn't even wanna speak to me?"

"Naw."

There's a brief knock at the door and one of them leaves the room to open it. Lee returns with another man; Lavelle recognizes him.

"Damn . . . I can't believe it," Lavelle says. "I can't believe I'm dying like this."

"Why? Didn't you say you taught her all she knew?" one of the soldiers asks.

Lavelle doesn't respond.

"Well, it looks like you did a good job."

A single shot to the head kills Lavelle instantly.

Cameron

"I love you, and everything I did was so I could be with you."

Cameron wakes up with an extreme headache. He rubs his head constantly, trying to rid himself of the pain. Moving around a little, he notices his surroundings. He's in the passenger seat of Toi's 2010 Yukon Denali.

"You a'ight?" she asks him softly. "You don't look too good."

"I—I guess I am. What happened?"

"You got fucked up," she tells him.

"Well, you look okay," he says, observing her. "Wasn't you drinking too?"

"Not like you."

When she says that, Cameron feels a pair of hands on his shoulders. He turns around to see who is behind him and cringes at Mercedes' battered face. He reaches for his gun.

"It's not there," Toi says calmly.

"Fuck is going on?" he asks.

"What you think is goin' on?" Yvette responds from the backseat behind Toi.

"Yeah, what you think is up, Cameron?" Kenyetta questions from the third-row seat.

"I think he knows what time it is," Carissa adds. She's seated next to Kenyetta.

Cameron swallows hard and looks back at Toi. "Why you do this?"

" 'Cause I can't stand bitch-ass niggas. You shoulda left well enough alone, Cameron. After Mercedes told me the story about Emerald City, I figured if you'd do your children's mother wrong, you'd do worse to me."

"So you would help them kill me?"

"Naw, you did that to yourself."

Cameron laughs a little and pulls the visor down to look in the mirror at Mercedes.

"Since we bein' real, so am I. I don't care about this bitch, Mercedes. I never have. I love you and everything I did was so I could be with you. So tell me. . . . Are you really gonna do this to me, baby?"

"What do you think, Cameron? You okayed some niggas to rape me!"

"I didn't know shit about that! That nigga lied!"

"You didn't stop it either," Yvette adds.

"This between me and Mercedes," he tells her.

"That's where you wrong," Mercedes corrects him. "They have everything to do with this. My friends have been with me every time you broke

284

my heart. All you had to do was keep a promise. That's it. And you couldn't do it. You sold me out twice, and there won't be a third."

With that, she removes a blade from her pocket and slices his throat open. And just like that, he's gone.

V-Burgers

"Let's just say, we use D.C.'s finest recipe."

V-Burgers is jumping as usual. The restaurant is jam-packed with police officers, and the phone is ringing off the hook with orders. Officers frequent the establishment because during lunchtime the restaurant gives them free burgers.

"What will it be, sir?" Lee asks.

"Give me two V-Burgers, with everything on it," Tath says.

"And what will you have, sir?" he asks Tath's partner, Kerry.

"I'll have the same." He smiles, rubbing his stomach.

"No problem," Lee says.

"I got to ask you, Lee," Tath remarks. "What do you-all put in your burgers?"

Lee smiles and says, "Let's just say, we use D.C.'s finest recipe."

What Lee doesn't tell them is that the meat from the burgers comes from all the bodies they are paid to remove around the city. The meat is grounded and seasoned to perfection right in the back of their store. And because sometimes the bodies are coming in quicker than they can cook them, the officers-eat-free promotion helps clean up their tracks greatly. So little do the officers know, but they are helping to keep the streets clean, after all . . . one body at a time.

Epilogue

A year later

Weeks after the war, the mayor ordered a full investigation because Officer Jones made a big deal about Emerald City receiving special treatment. But when the detectives visited, they turned a blind eye to everything. After all, Emerald City had many officers on its payroll . . . the detectives included. Shortly after the investigation concluded, finding that nothing was out of order, Officer Jones was mysteriously transferred out of the precinct and to another department. After a few complaints from people he arrested, he was later fired. He knew it had everything to do with him breaking silence, but he couldn't prove it.

Emerald City was up and running after a year. It wasn't easy getting order restored, and the women ended up putting millions into Emerald

City just to make it safer and stronger than ever. The guard's station was now farther inside Emerald, and the gate leading into the property was farther out. This way, the guard could see on the closed-circuit television who or what was entering before making a decision to open the gate. Security cameras were placed everywhere, and each building had a guard who worked for Emerald. Although the D.C. government owned Emerald City, it was the squad that made the rules.

Mercedes married Derrick and they lived happily in their home. Both of them were still very active in Emerald, and she never stepped out of her relationship again. What she didn't know was that from time to time, Derrick slept with a girl who lived in Virginia, who was catching feelings for him. Although he forgave Mercedes and would never leave her, he never forgot what he heard Mercedes say she did with Cameron. That changed his commitment to her, but not his love.

Lil C spent a lot of time in Emerald and was learning the ropes personally from his mother. All he thought about was money, and he trusted no one but his mother.

Yvette and Chris lived together, and Yvette was working hard to make the relationship successful. The only problem was, they argued constantly. Although they didn't always see eye-to-eye, their love for one another kept them together.

Carissa became bold with her sexuality and had sex with anyone she wanted, without regard for how that person felt. She'd become cold to the idea of love, but open to life. She sold the home she shared with Lavelle and purchased a yacht, valued at $5 million, which she kept docked in Southwest D.C. She lived there when she wasn't in Emerald.

Six months after the war in Emerald, Kenyetta sold her home. Realizing she didn't want to be alone, she took Carissa's offer to move into her yacht. Just like Carissa, Kenyetta had become turned off to love. When they weren't in Emerald, the two of them took trips around the world and were known as heartbreakers. It didn't bother them, because at least they were happy and their feelings were guarded.

Emerald City is back in order. The fort is stronger than ever, and the women opened a few legal operations to hide the money that is flowing. Life is good, but the war has left a lot of wounds.

Although they appear strong on the surface, a thought never leaves their minds. Can something as disastrous as that ever happen again?

Don't miss

Pit Bulls in a Skirt

On sale now from Dafina Books

Chapter 1

The Hustlers' Ball

December, Friday, 10:30 P.M.

Mercedes

It had been an hour since I hung up with my mother, and I was still pissed.

I couldn't believe she waited until the last minute to tell me she couldn't watch her own grandkids! Tonight was the wrong night for her to pull this bullshit on me. Mr. Melvin's yearly Christmas party, which we call "the Hustlers' Ball," was in an hour, and it was obvious I wasn't gonna make it.

Mr. Melvin, the property manager, started the parties at the community center in Emerald City to try to stop the violence. However, what he didn't realize was all he did was breed every hustler in D.C. that was in the game. It was the only time we allowed the security guards to open the gates for outsiders, but not without checking the list we provided for them first. We owned Emerald City and everybody in it. Nobody made a move without clearing it with us first. Even though D.C. government paid the guards, they received their *real* orders and *real* money from us.

With five buildings and twelve floors in every one of them, Emerald City was one of the largest projects in the city. Originally named the Frederick Douglass Housing Projects, the project acquired the nickname of Emerald City because all of the buildings had emerald green awnings.

Tucked behind the gates of Emerald City were Murry's food store, a barbershop, a beauty salon, and an arcade—everything you needed, including every kind of drug you could imagine.

"Ma, are you sure you can't watch them for me?" By now, I was begging my mother— something I normally don't do. But for the Hustlers' Ball, it was warranted.

"I'm positive. Bye, Mercedes!"

Click.

She hung up on me! I cannot believe she hung up on me! Man! I can't stand her sometimes!

I opened my bedroom door and walked into the living room. I started contemplating whether I should ask my son, who was sitting on the couch playing a video game, to watch his sisters for me. Asking Cameron Jr. was almost as bad as asking my mother. He had his own mind now, and that was somewhat scary. He was growing up very fast. I knew it was just a matter of time before he wanted in the game and in the life he'd been raised around.

Big Cameron already had him counting the cash we collected at the end of the week from the runners. And as long as he learned the ropes from his father, I had no problem with him dealing when he was ready, but he had to be *ready*. I loved this life and everything about it. Considering the power, the money, and the look on my man's face when he came through the gates and saw shit was still intact, this life excited me. There is no other feeling that can compare—outside of the way Cameron makes me feel when we make love.

"Li'l C, you sure you don't wanna make two hundred dollars tonight?" I asked him while he was playing *Madden* on our fifty-inch plasma-screen TV. "It'll help your momma out a lot."

I sat down and put my arm around him. He looked irritated, and I could tell he knew I was trying to butter him up.

"Doin' what, Ma?" he asked, never taking his eyes off the game.

"Watchin' your sisters," I responded, playing with his hair.

He looked at me with his big eyes and that beautiful curly hair like I had just asked him to do the worst thing in the world. Letting me know he wasn't going for it.

Cameron Jr. was thirteen years old and helped me out a lot with eight-year-old Chante and four-year-old Baby Crystal, but lately Chante was becoming too much for anyone to handle. And I made a promise not to force him to watch his sisters unless I was handling business, and I always kept my promises.

"Come on, Ma! All Chante gonna do is get on my nerves when you leave! She makes me sick sometimes! She cries the moment you go, plus she don't listen."

"Calm down, boy. I ain't gonna *make* you do anything. But you know the ball's tonight, and your Aunt Stacia and Dex gonna be here in a minute to pick me up."

Truthfully, I could've paid anybody to watch them, but I like them to be around their own things and in their own place. Plus I didn't trust just *anybody* in my apartment. And most of the muthafuckas I knew, who would have jumped at the opportunity to earn two hundred dollars for four hours, were fucking with that shit. So sending my kids with them or letting them watch them at my place was out of the question.

Between all of our clothes and our expensive furniture from overseas, I had over $200,000 worth of shit in my apartment. We did real well with the money the drug life gave us, so I didn't need anybody taking it from me because I messed around and let someone in my apartment who could later plot to rob us.

"If I say 'no,' you gonna be mad?" he asked.

"How can I be mad at you?" I rebutted. As I looked into my son's eyes, it never ceased to amaze me how much he looked like his father.

"I'm just gonna be upset, that's all." I continued hoping he'd change his mind.

"Well, I don't wanna do it," he said, continuing to play his game and avoiding my stare.

"All right, then," I said, walking slowly to my room, my tired attempt to give him time to change his mind. "Let me go tell your aunt the bad news."

I walked to my closet, which held Cameron's and my clothes. It was so packed that I could hardly find anything when I wanted it. Looking at the packed closet, I let out a frustrated sigh. I would be so happy when Cameron became a lieutenant, so we could finally move out of Emerald City. The bottom line was this: No matter how much money we had, we were still living in the projects. I knew it, even if the people around me chose to forget.

I grabbed my white Eddie Bauer ski jacket and zipped it up all the way to the top. I was just about to leave my room, until I remembered to grab my Marc Jacobs bag with "My Bitch" tucked inside it. My Bitch was the nickname I gave to the nine millimeter. I never left my house without it. I hadn't had to use her yet, but I was willing to . . . if need be.

I walked toward the elevators. As always, the stench that met my nose reminded me of how nasty my neighbors were. I could immediately smell the dirty apartments and the trash, which sat behind their doors for far too long.

While waiting on the elevator, Derrick, one of

the grimiest niggas on my squad, walked up to me. Derrick was a hard worker, but he had a tendency to try me from time to time. I was constantly putting him in his place. At first, I used to tell Big Cameron when Derrick got me wrong, but Cam started getting mad. He said that they'd never respect me if I kept running to him over everything they did. So I started handling stuff on my own, and I only came to him about the big shit.

"What up, Mercedes?" he asked as we both waited on the elevator.

"Nothin'." I did my best to keep my tone even, reminding him that we weren't friends.

"You goin' to the ball tonight?" he asked, still trying to spark up convo.

We stepped into the elevator and I met his stare with one of my own.

"Look." I paused. "You know I'm not with the small talk and shit. So unless we talkin' 'bout business, we ain't talkin'."

"Yeah . . . uh . . . I know," he said as we walked off the elevator. He looked all salty and shit. "I'm just tryin' to be cool with the female I report to, that's all."

I didn't respond. I let him walk ahead of me because I hated people walking behind me, especially somebody as grimy as Derrick. When we approached the exit to the building, I saw my girls on the steps.

Shit! They gonna be blown like shit wit' me.

Before he walked outside, I remembered I didn't find out the status of the dope fiend who gave him fifty dollars in counterfeit cash in exchange for some of the purest heroin in Southeast.

"Derrick!" I yelled before he pushed open the building's door. The cold air hit my face quickly before the door slammed shut again.

He turned around and walked over to me. "Yeah."

"What happened with that head? You handle it?"

"Yeah." He smiled as he smoothed the side of his face with his right hand and grabbed his chin. "We handled that shit. I think his funeral was last week."

"A'ight, but next time, get back with me."

"Yeah . . . okay." He stopped, clearly still upset that he had to take orders from me instead of Cameron, even though it had been over three years now. "I'll try to remember that."

"You *will* remember."

He nodded his head and turned toward the door. When he walked through it, the night air hit me hard. It wasn't a match for my Eddie Bauer jacket, but it was hell on my jean-clad legs. You'd think by now I'd be used to the cold air, since I had to man my post for twelve hours a day for the past three years.

The first thing I saw when I opened the door were tight-ass cars driving through the gates. *Damn! Rashawn from New York really did get the Lamborghini! She's a lucky muthafucka!*

There were all types of high-end cars navigating the streets. Mercedes-Benzes, which happen to be my favorite, BMWs, Range Rovers, Bentleys, and Acuras flooded Emerald City's gates, heading to the ball. Some playas had gone all out, showing up in chauffeured Navigator and Hummer limousines. Seeing the cars got me horny, and now I was even madder at my mother. For a second I even contemplated *making* Li'l C watch his sisters. But like I said, I never break my promise.

I saw my girls handling business as usual, in designer dresses and fur coats, while waiting for Stacia and Dex to scoop us up. The community center was a ten-minute walk because EC was so big, so we were better off driving, which only took about two minutes.

I laughed when I saw them dressed up while handing out orders in front of the building. And as always, Yvette was the loudest.

"*Look* . . . don't tell me you got it if you don't, Dramon! If shit ain't right when we get back, you might as well leave town. I'm not fuckin' around wit' you!"

"I got it, Yvette," he said, with his hands in his pockets, shaking his head with confidence. "Y'all ain't got shit to be worried about tonight. Me and my soldiers holdin' shit down."

Most of our soldiers were between the ages of sixteen and twenty-one. Cameron said Dex liked them that way because they showed respect; and above all else, they were hungry for that money. He said the older they got, the more rebellious they became and wouldn't take kindly to women giving them orders. Once they reached that rebellious age, he'd cut 'em off. However, if they were good, he'd put them to work outside Emerald City. He wanted as few distractions for us as possible. I respected his plan, but Yvette didn't give a fuck. She was ready to handle them no matter how damn old they were. And most of the soldiers, if not all, *feared* or *respected* Yvette. She could handle shit with the best of the men.

While Yvette was briefing the soldiers, the others turned around and saw me standing there not dressed for the occasion or the night.

"What you doin'? Why ain't you dressed?" Kenyetta asked as she looked me up and down.

I had to give it to my girl. She was killing a red dress, Fendi heels, and the red-and-black lace mink Fendi purse to match it. Kenyetta was five-seven, with dark, pretty skin and Indian hair, which fell to the middle of her back. Tonight she had it up in a classy bun. Men killed for Kenyetta, but she belonged to Dyson, one of the members of the Emerald City Squad.

"Yeah . . . what's up wit that, Cedes?" Yvette asked after finishing with the workers, who were now at the bottom of the steps manning the gates. "Go put your shit on. Dex and Stacia will be here in a minute," she continued as she pulled out her compact to check her lipstick.

Yvette wasn't the prettiest—but with the money she earned, and the power she had, she quickly became one of the most wanted women in the projects, along with the rest of us. She was a shortie with big titties and a phat ass to go with it. We joked all of the time about her being one sandwich away from being overweight. She hadn't always been that way. I guess running Emerald City's gates and leading the soldiers took its toll on her body. She had a smooth amber complexion, and sported a short, spiky haircut. Her hair was always fierce, regardless of what she had going on.

At five feet five inches, she was the meanest bitch you could ever come across. I gave the soldiers leeway on *certain* shit, but Yvette didn't give them any on anything. She was in charge of security and made it clear that she wasn't the one to be fucked with, skirt or not. She would carry any nigga anywhere if the money was fucked up or if they were caught slippin'. Being the baddest bitch, it was only fitting that she fucked with the meanest nigga of the Emerald City Squad. And Thick was the only man who could handle her.

When he came into the room, you couldn't help but respect him. Even the scar on his face made you wonder about the life he led.

"Don't start with me. I'm mad enough as it is," I said, brushing off their comments. I wasn't in the mood to go into what had happened with my two-faced mother.

"Don't start with you? Bitch, tonight is *our* night! This is the only night we get recognized for the shit we go through in EC! Ain't no otha project, outside of Emerald, being held down by bitches!" Carissa insisted.

Carissa was usually laid-back, but not when she felt passionate about something. She looked just like a young Salli Richardson, only better. Her skin was the color of copper, and she didn't have a flaw on her body. Not even a mole. She wore her hair in a jazzy bob, which brushed her cheeks every time she moved. She was beautiful.

The niggas gave her the most shit because she was short and cute; and when they saw her, all they thought about was fuckin'. But just like we all dealt with members of the Emerald City Squad, Carissa was no exception. She was messing with Lavelle. And the niggas around here knew if anybody loved their woman, he did. He wouldn't have a problem putting two to the heads of any niggas who disrespected him or her.

"Go and get dressed!" Yvette insisted. "Stacia just called and said she'll be out front in a minute. They comin' through the gate now."

"I can't roll, y'all. I'm serious," I said, tucking my hands back inside my warm pockets. "My mother can't watch the kids tonight."

"Please say you playin'!" Yvette yelled. "Damn! Call her! I'll see if she'll do it for me."

"Don't waste your time. I tried offering her four large and she still said no."

"So you ain't playin'?" Yvette asked in disbelief.

"Naw, I'm not playin', but I wish I was. She messing with Mr. Brown again and she think I don't know that shit. You know his wife's out of town this week at that Mary Kay convention."

"Mom's wrong as shit," Kenyetta said, shaking her head.

"Tell me about it. But y'all go ahead. Just tell me how it was," I said, trying to hide the fact that I really didn't want them to go without me. We did everything together. And I wanted to see if they would ride or die with me for real.

"Look . . . why don't you let Tina watch 'em?" Yvette suggested.

She already knew the answer to that, so I don't even know why she let it fall out of her mouth.

Tina and her badass kids lived with Yvette from time to time when her mother, who lived across the hallway, put her out. Regardless, there was no way in hell I was letting her watch my kids. Besides, Yvette's apartment was nasty and too junky for my taste. The last time I let Crystal stay over Yvette's, she came back with bumps all over her arms and face. I think they were roach bites, and I was mad as shit with Yvette. I got over it after a while, but I made a promise that it would never happen again. Yvette's my girl, but she could take better care of her crib. I'm surprised Thick's big ass ain't put her in her place yet.

"Naw, I can't do that. You know I like Li'l C to be at his own house, around his own things."

"You spoil those kids rotten!" Kenyetta said. "And Li'l C damn near runnin' the place." She giggled.

Before we could get into anything else, Stacia and Dex pulled up in front of the building in his silver Hummer. Stacia looked beautiful. Her white fur coat was the first thing I saw before her glossy lips started moving.

"Party night!" she screamed through the open window.

"No, she didn't get the white mink I wanted!" Carissa said. "Dex stay lacing her up!"

"I know. Don't she look beautiful?" I added, trying to hide the fact that I was slightly jealous.

The cold air blowing through the window pushed her long hair into her face and teased her fur coat. Her honey brown skin was flawless. She was so beautiful that no one questioned why Dex chose her. We walked down the steps and by the soldiers who were already guarding Emerald City.

"Hey, baby!" I said as Stacia jumped out and gave us all hugs.

"Hey, you!" Stacia yelled back.

Dex came around to the passenger side to open the doors for us and we hugged him too. Stacia and Dex was livin' it up for real. They were the Beyoncé and Jay-Z of Emerald City and we adored them. Their relationship was the example we used when we talked to our men. They all made promises to move us out of Emerald City, once we got things tight, but Dex had kept his promise to Stacia.

Stacia and Dex used to live here in Emerald City until he became the chief in command and started pulling in six figures a month. Although

Dex got put on and eventually moved, he didn't stop showin' love to the rest of us.

He was here so much that we started forgetting he even moved with Stacia to their eight-bedroom castle-style home in Alexandria, Virginia.

Dex showed his loyalty, but Stacia was another story. She used to come by all of the time to sit with us on the steps of Unit C, like we did before they moved from the projects. We could talk to her about anything—from our relationships to our dreams. And if Stacia could make it happen or help us, she would. She always had the answers. When she left, it kinda hurt. Our group had been dismantled, and it hurt even more when she stopped coming around as much. Dex started getting kidnap threats about Stacia, and he told her to cut the visits short. Sometimes she didn't listen.

Instead, she'd just dress down so people wouldn't recognize her if they saw her sitting with us. But the moment anybody saw the fifth girl posted up in front of Unit C, they'd know exactly who she was, no matter how she tried to disguise herself. We all missed Stacia but understood that Dex kept his promise. We wanted her to be happy.

Dex didn't always have it that way. At one point he ran hand in hand with my boyfriend, Cameron, Dyson, Thick, and Lavelle. But after Dreyfus, our supplier, came in blasting on Tyland Towers, a project a few blocks over from ours, Dex came up with a plan that sealed his position as the man of Emerald City.

They say Dreyfus is six-three, dark-skinned, with smooth black hair. But no matter his looks, he was ruthless. He didn't get involved with every little detail that happened in the projects and hated being bothered with bullshit. The only thing he demanded was his money be right and on time, *every time*. About three years ago, the crew over at Tyland Towers failed to heed his warning.

When some stickup kids from uptown D.C. got the inside scoop from somebody on the inside as to where the warehouse was in Tyland Towers, they took full advantage. They got into the crew for over $200,000 in cash and product that night. And all of that shit was on consignment. When Dreyfus found out that Jamal, who ran Tyland Towers, let some niggas get into him for that much cash, he came through with ten niggas blastin' on Thanksgiving Day.

He killed off all of Jamal's troops and sliced his throat in front of his pregnant girlfriend, Patricia. Then he called a meeting with the captains from all of the spots he supplied. Dex went to represent Emerald City because there was no lieutenant at that time. While they were there, Dreyfus reminded them of his policies, particularly not having his money fucked with, using Tyland Towers as an example. He vowed that shit would be worse if it happened again.

After the meeting Dex came up with the idea

of the gatekeepers. He called Cameron, Dyson, Thick, and Lavelle, also known as the Emerald City Squad, and told them about his plan. Instead of them hating, they put the plan into action to ensure what happened to Tyland Towers didn't happen to Emerald City.

The plan consisted of four gatekeepers running the largest unit, Unit C, at all times. Since all of Emerald City could clearly be seen from Unit C, one responsibility of a gatekeeper was to handle "the approach."

The approach happened the moment the security gave the wave that something wasn't right with whoever was coming through. Two people handled that function. The other person handled security and the fourth handled the collection of the funds.

Dex's plan worked so well that Dreyfus made him the chief of Emerald City. But when the money really started flowing, it became difficult for the EC Squad to man the gates alone. More fiends were coming through, which meant more product and more responsibility. They hadn't anticipated what would happen if things worked out so well. Because of that, they never trained anyone else on the gatekeeper plan, since they didn't trust anyone.

That's when Thick came up with the plan to put us out there. Since we were around them all of the time, they trusted us and we knew Emerald City inside out. That was three years ago, and we've been manning the gate ever since.

* * *

"Wow, girl, you wearing jeans?" Stacia asked, tugging at the loop on my belt. "That's different."

"I'm not wearing jeans. . . . I can't go," I said, avoiding the disappointment on my friend's face.

"What? Why?" she asked, looking at Dex, who looked more and more like money every time I saw him. The diamond earring in his right ear was so bright that it almost looked like a flashlight.

"Damn, girl! Does your man know that? I just saw him and he ain't say shit about that," Dex asked with his raspy voice.

"Not yet. I can't find him anywhere. You know how y'all take all day to get ready for the ball. He put more time into tonight than he did on me." I laughed. "Well, look, go ahead and have fun!" I didn't want to continue to throw a pity party outside of Unit C and bring everyone down. "I'll be a'ight."

"We can't leave you," Yvette said. "You know that shit. How we gonna go to the Hustlers' Ball with one of the gatekeepers missin'?"

"But y'all look so nice. Seriously, y'all can go without me." I really wanted them to stay and chill with me, but I knew how bad they wanted to show off their outfits.

"Naw . . . we chillin' wit' you tonight!" Kenyetta said as she hit my arm. "But damn, girl, I was gonna kill them in this dress tonight!" She pouted. "Dyson woulda been mad at my ass when I came through them doors. He needs to be thankin' you," she continued as she opened her fur coat, revealing her red dress. I could tell that if you shined the right light on it, you would've been able to see right through it.

"You? I wanted to show mine off too!" Carissa opened her coat, revealing her short black Missoni dress under her fur coat, which cost over two grand. "They wasn't gonna be ready for what I was gonna give."

"Well, since we're having a fashion show," Yvette said, "I was gonna kill 'em in my dress too." Yvette's white-on-white look made her look sexy and sophisticated. The full-length fur coat set off her Emilio Pucci dress gracefully. They all looked like a million bucks. And for what? To stay home. "Anyway . . . go ahead, Stacia. We'll see you later."

"Well, okay, guys!" Stacia sighed. "I hope y'all know you're breakin' my heart. How you gonna leave me with the guys alone?"

"You can handle 'em." Carissa laughed. "And keep a close eye on my man."

"I'll try." She laughed back. "I'm gonna call y'all tomorrow!" Stacia said as Dex hugged us, then opened the door for her. "Don't forget about the cookout, and bring my babies! *All* of them, Mercedes!"

"Okay . . . I will." I waved.

"I have a surprise for them too," she continued to say as she jumped into the truck, and Dex got behind the wheel. "I love y'all!"

"We love you too! Have fun!" We waved as they drove to the party.

"Sorry, y'all. I know how bad you guys wanted to go," I said, happy they decided to stay. I figured the least I could do was get them high. "Well, since we got the soldiers at the gates tonight, let's crack open the Ace of Spades I have in my apartment on chill. Plus Big Cameron left me a phat-ass J too," I said as we walked up the steps.

"I'm wit' that shit!" Carissa said, smiling.

"Me too," Yvette added, linking her arm with Kenyetta's. "As long as we got each other, I'm good."

Even though we didn't make it to the ball, we still had a nice time laughing and talking about old times.

We were still up at four in the morning when the phone rang. No one expected to hear what we did when I answered the phone.

And the news would change our lives forever.

Everyone's got a "hate list"—but in these
explicit street tales, one woman plans to do
something about it . . .

Don't miss Reign's

Hate List: Be Careful Who You Cross
and
Hate List 2: Loose Cannon

On sale now from Dafina Books

From *Hate List: Be Careful Who You Cross*

1

Hood Love at Its Best

The summer air was hypnotic, and a perfect breeze was blowing through and around the inner-city buildings that night. Nineteen-year-old Yvonna's red Prada stilettos clicked quickly against the concrete pavement, which led toward her block.

She was irritated that the gum she was chewing had lost its flavor and that the thong she was wearing had run so far up her ass, it was difficult to walk. She would've freed herself from the uncomfortable feeling, but she was almost at her building in Southeast D.C. Not to mention her hands were occupied with grocery bags filled with food.

"You need help, shawty?" yelled a neighborhood blockhead.

"Naw, I'm good," she responded as she passed him, walking seductively. She added a little extra in her step because she knew he was watching. "Boy, don't waste your time dreamin' 'bout it"— she paused, turning around to catch the lustful look in his eyes—"'Cuz it's never gonna happen." She winked and continued her stroll to her apartment.

"Man, ain't nobody payin' you no mind," he replied as he cupped his dick and balls. "Wit' yo' half-crazy ass," he mumbled.

"Crazy" was a word she hated. Yvonna contemplated smacking him for the disrespect, but she thought better of it. Instead, she shook her head and cut the corner of the fenced-in entrance. She knew he wanted to fuck her, just like the rest of the hustlers 'round her way.

As her mind wandered, she thought about Cream, one of her best girlfriends. She was mad at her for dropping her off two blocks from her building. If Cream hadn't fucked Yvonna's neighbor's husband, she would've been able to drop her off out front.

But Treyana swore that if she saw Cream anywhere near her block, she'd stomp a mud hole in her ass. And since Treyana had six brothers and sisters, Cream knew Treyana meant it. She didn't stop at just fucking him; she went as far as to shack up with his bum ass in a run-down motel off New York Avenue in D.C. Best believe the dogs were called out on her, so Cream hid out.

When Yvonna reached the apartment building she shared with her six-year-old sister and, as she would say, her senile veteran father, she managed to free three fingers to grab the building's door. Once inside, she cracked it open, stuck her foot in to hold it steady, and twirled her body inside. The glass door bounced on her ass once before she took two steps forward and allowed it to close fully behind her. She briefly placed the bags on the floor to catch her breath and looked up at the two flights of stairs she had to tackle before *finally* getting some rest.

"Damn! Maybe I should've let his ass help!" she said out loud.

Picking the bags back up, she forced herself up the dimly lit stairway. She smiled when she saw her door, realizing in a minute she'd be able to get naked, sit on the couch, and munch on the oatmeal crème pies she had in one of the bags.

Now upstairs, Yvonna placed the bags on the floor and reached for the keys in her pocket. Before letting herself in, she dug in her ass and adjusted the thong, which had been holding her hostage for the past few minutes. So caught up in bullshit, she hadn't heard or sensed the person in the dark hallway behind her.

"Don't scream," he whispered heavily in her ear as he placed his left hand firmly against her mouth. Yvonna could smell the faint scent of cocoa butter, since his index finger was directly under her nose. "You fuckin' hear me?"

She nodded her head yes.

"Open the door."

It took her a minute to find the right key on the Burberry key chain. The jingling sound resonated in the hallway. When she located the key, she did as instructed and allowed him in as she wrestled with the bags.

"Hurry the fuck up!" he whispered again.

With the bags against the living-room wall, they walked in and he locked the door behind them.

The apartment was totally dark, with the exception of the light that illuminated from the huge fish tank against the living-room wall. Just as she expected, her six-year-old sister, Jesse, was asleep; and she saw no signs of her father.

With his hand still over her mouth, he mumbled, "Now walk over to the couch! You betta not scream. You hear me?"

She nodded yes. When she reached the couch, she bent over the edge, as he demanded. With her ass in the air, and her knees slightly bent, he reveled in her sexiness. The red Baby Phat shorts looked as if they were painted on. Still, they were in the way for what he had planned. With that, he tugged at them until they hung loosely at her ankles.

"Dayyyuummm!" he said, focusing on her honey brown ass in the purple thong. Then he ripped that off too. Yvonna squinted in pain, because the thong had rubbed her raw.

"Don't hurt me," she begged, looking back at him. "I'll do anything you say. Just, please, don't hurt me."

"Didn't I tell you not to say shit?" he asked as he pressed up against her back to reach her ear. He placed more force on her than necessary.

She nodded yes.

"Then why da fuck you speakin'?" Sprinkles of spit touched her face.

She didn't respond.

"Don't say shit else!" he said as he busied himself with the pussy he was about to take.

As he captured her silence, he entered her raw. His dick had grown to a solid seven inches. He was so hard that if he'd been any harder, it would've felt like a bat going in and out of her tiny body. The veins on his dick were pulsating as he fucked her without remorse—not caring about what she was feeling. Licking his lips, he caught a brief glimpse of his balls slapping against her phat ass. When he realized he was being turned on even more, and on the verge of cumming before he wanted to, he allowed her ass cheeks to drop against his stomach. With one hand pressing on the small of her back to keep the arch, he grabbed her hair and used it as a rein to ride her from behind.

"Shit! I'm 'bout to cum!" He moaned. He had her in the perfect position and could no longer hold out.

Hearing this, Yvonna decided there was no way she was about to be left hanging. She slyly backed up into him and twirled her hips with each motion he made. But when she did, he was brought closer to his point.

"I'm about to cummm! Shit!" he yelled.

"Shh!" she managed to answer, thinking her little sister might overhear them.

"Fuck that," he responded. "Your pussy shouldn't be so good."

Yvonna didn't care what he did now. While he was yapping off at the mouth, she'd already gushed her wetness all over his dick. Unlike him, she was able to moan hers out, giving off the impression that she hadn't cum.

"Stay right there," he informed her. "Don't move!"

When he took his slippery dick out, and aimed for her back to release his cum, it reached the glass coffee table instead. Yvonna burst out into laughter, seeing the mess he'd made. He chuckled and fell into her, his cold platinum diamond chain pressed against her skin.

"You know you crazy, right?" he asked, sounding out of breath.

"I'm crazy? How you figure?"

"'Cuz you stay likin' this rough shit," he replied before pulling up his True Religion jeans. He then disappeared into the darkness of the apartment and returned with a warm washcloth.

"And you love that I like it rough. Anyway, I thought you couldn't come over tonight," she responded as she rose so he could clean both of their wetness from her body. When he rubbed her exposed vagina with the washcloth, she tensed up due to the rawness she felt.

On the sly, he stuck his finger inside her. "Damn! You still wet! Let me hit it again real quick!" He reached for himself.

"Stop, boy!" She snatched the washcloth from

him and cleaned the mess off the table. "I'm already in pain, messin' wit' yo' silly ass!" She slid back into her shorts, leaving the zipper open so her tiny belly could breathe. She didn't see her panties and wasn't searching for them either. She flipped on the kitchen light. "And put them groceries on the counter." She continued talking as her tiny feet slapped against the cold hardwood floor. "Might as well make yourself useful."

Yvonna wondered why he had popped up the way that he did. "I thought you were goin' to the party tonight." She grabbed the black rubber hair band that she kept on her arm, and pulled her hair into a ponytail, which sat on the top of her head. "You act like you ain't have no time for me earlier when I called."

"I always got time for you." He pinched her ass.

"Move, boy!" she yelled, secretly loving his aggression. "And how you know what time I was gonna be home?"

"I waited on you. Plus you always go to the store at night. You betta switch your routine up."

"I ain't changin' shit! I hate waitin' in dem long-ass lines. At night I'm in and out. And don't try to skip the subject, B. What's up wit' the party?"

"I'm still goin'." He placed the bags on the counter and looked as if he had something on his mind. "I just came to check you before I left. Plus I wanna talk to you about somethin'."

"Everything okay? Besides the fact that you're standin' me up for the movies again?"

"I'll make it up to you, shawty."

"Oh, I know that," she said, curling her lips. "But you betta know it too!"

He walked up behind her and placed his arms around her waist. The diamond-studded belly ring she wore scratched his arm lightly.

"So you really gonna do it, huh?"

"Yes, Bilal," she responded, stealing a piece of his apple, which he'd taken from the grocery bag. She already knew what he was talking about. Her transporting drugs from D.C. to New York for the gang he belonged to. "And don't start with me .... because I don't want to hear it."

"What if I tell you I don't want you doin' it? Then what?"

"We already talked about this, Lal!"

"I know we talked about it," he said as a look of concern overtook him. "But I don't think you should do it. Once you get involved in this shit, you stuck."

Yvonna stopped what she was doing and looked into his eyes. His long eyelashes added softness to his rugged features. His black and Spanish heritage made him look exotic. And because he stayed in the streets, the sun caused his skin to bronze.

To hear Yvonna tell it, everything about him was perfect: from his six-foot-two height, to his large dick. And no matter how much he loved wearing plain white T-shirts, baggy jeans, and Nike boots, he still looked like a model with a thuggish quality. He was tatted up. His favorite was the one on his arm that read *LalVon* inside a coffin. It represented his motto that it would be Bilal and Yvonna—the two of them together—till death.

"I hear you, Bilal." She smiled, walking over to him before stealing a passionate kiss. She then ran her hand over his silky goatee. "But I'm a big girl and I been wantin' to get with the Young Black Millionarz before I met you in high school. You act like I'm an angel or somethin'."

"Oh, I know you be throwin' them bows." He chuckled. "That's one of the reasons I love you." He looked into her hazel brown eyes.

"But shit has changed with the YBM. It ain't how it used to be," Bilal cautioned. "Ever since Crazy Dave and his stepbrother Swoopes got put on, niggas been lunchin' out. Some dudes doin' stuff we ain't used to do. Like stickin' up motha-fuckas and shit. They fucked up all the game."

"Why they even let them in?" she questioned.

"Because they thorough and don't give a fuck," he advised. "And you need a few niggas like that on the squad."

"I don't know 'bout Swoopes, but I think Dave's a punk for real," Yvonna said, fanning her hand in the air. She hated his fucking guts. "Plus I don't appreciate him telling people Sabrina's pussy smelled like cat piss. It ain't like he fucked her! So how would he know, anyway?"

"How you know he ain't hit?"

"I *don't* know." She removed the black shirt she was wearing and allowed her titties to show. She hated clothes. "But he don't eitha."

"No lie—your girl do need a lesson in hygiene." He laughed, pinching her nipples.

"And how do you know?" She hit him on the hand. "Don't be talkin' about her. That's my friend!"

"Everybody know that girl's pussy stink! Every time she get out a car, niggas turn the other way. I mean, she a big girl and all, but she still can wash her ass. That's ree-dic-ulous!"

Yvonna couldn't say much; because although Sabrina was one of her best friends, Yvonna knew what Bilal was saying was true. On many occasions she had pulled her to the side to have a conversation with her about her odor, and she still couldn't get it right. Most women wouldn't have the heart to tell their friends, but Yvonna did. She felt sorry for the nigga who fucked and got her pregnant.

They were still talking when Bilal's cell phone rang.

"Hello," he said, walking away from her. He looked back to see if she was watching. She was. "I can't hear you," he said as he walked farther away. He was trying to space himself away from Yvonna, since she was always sweating him about his calls.

Picking up on the cue, Yvonna walked back into the kitchen. *Why the fuck he got to go in the other room?* she thought. *I hope he ain't fuckin' around on me again!*

Bilal was a good dude. However, just like most, he made the mistake of stepping out on her every now and again. And ever since the last time, Yvonna didn't trust him. It didn't make her feel any better that he wasn't with the Young Black Millionarz right now, and he was at her house. It didn't help that he slept over there almost every night, despite living on the Maryland side of town. In her book: once a cheat, always a cheat. Still, love wouldn't allow her to leave him alone.

"Who dat?" she asked, walking up to him while he was in the living room on the couch. She could no longer bite her tongue.

"I'ma hit you later, man," he said as he ended the call. He didn't want her going off like she had many times in the past. Yvonna had a temper so bad that when she got angry, she would get violent and not remember doing it.

"Bilal, who the fuck was that?" she yelled as she took the black New York Yankees cap off his head and hit him with it.

"Stop trippin', girl!"

"Don't tell me to stop trippin'!" she yelled as she snatched the BlackBerry off his hip and hit send to connect to the last caller. Bilal tried to get ahold of her, but she was too quick. When the phone rang and someone answered, she asked, "Who's this?"

"Why you got his phone?"

When she realized it was a *he*, she suddenly felt stupid for violating Bilal's privacy.

"Oh . . . ," she said, feeling slightly dumb. "It's *just* you."

"Yeah, it's me," Dave responded, irritated. "Why you bein' pressed?"

"Give me my phone, girl," Bilal said, snatching the BlackBerry from her. "How you feel now? Stupid?"

Silence.

"Hello," Bilal said, placing the phone back on his ear.

"You gotta get your girl in check, man. She can't be goin' through your shit."

"Don't worry about me, partna!" He smiled. "I got this over here."

"No, you don't!" Yvonna yelled, still up in his biz.

"I hope you're not serious about what you gonna do either," Crazy Dave said, reminding him of their last conversation. "Real niggas don't go out like that."

"I *am* serious, and just 'cuz I know what I want, don't mean I'm not real."

"Yeah, a'ight, man!" He laughed. "You betta hope she don't find out, 'cuz marrying her ain't gonna change the fact that shawty on the way."

Bilal looked at Yvonna, hoping she couldn't hear what Dave said.

"Like I said, let me do me, and you do you."

"Yeah, whateva. Don't forget 'bout dem dudes neitha. Swoopes owe a lot of money to some cats, and that'll be enough to settle all debts."

"I told y'all, I ain't wit' that shit." He was mad he brought it up.

"Nigga, ain't nobody sayin' you got to do shit." Dave felt Bilal was being soft and his voice was as deep as Method Man's when he addressed him. "But you the only one they trust. You get 'em to the club, and me and Swoopes will do the rest."

"What I tell you 'bout talkin' 'bout this shit over the phone?"

"Yeah, whateva, nigga," Dave replied. "Just don't try and back out."

After he hung up, Bilal placed his phone in his pocket, instead of the clip. He had a few females whom he hadn't fucked in a while lingering around, but nothing serious. Sitting down on the couch, he removed his boots as if nothing had happened.

"Where my slippers, ma?"

"Fuck dem slippers." She frowned. "What his hatin' ass say, 'cause I know he was talkin' 'bout me?" She plopped on the couch next to him, and his hand fondled her breasts. "You know he wanna fuck me, right?"

"Did he tell you that shit?" he asked like he was on his way to confront him. Sitting up straight, he awaited her answer.

"No . . . I can just tell. Whenever he come around, he got to say somethin' to me—even if I ain't speakin' to him."

"You be on his shit too. Don't get dude fucked-up. Dave ain't tryin' to get at you. He just not used to girls speakin' their minds. But I'ma need you to stop clockin' my calls, Yvonna. That shit ain't cool no more. We ain't kids."

"Fuck that!" Yvonna said, slapping his hands off her. "You just betta not be cheatin' again, Bilal. 'Cuz dis time I'm leavin' you!"

"Stop comin' for my head 'bout dat cheatin' shit! You know I ain't fuckin' you over no more."

"Well, you did! You fucked me up, 'cuz I would've never thought you'd step out on me."

Bilal sighed. Once a week he had to prove to her that he was a changed man.

"I don't wanna talk 'bout that shit no more, Yvonna! You can't be monitorin' my phone calls and shit. It's bad for bizness."

"As long as we're together," she responded, reaching for his phone—only to realize it wasn't on his hip. "Nothing's off limits."

With that, she went for his pockets. He didn't fight. Instead of grabbing his phone, she felt a tiny velvet box. As she pulled it out, her eyes got as big as saucers. When she opened it, a diamond solitaire ring stared at her. Without waiting, Bilal got on one knee as she began to fan herself anxiously with her hands.

Taking the box from her, he said, "Yvonna, I fuck wit' . . . I mean"—he paused, clearing his throat and trying to avoid using slang—"I love you. You're the only shawty I can see spendin' the rest of my life with. And I'm bein' real when I say that. I can have fun wit' you, ride or die wit' you—and most of all, I can see havin' kids wit' you. There's nobody out here for me but you."

"Bilal, I can't believe—"

"Don't say nothin', baby," he said, rubbing the tears from her eyes. "When I see how you look afta your sister—despite your father being fucked-up—I smile because I know you would hold me down if shit got rough. We got each otha, and that's real. I don't care what people say 'bout you, or 'bout us bein' together. Everything I do is for you.

"You a dime, Yvonna. You fuck me like I like to be fucked. You can cook your ass off, and you understand the game I'm in and respect it. Fuck dem hatin' mothafuckas out there! I know what I want, and what I want for the rest of my life is you. So what I'm askin' you, baby, is . . . will you do me the honor of being my wife?"

Yvonna jumped up and down and kissed him on every inch of his face before she mumbled what appeared to be a "yes." As she thought about their new life together, she also thought about all the bullshit she went through to get to this point: the cheating, the late-night calls on his cell phone, and the nights she went looking for him—only to find him with another girl.

Bilal stayed fucking around on her in the beginning; but no matter what, he always let it be known that he wasn't leaving her for another bitch. There were females who tried to get him to change his mind, and one in particular took it all the way by telling Yvonna about it. Bilal was known as a "ruthless mothafucka" with manners. He took it as far as it needed to be took, and no further. If he was coming for you, you'd know why; and that was a turn-on for a lot of the chickenheads around the neighborhood.

After Yvonna fucked up the female who told her about Bilal, she approached him about it. And instead of him being a punk, he manned up and told her the truth. But Yvonna wasn't a slouch, and she didn't forgive easily. For six months she cut his ass off. She drove him crazy—not accepting his calls or visits. Little did he know, she was hurting as much as he was. But she decided that she wouldn't take him back until she made him sweat.

That's when she started dating this nigga named Lucy. He was known around the way for being a player. She had the neighborhood buzzing when word got out that the LL Cool J look-alike wanted to give up everything for Yvonna. When Bilal found out, he stepped to them both at Jasper's restaurant. Because Lucy wasn't no busta-ass nigga, Yvonna knew that Bilal was ready for war; and most of all, he was ready to die for her. At that time she missed him so much that she stopped the games and walked out with Bilal, leaving Lucy behind.

"So what up, ma?" he responded as she continued to bombard him with kisses. "You gonna marry me or what?"

"Yes! Yes! Yes! You know I'ma fuckin' marry you!"

"I wanna tell your father," he said, standing up and moving to his room. In all this time he had never gotten to meet him. "I need his blessing."

"No!" She jumped up. "He'll find out soon enough."

"Why you don't want me to meet the man? We been kickin' it for three years and you *still* don't want me to meet him. Why?"

"You marryin' *me*, so that's all that matters,"

she said, kissing him again. She *really* didn't want her father embarrassing her. Ever since he'd been back from the war, he hadn't been the same.

Needless to say, Bilal didn't leave her that night. Like always, they crawled in the bed that Yvonna shared with her six-year-old sister, Jesse. One of the things Yvonna hated about the apartment was not having her own space. She knew Jesse was just as frustrated.

Needing a bigger place was one of the main reasons Yvonna wanted to get with YBM. She needed the cash to get Jesse and herself out of the two-bedroom apartment and into something bigger, without her father. But now it looked as if the three of them would be a happy family.

"I love you," Yvonna said as she lay on her side, and turned her head to kiss Bilal, who was behind her holding her tight.

"I love you too, ma."

When she looked at Jesse, she smiled when she saw her sleeping heavily in front of her. She thanked God for finally bringing her closer to something she always wanted, a family of her own. What she didn't say out loud was that something told her that the happiness wouldn't last.

From *Hate List 2: Loose Cannon*

Prologue

Yvonna looked at her nude body in the full-length mirror on the bathroom door. She examined herself, as she had many times before.

"Who am I?"

That question wasn't about the curves in her hips or how her breasts were still as perky as they were months after cosmetic surgery. The question was about her mental stability and why it always seemed that everyone she loved—for one reason or another—could never love her back.

She turned around and, through the open doorway, stared at Dave's body on the bed. A single tear fell down her face as she realized a love lost. The glossy blood from his throat dripped out of his body and fell against the wooden floor.

She loved him with the kind of love she had as a child, when she played with a brand-new doll on Christmas Day. This was before her father had raped her, stealing any innocence or understanding she had of life. All she wanted was love. Yet, a part of her—the part she called Gabriella—loved nothing more than to *cause destruction to those who crossed her path. Gabriella was how she protected her feelings.*

As the steam from the running shower filled the bathroom and covered the mirror, she smoothed it off with her left hand. Another tear fell down her cheek as she readied herself for what she was about to do. Kill again. Feeling extreme contempt caused Gabriella to appear behind her wearing a one-piece tight red dress.

She placed a hand on her shoulder and whispered in her ear: "Think of it this way. Once they're gone, you'll be happy. Isn't that what you want?"

"Yes." She nodded.

"Good." Gabriella kissed her cheek. She looked just like Taraji P. Henson from the movie Baby Boy. "Now do it. Get mad. And get even. Let's finish what you started."

Yvonna wiped the onerous tear off her face and grabbed the knife off the edge of the white porcelain sink.

With revenge and malice overflowing, she carved into the flesh of her right shoulder the names of the people she hated most. Although the blade tore through her soft skin, she didn't flinch. The pain was pleasurable as she watched the names of the people she despised appear with oozing blood. When she was done, she wiped the red fluid off her skin with her free hand and smiled:

Bernice
Cream
Jhane
Swoopes

HATE LIST 2: LOOSE CANNON

Yvonna was beyond crazy.

Yvonna was beyond mad.

Hate consumed her so much that it was difficult to breathe at times. And with Gabriella being unleashed, it was impossible for her to be controlled.

Catch a Co-Conspirator by Her Toe

Yvonna and Gabriella stand quietly backstage as they watch the middle-school children act out a scene from a play the students wrote called *A Midwinter Night Scream*. Colorful costumes dress the floor, empty chairs, and equipment as they run from the stage to the back to prepare for each scene.

Like snakes waiting to attack, *they* remain still. Their eyes are fixated on two children—and nothing or nobody would stand in their way. They *have* to get them.

"Hi, I'm Mrs. Princely. Can I help you?" asks a beautiful black woman with soft, curly, shoulder-length hair. Her face is stern when she approaches Yvonna from behind.

"No, I'm just watching my niece. Isn't she

beautiful?" Yvonna looks at the stage, at no child in particular.

The woman's face softens immediately. After all, Yvonna looks nothing like the average abductor. In fact, she looks stylish in her dark blue custom-made jeans and red leather jacket. Her hair is styled in her trademark short, spiky cut. Just the way she likes it.

"Oh . . . which one is yours?" The teacher smiles, looking upon the stage with Yvonna as the children sing a wretched ballad.

Yvonna doesn't have an answer for the nosy bitch and she wishes she would just leave her the fuck alone. She doesn't, though.

"Tell the bitch her name is Lil Reecy or some shit!" Gabriella yells from the sidelines. She is wearing an all-red leather jumper by Baby Phat. "Make somethin' up! Think on your feet! Haven't I taught you anything?"

"Be quiet! You makin' a scene, and shit!" Yvonna tells her.

"Are you okay?" the woman asks.

"Oh . . . uh . . . yeah."

She scrutinizes her. "Well . . . who are you talking to?"

"No one. Just had an outburst. That's it."

Yvonna has worked so hard to control Gabriella, but nothing succeeds. She is still convinced that Gabriella is real; it's just that other people can't see her.

"If you say so. Well, which one is your niece?"

Yvonna scans the crowd of brats and picks the homeliest-looking one she can find. If truth be told, not a one of them looks like she's seen any parts of a tub, soap, or water—ever.

"That one right there." She points at a girl with pink barrettes in her hair and a bright yellow sunshine costume. "She's my niece."

"Who? Tabitha?"

Yvonna can tell by the woman's expression that she could not imagine a child so afflicted being related to her in any form or fashion.

"You just had to pick 'Snot-Nosed-Nancy,' didn't you?" Gabriella laughs. "Don't be surprised if she don't believe you now."

Yvonna ignores her and says, "Yes. She's my niece. I just got back in town and wanted to surprise her. So when I found out at the last minute about the play, I ran over here. I wanted to be the first person she hugs when she steps off the stage."

"Wow! Oh . . . uh . . . I can't wait to see the look on her face!" The woman beams. "No one ever supports her in school. Not to say anything bad about your family."

"No worries," Yvonna reassures her, touching the teacher lightly on the arm. "My sister's a hot-ass mess, I know it."

The woman gasps. Yvonna ignores her reaction.

"But you should get on out of my face." Yvonna stops and clears her throat and says, "I mean, you should go back out there. The kids need you."

"They're fine. I want to be here to see Tabitha's face when she sees you."

This woman is causing Yvonna's blood to boil.

If this bitch knows what's good for her, she'll get lost before she shows up missing . . . permanently. Because nothing or nobody would stop Yvonna from snatching Treyana's kids; and she would not mind covering her tracks *and* witnesses if they got in her way. She never thought deceiving Treyana's sons into leaving out the back door with her would be so difficult.

"Hurry up and get rid of her! They almost done!" Gabriella yells.

Gabriella is growing agitated, so Yvonna has to think quickly. Her mind wanders and she grapples with choking the fuck out of the old-ass crow or smacking her down. She decides upon smacking her, until she sees a little girl holding her hands between her legs, running toward the restroom. The glittery purple shoes she wears cause a devilish idea to enter her mind.

"Excuse me," Yvonna says to the woman. "I have to go to the restroom before my niece comes out."

"No problem! I'll be waiting right here when you get back. I can't wait to see the look on her face!"

Man, this whore is about to make me unleash! Why she gotta be all in my fuckin' business?

Yvonna makes her way past the children who are roaming around backstage. She sees a small bucket on the floor filled with costume jewelry for the performance. She takes one look behind her to see if the woman is watching—she isn't. A little girl who needs help changing a costume has taken her attention.

So Yvonna dips inside the restroom and looks under the stalls until she sees the purple shoes the little girl is wearing. When she spots them, she goes into the stall next to her and dumps the jewelry on the floor. Afterward, she uses the bucket to scoop out some water from the commode. There is shit and piss inside, but Yvonna doesn't care. She stands up on the commode and dumps the foul feces all over the little girl, who screams in terror.

Yvonna's laughter prohibits her from running as fast as she wants to while exiting the bathroom. She manages to calm herself down moments before approaching the woman.

"I think something's wrong with one of the children in the restroom. I saw another little girl playing an awful joke on her. Hurry!" Yvonna appears frantic. "Go help her! Please!"

The woman drops the clipboard she's holding and runs toward the bathroom. When she leaves, Yvonna regains her focus as she watches Treyana's kids come backstage after their roles. She's amazed at how cute they are—with their fluffy, curly hair and wide-eyed smiles—despite the costumes they are wearing that make them look like two fruity bitches. In her opinion they don't look like Treyana or her husband.

"You boys were wonderful!" Yvonna cheers. "I'm so proud of you."

"Who are you?" one of the twins asks. "You look familiar."

Yvonna has been around them, but not often, and she is surprised they remember. One of them is slightly taller than the other, but they are otherwise identical.

"I'm your aunt Paris! You don't remember me?" Yvonna touches her heart and appears hurt.

"No," the other one responds. "I never heard of you."

"That's awful! You really haven't heard of your aunt Paris from Texas?"

The twins look at each other again and shake their heads no.

"Don't worry about that right now. We'll have plenty of time for catching up." She smiles. "But right now, I need you to come with me. Your mom wants me to take you home. We'll talk about everything on the way there."

"But Momma said never to leave with a stranger," one of them says.

"A stranger?" Yvonna folds her arms and stands on her back foot. "I doubt very seriously that a stranger would be dressed as good as I am. Now, are you coming or not? It don't make me no never mind," Yvonna lies.

Whether the boys know it or not, they are leaving that school with her—even if she has to snatch them by their undeveloped balls.

They look at each other and then at her. She knows they're examining her stylish shoes and her pretty face. She smiles. She doesn't look harmful, and she does everything she can to conceal her pleasure. Men always become her victims.

Little do you know, but the Devil has many faces, she silently says.

The taller one shrugs his shoulders, looks at the shorter one, and replies, "Okay. Let's go."

"Great! And I brought some candy for you too. I figured you'd like it."

Like all kids experience, when they come into contact with sweet poison . . . it is lust at first sight.